HE

PRE

BONES

C000225071

BOOKS BY CARLA KOVACH

The Next Girl
Her Final Hour

HER PRETTY BONES

CARLA KOVACH

bookouture

Published by Bookouture in 2019

An imprint of StoryFire Ltd.

Carmelite House
50 Victoria Embankment
London EC4Y 0DZ

www.bookouture.com

Copyright © Carla Kovach, 2019

Carla Kovach has asserted her right to be identified
as the author of this work.

All rights reserved. No part of this publication may be reproduced,
stored in any retrieval system, or transmitted, in any form or by
any means, electronic, mechanical, photocopying, recording or
otherwise, without the prior written permission of the publishers.

ISBN: 978-1-78681-667-2
eBook ISBN: 978-1-78681-666-5

This book is a work of fiction. Names, characters, businesses,
organizations, places and events other than those clearly in the
public domain, are either the product of the author's imagination
or are used fictitiously. Any resemblance to actual persons, living or
dead, events or locales is entirely coincidental.

This book is dedicated to those who care for relatives or work in the care industry. What you do is truly amazing and I firmly believe caring to be one of the hardest jobs ever. The physical and mental strength you have really is your superpower.

PROLOGUE

'Give it back,' I yelled as I ran into our shared room and wrestled my stupid sister to the floor. She grabbed the doll harder, pulling it close to her heart. My sister wasn't having it, she always got what she wanted. My mother made it and I wanted it. I forced my fingers into the protective ball she'd formed with her body. That doll was going to be mine. Even though she was a whole year older, she was clumsier and tinier – born too early, they all said. I was cleverer at six than she'd ever be, stupid child. I'd show her just how much. She needed to know her place. What was hers was mine, and that's the way things would always be.

As I snatched the arm of the knitted doll, the sound of its button eye pinging against the bed frame stopped us both. All I could hear was the music Daddy played on the wireless, something about the devil in disguise. My stupid sister was the devil in disguise.

She gave me a teary stare as she hugged the disfigured toy. 'Don't you dare cry! You know what you'll get if you cry.' It wouldn't be the first time my idiot sister had got me into trouble by bawling her eyes out for nothing. She was always Mummy and Daddy's favourite with her strawberry blonde curls and her stupid sickly pale face. With a trembling bottom lip, her tears turned into loud sobs. I pinched her hard. 'Stop it, stop it, stop it,' I yelled.

My heart began to hammer as I heard the music stop, followed by Daddy's footsteps thundering up the creaky old stairs. 'Your mother goes out for five minutes and you just can't be a well-behaved little girl. What's going on here? I should tan your bloody hide,' Daddy shouted. I realised I was gripping her so hard that she was turning red.

'She broke her doll and she's upset,' I said as I pretended to hug her. Feeling her pulling away from me, I gripped her closer until I was pinching her again. 'Don't you dare move,' I whispered in her ear as I stroked her hair. Her tears began to wet my sleeve, all because of her stupid doll.

'Are you all right, my lovely?' he said as he kneeled down, prising my arms from her. Always her, she could do no wrong.

I pulled her back towards me and squeezed her harder, pinching the skin on the back of her arm, and she nodded. Her expression was betraying me as her bottom lip began to quiver again. Daddy's gaze moved from hers to mine. 'I've told you about this before, haven't I?' he yelled as he pulled me from my sister and dragged me along the wooden floor and down the landing, the floral dress Mummy made me riding up towards my chest.

'Not the cupboard. Daddy, please. I'm sorry, I'm sorry.'

It was no good pleading. After slapping the top of my leg and flinging me to the back of the dark cupboard, he turned the key in the lock, leaving it in so that no light could filter through. I shivered in the darkness. It was all her fault, it always was. As soon as Mummy came home, she'd let me out and I'd show my horrible sister exactly what I could do. The wireless was switched back on. Daddy was downstairs again singing along to some old song that Grandma likes, probably resting in front of the fire, awaiting Mummy's return.

'Let me out,' I called. A shaft of light replaced the darkness. My sister's green eyes stared at me through the keyhole. 'Let me out.'

She took a step back, the torn knitted doll, gripped in her arms, unravelling a little more with each step. Her red puffy gaze met mine and she shook her head as another tear slid down her cheek.

'You wait. You just wait, you naughty little girl.' I kicked the inside of the cupboard before realising I'd just disturbed all the spiders. The light was taken from me as she placed the key back in the lock. 'Leave the key out,' I yelled as I kicked harder. Daddy turned the music up even louder until my cries could be heard no more.

I hate her, I really do. I will always hate her.

CHAPTER ONE

Saturday, 14 July 2018

Toby sucked on the last of his roll-up. In fact that was the last of his tobacco, his pouch was well and truly empty. Maybe he could scrounge a smoke during his break time, some kind person might help him out. He shook his head, dreading actually arriving at his new job, the job he never wanted in the first place. If it wasn't for the cowbag at the job centre penalising him for turning up late, he'd have received his benefit money. Instead, him turning up to explain that he'd fallen out of bed, hurting his ankle, hadn't been convincing enough. It was an excuse, he knew that, but *overslept* isn't a reason they take pity on and he had genuinely overslept. Alarm didn't go off – yeah, right. He'd left with a lecture on timekeeping and information on a lead for work with a local job agency.

He shook his head as he flicked the nub end onto the grassy verge. Whizzing around the bends of the snaking Warwickshire roads in his trusty old car felt like freedom. That freedom was soon to end and be replaced by some jumped-up line manager shouting orders all day. A little weasel of a human who was way less qualified than him. He pulled the sun visor down. Seven in the morning on a Saturday. Who works these kind of anti-social hours? Him, apparently – for at least the next six weeks. That's when the dreaded minimum wage contract finished, unless his nightmare was to come true and they'd offer him a permanent job. No, the strategy was to go in, do the minimum required, show no aptitude for more, don't be too productive, and escape to the toilet as often as possible. Steal a toilet roll. He'd run out and no benefit money meant no toilet rolls. He'd come back with a few tins from the food bank last night but no toilet roll. It wasn't thieving, it was survival. Besides, he'd make it up to society when he discovered himself and finally decided what direction his life was going in.

The July sun already made him sweat. At least it would be cool at the meat packing factory. If the heat or lack of breakfast didn't make him queasy, the sight of portioned up dead animals and being surrounded by the metallic aroma of blood certainly would. It was gone seven fifteen and he was meant to be there for his induction in a few minutes. He pushed the tape into his old cassette player and 'Ace of Spades' by Motorhead filled his little car. With every stretch his speed increased. There was nothing on the road. It was fun time. As he sped out of the bends he shouted the lyrics as the chorus came on and banged his fingers on the steering wheel to the beat.

His dad would be so proud – not. He imagined his dad giving him that father to son lecture about wasting his degree. He never wanted to be a dentist anyway. He hated people's yellow teeth, their gingivitis and their chapped lips and gumboils. His father may have bullied him into doing dentistry, but he was a man now and he'd make his own choices. Right now, he chose to live alone in his bedsit, run his banger of a car, and take odd jobs followed by long stretches of free time. That suited him just fine. 'Up yours, Dad,' he shouted as he sped around the last bend where the road merged into Laurel Lane.

Lemmy's voice boomed through his car for the finale chorus as he came out of the bend. As the low sun dazzled him, the back doors of the white van in front suddenly opened. Slamming his brakes on, he skidded as a person slipped out, landing on the road just in front of Toby's car. The van continued at speed along Laurel Lane with the back doors flapping open. Lemmy stopped singing and birdsong broke the silence before the next track came on. Toby rolled his window down further and listened for any sound of human pain but there was nothing.

Gasping as his heart hammered, he peered through the windscreen. The person was no longer there. He wiped his sweaty brow with his sleeve and Alice Cooper began singing the opening to 'Poison'. He slammed the flat of his hand into the tape player and the tape ejected.

Shaking, he opened the creaky car door, giving it a shove to widen the gap enough for him to get out. He checked the time, seven thirty. He'd really blown it. With reporting the incident and making a statement, there was no way on earth he'd be making work today. A murmur came from the front of the car. With wobbly legs, he took one step followed by another until he spotted the girl. 'Shit.' He kneeled down as comfortably as his lanky frame would allow and grabbed his phone, calling the emergency services. The girl tried to speak but instead of words, flecks of blood came from her mouth, spraying his T-shirt.

'Ambulance, and police, Laurel Lane, Warwickshire. There's been an accident and a girl has been hurt. You need to get someone here quick, mate,' he yelled as he tried to stop the bleeding from the girl's abdomen. Blood flowed over his quivering hands. He let her go and removed his T-shirt, rolled it up and pressed it against the open wound on her side, stemming the flow. 'Talk to me,' he yelled as the girl drifted in and out of consciousness. He wanted to turn her over into the recovery position but he knew better. He might make her injuries worse if her bones were broken.

The young girl was covered in dirt and the smell coming from her almost made him want to gag. Her straggly hair half covered her gaunt face and he cringed at the sight of her plaque covered teeth. As he held the T-shirt to her bony side, he could feel that there was nothing to her. He wished she'd come around again but it wasn't looking good.

His mind flashed back to the white van. He had to remember as much as possible. Had he run her over? No, he hadn't heard a bump and there was no sign of damage on his bonnet or bumper. He had been speeding. He knew he had. There was a forty sign on the stretch before and he'd been going at least fifty coming out of the bend. He hadn't run her over though, she'd fallen in front of him, came from nowhere out of the back of a large van.

He had no MOT on his car. Was his insurance still valid? He racked his brains but couldn't remember. The MOT was a month overdue. Damn, he wouldn't escape this without a fine, points and a ticking off, all because of someone else, nothing to do with him.

No one knew his name; he could just get back in, turn Alice Cooper up to full volume and keep driving.

He looked at the girl and thought of what his dad would say and he knew on this occasion his dad would be right. He would stay with her and take whatever punishment came his way. It's not like he had any prior convictions and he hadn't hurt her. He'd just tell the truth. With his other hand, he stroked her thin wisps of red hair and whispered, 'An ambulance is on its way. Just hold on.'

The heat from the sun was burning his lily-white bare back. He really needed a smoke to calm his nerves but now he had no chance. The more of her features he took in, the more he noticed how unusual she looked. All skin and bone, blemishes and chapped lips. She had a starved, dehydrated look about her. 'What happened?' he asked as he continued stroking her hair to the sound of the approaching sirens.

As the ambulance pulled up, the girl's body jerked. Trying to hear what she was saying, he leaned in closer feeling her desperate breaths on his neck.

'Help her,' the girl managed to whisper before her body flopped in his arms.

'Wake up. Wake up,' he yelled as her body began to jerk and fit.

CHAPTER TWO

Gina's mobile buzzed across her bedside table. She reached out with closed eyes, searching for the phone with her fingers. As she grabbed it, Gracie called out. 'Nanna. It's morning, Nanna.'

She prised an eye open and accepted the call. 'Hang on a minute, chicken. What's up, Jacob?'

'We've had an incident, guv. I know it's your weekend off but it's a biggie. A young man named Toby Biddle reported an incident just before seven thirty, saying that a woman jumped out of a van on Laurel Lane. Looks like she's malnourished. Her hair and teeth are in an awful state. Something bad has happened to her by the looks of it as why would she jump out of the back of a van? Officers at the scene checked his car over and concluded that there hadn't been any impact between the girl and his car. Paramedics are just attending to her at the scene and then heading to Cleevesford Hospital. It doesn't look like she'll make it from what they're saying. If she doesn't we could be looking at a murder case. Shall I meet you there?' Jacob asked.

'Nanna?' Gracie giggled as she tugged on the curtains and began to sing.

'Sounds like you have company.'

'My granddaughter, and she kept me up half the night – I seriously feel like death. I feel even more like death now I have to call my daughter to say I'll be dropping her off at this time on a Saturday morning. She's going to be well thrilled with me. I'll be there as soon as I can, within the hour.'

She ended the call and watched as Gracie began pulling the curtains harder. 'Gracie, don't do that, chicken. You'll hurt yourself.' Gracie returned her warning with a mischievous smile and yanked the curtain, dragging the pole down, which narrowly missed her head. The little girl began to cry as she realised she'd had a near miss. Gina stepped out of bed and lifted the child out of the chaos. 'I told you not to pull it. Let me see.' She ruffled her hand through Gracie's light wisps and smiled. 'Has Gracie hurt her head? Has Gracie hurt her arms? Has Gracie hurt her feet?' Her granddaughter's cries turned into shrieks of tear-sodden laughter as Gina touched her sensitive toes.

'No,' Gracie yelled. Gina moved her fingers away from Gracie's foot and gave her a kiss on the cheek.

'Right, Nanna has to go to work and I have to take you back to Mummy. We had a lovely night though, didn't we?'

'Want to stay, Nanna.'

'So sorry, darling. We'll do this again soon. You know Nanny loves you, don't you?'

Gracie chuckled and held onto a strand of Gina's frizzy brown hair. 'I want to stay.'

Gina knew Hannah would be disappointed. Her night off would be ruined by the lack of a lie in. Nanny Hetty had never sent Gracie back early. They always reminded Gina about how good Nanny Hetty was, but Nanny Hetty, Gina's ex-mother-in-law, was a lot older than Gina and had retired many years ago. She could never compete and she wasn't about to start. She had a busy job that she loved and an incident had come in.

'I promise we'll do something fun very soon,' Gina said as she fed Gracie's dress over her head, pulling her chubby little arms through.

As she led the toddler to the bathroom, she phoned her daughter.

'Mum? It isn't even nine. Has something happened?'

'I've had a call. So sorry, love. I need to drop Gracie home on my way to the station.'

'For heaven's sake. It was one night. One measly night and you have to go to work? I thought you'd booked the weekend off. I thought we were all going out later. I thought things were going to change – you promised. I even booked cinema tickets to watch *Incredibles 2* this afternoon and was going to surprise you.' Gracie began to laugh as she pretended to gargle while playing at brushing her teeth. 'No, you're not being fair with us.'

'Sorry, love—'

'You always say sorry. Even after what happened with your last case. You've let me down but this isn't all about me or Gracie. What case is it? Not another where you're going to be in grave danger or some madman is going to force his way into your home and try to strangle you? You're really selfish, you know that? I don't want to lose another parent and I don't want Gracie growing up without her nanna.'

The moment she broke down in front of the workplace counsellor flashed through Gina's mind. Hannah was right, the last case had hit her hard and Hannah had seen her slowly withdrawing afterwards. Their relationship had never been the best but deep down neither wanted anything to happen to the other. Hannah and Gracie were all Gina really had when it came to family. Her parents had passed away a long time ago and she had no siblings. The moment when her attacker was throttling her on her kitchen floor filled her mind and her heart began to bang as her throat constricted.

'Mum, Mum—'

'Sorry. I was just err…' She was just what? She didn't know how to respond to Hannah as she opened her mouth to continue speaking. The incoherent jumble of words remained in her head, unable to escape.

'I was just saying, I've already lost a dad. I know things happened between you and Dad, and I know he wasn't good for you—'

'Good for me? He would have killed me if he'd had the chance. We've spoken about this!' She began to tremble with rage. Had her daughter not understood a word she had said when she told her how severely Terry used to beat her? How he'd broken her ribs, thrown her around and kicked her, mentally chained her to their house. All those years it took her to finally confide in Hannah were now being repaid with a total lack of understanding. She wished she'd never said a word. *Sometimes the truth is overrated,* she thought.

She heard Hannah sighing. Gracie stared up at her, tap running and her toothbrush tickling her teeth in a poor effort to clean them. Gina pulled the little girl close to her, not wanting to upset her granddaughter.

'I'm sorry. I shouldn't have said that.' Hannah began to weep. 'It's just… I can't lose you as well. I know I can be a bitch sometimes but don't you ever put me through what happened last time, again. You shouldn't be doing this any more.'

'Are you telling me I should give up my job? I can't do that. You can't expect me to give up everything I love or else what the hell have I got to live for.' Gina gripped the phone as she awaited her daughter's response.

'Now I really know where Gracie and I stand. Say no more, Mother.' Hannah ended the call. The little girl wriggled free and began singing as she played with her toothbrush.

'Bloody hell,' Gina said as she dragged the brush through her tangled hair, and then tied it back. She realised what she'd just said to Hannah and wished she'd kept those thoughts to herself.

'Bloody hell,' Gracie said mimicking her angry expression. Gina smiled through the tears she was holding back and the toddler dabbed toothpaste on her button nose.

'Whatever you do, chicken, don't say that to Mummy, okay? Nanna said naughty words.'

'Bloody hell,' she shouted as she giggled. Gina knew she'd be in more trouble now.

She tied Gracie's hair back. 'There, you look lovely. Let's go and grab your bag and get in Nanna's car.'

'Is Nanna crying?'

'No, chicken. Nanna just has something in her eye. It's nothing.' She wiped the tear running down her face and kissed Gracie on the head. As she turned to the landing, a message from Jacob pinged on her phone.

You need to get here, quick. Things aren't looking good.

She lifted Gracie, grabbed her bag from the bedroom and ran down the stairs and out the door.

CHAPTER THREE

Gina hurried through the hospital reception area, arriving at the Accident and Emergency desk. 'DI Harte. A girl was brought in a short while ago following an incident.' She held up her identification.

The young male receptionist tapped a few buttons on his keyboard. 'Head over to that door. I'll buzz you through.' The room was half filled with people. A woman was comforting a child who was clutching his swollen ankle and a man stood against the wall holding his head while balancing an unlit cigarette in his lips.

The door buzzed. She entered the ward and watched as medical staff busied themselves, pushing mobile monitoring equipment around, taking blood samples from patients in booths and attending to a screaming child with what looked to be a dislocated shoulder. Gina flinched as they pushed the shoulder back in its socket.

'DI Harte. I'm here about the incident,' she said to the nurse at the central desk.

The woman pulled her ponytail tighter and pointed to the far end of the ward. 'Go as far as you can that way, it is the last booth on the left.'

'Thank you.'

As Gina walked through the maze of booths, taking in the sounds of pain and misery, her eyes fixed on the end of the corridor. The curtain was pulled together and a nurse dashed through with a medical trolley. PC Smith sat outside on a chair, reading a paper while scoffing a pastry.

'Coffee?' Jacob asked, coming up behind her. His waxed hair was shaped neatly around his ears and forehead. In the past his hair had always slightly resembled that of an Action Man, but more recently he'd grown a bit more on the top and waxed it with a side parting, making him look a little more sophisticated. She'd also noticed he'd started wearing better fitting suits and tailored shirts. Since he'd become loved-up with Amber, he'd smartened up his act.

She took the machine coffee from him and sipped from the plastic cup. 'I gather we have to just wait for an update.'

'That's about the size of it. They said a doctor would be here soon. I was here when they brought her in. It's not looking good, guv. Here's me hoping we might be able to ask her a few questions but she got worse, and it was quick. Her eyes opened when I arrived and I could tell she wanted to say something, but she couldn't.' Jacob stared at the curtain. The shape of a person's rear protruded through the material.

'Can we deduce anything from the scene?'

'The area where the incident took place was cordoned off before I came and I got word back that Keith has arrived at the scene, ready to check for any forensic evidence. Elimination prints etcetera were taken from the car driver and the ambulance staff. The first officers who arrived at the scene escorted the ambulance to the hospital. Smith took a ride in the ambulance and kept a log.'

'Great.'

'The lad who called the incident in is at the station, waiting to be interviewed.' Jacob swigged his coffee as their gazes wandered to the booth, hoping that a doctor would see them soon.

'So our witness claims that the girl appeared out the back of a van. Serious stuff, if that's the case. Could she have been kidnapped? Had she managed to escape? I mean who just jumps from the back of a van, and in the state she was in?'

'From what I've heard and seen, the poor girl had been suffering for a long time. Maybe she was being transported,' Jacob replied.

'Maybe. But why do that and not lock the van doors? I really hope they hurry up so that we can speak to her.' Gina checked her watch. She'd rushed Gracie home and faced her scowling daughter so that she could wait around in a hospital. She should have known that nothing would happen speedily. Her stomach rumbled as she caught sight of the vending machine. A bar of chocolate would fix a lot but she'd resist. Jacob stared at the messages on his phone, passing time. 'Reading your love notes?'

'Might be.'

'How's things with Amber?'

'Tinder came up trumps when they suggested her. Seriously, things are going really well. The past couple of months have been a dream.'

'I never thought I'd hear you say that. I'm glad you've found someone who makes you happy. Here's to it lasting.' Gina held her coffee cup up and tapped it against Jacob's.

'We're virtually living at mine, we have breakfast together and, oh my goodness, she doesn't whinge at me doing my job. I may well be on to a winner. How's things with you? No secret men on the scene?'

'I never have secret men on the scene. What do you take me for?' Gina was aware he knew there had been someone and he was right. Chris Briggs, their DCI, who had been the source of all her thoughts for months after their brief affair. Ending it had been hard but their friendship had recovered well. There was no way she wanted to put that in jeopardy again and neither of them wanted to risk being transferred from Cleevesford.

A man in glasses and a white coat walked towards them. She finished her drink and threw the cup in the bin. 'Doctor Nowak. We meet again.'

'Detective…'

She could tell he was struggling to remember her name. She'd met him a few months back on a previous case. He'd been working in the maternity ward back then.

'DI Harte, and this is DS Driscoll. We're here about the casualty in that booth. Have you made an assessment yet?'

The doctor brushed down his coat, squinted through his glasses and spoke in his gentle Polish accent. 'In brief, your patient isn't in a good way at all, I'm afraid. We're in the process of inserting a chest tube thoracostomy, or a lung drain, due to fluid on her lungs. It appears she has a severe infection – pneumonia, to be exact. When she arrived we did the initial assessment, we sent her down for an X-ray and soon after we had to sedate her. Her organs are failing, although we'll be able to tell you more in a short while. What is also concerning is the state of her body. There are track marks all up her arms and around her groin area, suggesting long term drug use and that comes with even more problems as I'm sure you're aware. She has a gash to her abdomen, which we've had to attend to. I don't know how she's still alive. She's extremely thin, malnourished. Do you know who she is? We don't even have a name for her.'

'We don't, I'm afraid,' Gina replied. 'I was hoping to ask her.'

'I don't think you'll be asking her anything. The next thing I was going to say was we've just made the decision to place her on a ventilator. The medical team are doing that now. If we don't she won't make it. The chances are slim anyway, even with all that we're doing. She's a very sick girl.'

Gina looked down. She'd rushed over and she wasn't even going to be able to speak with the victim. 'Can we try to talk to her before you carry on?'

'I'm afraid I have to put the welfare of the patient first. No one will be talking to her. She isn't capable of talking, Detective.'

She wiped her brow. The hospital felt stuffy and their main lead had led to nothing. 'Jacob, please give Bernard in forensics a call. Ask him how long he'll be.'

Jacob nodded. 'Will do, guv.' He left along the corridor in search of a phone signal.

'We will need to identify the victim, Doctor. We know she wasn't carrying any identification so a forensics officer will arrive soon. We'll need to take all her clothes and various samples to run through our DNA database.'

'With all due respect—'

'With all due respect, this girl has a family somewhere. Something has happened to her and we need to contact them, so I thank you for your cooperation. It won't be invasive, it will just be a swab or a few hairs.'

The doctor removed his glasses and they dangled loosely on a chain, landing just above his chest. 'Right you are, Detective. I'm going to head back to attend to my patient now.' He turned and walked towards the booth.

'Wait.' Gina followed him and handed her one of her contact cards. 'If her condition changes or if you manage to bring her round – whatever happens, please call me?'

'Will do, Detective.' He continued down the corridor, pulled the curtain aside and entered the booth in which their victim lay.

Smith looked up from his paper and waved. 'I have a stack of paperwork to wade through and drug dealers to investigate. Do you know how long I'll be here?'

Gina shook her head. 'No idea.'

'Not your fault, guv. But let me know when I can leave. I'm slowly sinking in it.' Smith shrugged and continued reading the paper. She knew someone would be there to relieve him soon.

One of the nurses exited the booth and the curtain opened to reveal a young girl lying in the bed with a tube inserted in her mouth. Gina took a few steps forward and took in her features. Straggly dyed red hair, stuck together in tangled clumps, framing her pale face. Dark circles accentuated her sunken eyes, giving her a deathly look. The corners of her mouth were blistered and cracked. Gina looked away, not knowing how someone so thin could still be alive. The skin on her chest stretched over her collarbone, looking like it could easily tear. She could be no more than sixteen years old.

'Bernard's on his way.' Gina flinched and turned to see Jacob behind her.

'Right, let's go and see what our witness has to say. We won't be able to ask the girl a thing so he's all we have to go on at the moment. Let's make it count.'

'Yes, he said her last words were "help her".' We need to find out who *her* is.'

'God help us if there's another poor girl out there being kept in that state.'

CHAPTER FOUR

Elisa wiped the jam from her navy tabard. She wished her uniform had been a bit shapelier. Turning to the side, she checked her reflection in the window. The tabard hung down from her breasts and that's where it stayed, sticking out, making her look like her stomach came out as far as her chest. Then her thin legs stuck out the bottom, from the knee down. She was sure the uniform was meant to fall a little below waist level, but at five feet and half an inch tall, it swamped her. She'd do anything to add a couple of inches of height onto her body so that she didn't always have to look up at friends or get a stepladder out to reach the cereal in the cupboard at home. At least most of the shelves in the shop were within her reach, although she'd been given a wooden box to use as a step, if she needed it.

She screwed the lid on the sample jam after filling up the ramekins. Tipping a few broken crackers onto the plate, she stood, waiting for business. That's what she did all day, waited. There were occasional customers but never a queue. Two weeks she'd been working for the Taste of Nature farm shop while she decided what to do with her life. Her stomach flipped as she thought about her GCSE exams, not sure if she'd really done her best. All those nights spent with her boyfriend Ethan could have been put to better use until the exams were over, but she had no regrets.

She had a plan. As soon as was old enough, she was getting her provisional driver's licence and the money she earned from this job would be spent on driving lessons. No more would her mum have to drop her off or pick her up all the time, like she had that morning.

Elisa grabbed her phone and started to walk out of the shop. Her employers wouldn't notice and it would only be for a couple of minutes. She wanted to enjoy the sunshine and read Ethan's texts. Closing the door gently, she crept around the side of the building and leaned against the wall. As she scrolled away, she laughed. If her mother were to ever see some of the texts, she'd go ballistic. They had been sexually active a while and the texts showed that this had been going on way before her sixteenth birthday.

She fluffed up her hair as she pouted for a selfie. Quick edit, dog ears and cute nose, she'd then message it to Ethan and he'd receive it during his break. As she began to creep back towards the front door, finger on the send button, she glanced up and spotted a car parked at the bottom of the drive, a silver saloon. A customer. She hurried back to the main entrance and brushed her tabard with her hands. She turned around; the car was still there. If it was a customer, he'd pull up into the car park, not pull up on the road that led up to it.

She held a hand across her brow to block out the sun and focused. There was a man sitting in the driver's seat. She trembled and her heartbeat began to quicken as she saw that he was looking right at her. She couldn't make out his features. She held her hand up and smiled, hoping that he'd respond and put her at ease, but he didn't. He remained still. She swallowed and felt sweat prickling under her armpits. She wasn't alone in the shop and that made her feel safe enough. If anything happened, someone from the office would come down and help.

Flinching as the engine was turned on, she grabbed the door handle and watched as the man did a three-point turn along the gravelly road and accelerated away, turning right towards Cleevesford. She exhaled and opened the main door, heart pounding as she almost hit Mrs Hanley in the face with her phone.

'Elisa, it's the third time I've caught you playing with your phone while you've been on duty here. Put the thing away and look like you're ready for customers. If I catch you outside, messing around when you're meant to be working, we may have to review your position here. Go on.' The woman ushered her forward. 'Back behind the counter. The sweets need topping up. Grab some cola cubes from the Welsh dresser.'

'Sorry. It was so quiet. I just wanted some fresh air—'

'You can have all the fresh air you need at five o'clock this evening.'

The woman tottered on her ridiculously high heels and straightened a few jars of jam, before stepping back and admiring her work. As she searched the room for more jobs that might need doing, she adjusted her breasts in her bra and undid the top button of her blouse.

'Mrs Hanley?'

'What now?' The woman checked her reflection in the window, smiled at herself and looked at Elisa.

'While I was out there, I saw a car parked on the driveway up here, a silver car. There was someone in it and the driver was just sitting in his car. I think he was watching me.'

The woman shrugged her shoulders. 'That sounds a little melodramatic. Maybe he'd taken a wrong turn, was making a phone call or having a break from driving.' She pulled a piece of fluff off her shoulder and dropped it to the floor. 'Right, back to it and I want that phone turned off while you're working.'

Back to what? They had no customers. She'd top up the sweets, then what? The woman watched as she held her phone. She quickly pressed send on her message to Ethan and turned the phone off. Mrs Hanley passed her and went upstairs.

Elisa crept along the tiled floor in her flat shoes and stared through the glass door. A shudder flashed across the nape of her neck, making her shiver again. She was sure the man in the car had been watching her. She shook her head, checked back in case Mrs Hanley had crept back down, then she popped one of the loose sweets into her mouth. In hindsight, she wished she had walked a little closer to the car, had a proper look at the man. Her mind replayed the moment she saw the car. He had been looking in her direction. She was sure of that.

CHAPTER FIVE

Gina and Jacob sat opposite the young man. He must have been at least six foot tall and was hunched over, awkwardly playing with the frayed cotton T-shirt they'd given to him when he arrived.

'Is she going to be all right?' he asked. 'I held her, there was nothing else I could do.'

'You did all you could, Toby. She is being cared for at the hospital now. Can you please confirm your full name?' Gina asked.

Jacob gripped the pen, ready to note down any details.

'Toby Benjamin Biddle.'

'Where were you going this morning?' Gina watched as he picked his nail. His slightly greasy dark hair was starting to stick to his acne-scarred forehead. Although he'd washed since his initial examination by the station medical officer, she spotted a fleck of blood to the left of his ear. After speaking to Nick, the desk sergeant, she knew that he'd arrived in a state after trying to stem the blood that had been flowing from the girl's abdomen.

'I had this job to go to. An agency sent me to Rashers Meat Packing Plant on Cleevesford Industrial Estate. I was meant to be having an induction at seven thirty. I haven't even managed to call them yet.'

'We can do that for you.' Gina knew they would be verifying that information anyway.

'Thank you. Although, I doubt they'll want me after not turning up. The only excuse these crap employers accept for not turning up is death.' Toby thought about what he'd just said. 'I'm so sorry. What an idiot, I shouldn't have said that—'

Gina leaned forward. 'Toby, it's fine. You may have saved her life. Please tell me everything you can remember. Start from the beginning.'

'I was just driving, enjoying the quietness of the roads. There's not much in the way of traffic around when you take the scenic route early on a Saturday morning. I wasn't looking forward to arriving at work, I mean, who would look forward to packing meat all day on a day like this?' He wiped the sweat from his brow and took a sip of water. 'All I remember is going around the bend on Laurel Lane and seeing a girl falling out of the back of a van. It happened so quickly, I don't know what more I can add.'

'Describe how she fell out of the van.'

He closed his eyes as if trying to recall what had happened. 'From what I remember, it looked as if she had pushed the door open and was trying to slip out. No, it was more like she was leaning against the door and fell out, I think… oh, I don't know. She wasn't poised to jump. It happened too fast. Sorry, I don't know. All I know is that I literally had to do an emergency stop. I thought I might have hit her but when I checked, I hadn't.'

Gina glanced at her notes. One of the officers had noted that there had been no marks found on the front of Toby's car that were consistent with hitting her. There had been dried mud over the bumper, the bonnet, and indeed most of the car. Not washing his car had shown him to be telling the truth. The dirt had remained undisturbed. She also spotted a further note about his car boot being full of old clothes in bags, and the back seat of his car had been littered with fast food containers mixed with shoes and old bags of books. There had been nothing to suggest the girl had been in his car and, given his collection of clutter, there would have been no room for her.

'What happened then?'

'I was scared. I think I felt sick but wasn't sure what to do. I kept thinking, what if I'd run over her? What would I see? Was she going to be covered in blood on the road? I got out and walked around the front of the car. I hadn't hit her, thankfully. She was just lying there, eyes slightly open. She was trying to say something but it just came out as a murmur.'

'Could you make out anything she was trying to say?' Gina hoped he'd remember something. The girl had been trying to tell him something.

'It sounded like, "help her".'

'Did she say any more, like who she was referring to?'

'No, she started fitting and passed out. The ambulance turned up and took her from there. She didn't try to say anything else. I did notice she was bleeding from her side when I went around to help her. I pulled off my T-shirt and held it to the wound, hoping to stem the flow of blood. That's when I called you guys. I really don't have any more to add. Shit, I can't believe this has happened.' He leaned back on the plastic chair and rubbed his eyes. The emergency T-shirt they'd issued him with rode up, revealing his hairy stomach. It was far too short for his elongated torso.

'Going back to the van. Can you describe it?'

'The van. It was definitely white and it was Transit size. Quite a high roof. I saw some signwriting on the side as it drove away. I couldn't make out what the text said but I could see that the letters were dark green.'

Gina knew that searching for all the owners of large white vans would be a lot of work. They were one of the most common work vehicles on the road. Green signwriting would narrow any suspects down a little bit.

'Anything else about the van?'

'No. I wish I saw more. At the same time I was trying to do an emergency stop and was panicking as I thought I might hit the girl.'

Gina looked up and smiled. 'You've done really well. If you think of anything else later or even tomorrow, give me a call. We may need to speak to you again and we will be keeping your clothes, I'm afraid. Is there anything further you remember?' She passed him a card. His clothing had already been bagged and sent to forensics for analysis.

'No. I can't think of anything. The copper who brought me in, they took my car. What do I do?'

Gina checked her notes. 'We'll explain that to you soon. We've found that you haven't got a valid MOT certificate but, luckily for you, your insurance was still in date. Unfortunately this will be passed to the traffic department. This will be explained to you later.' Gina thought about mentioning the dangers of driving a vehicle that wasn't roadworthy but she could see that he'd been through enough for the day. If the poor girl lived, it would be down to him stopping and administering first aid at the scene. He'd potentially lost his job and he'd had to call his mother to pick him up as his car had been impounded. 'DI Driscoll will keep you a little longer while he completes your witness statement. He'll ask you to sign it, then you can go home. Your mother is in the waiting room.'

The young man exhaled and slumped over the table while he waited. Gina smiled and left the room. Detective Constable Harry O'Connor walked down the corridor. His shiny bald head reflected the strip light above. 'Bakewell tart in the main office, courtesy of Mrs O,' he said as he passed. Her stomach rumbled. She was definitely heading over to get a slice before it all went.

'Before you settle, call Rashers Meat Packing Plant on Cleevesford Industrial Estate. Tell them that we have their most recent recruit here, which is why he didn't turn up for work. Explain that he's been helping us with our enquiries following an incident in the area, this morning. I hope the poor kid doesn't get laid off before he's even started.'

Harry put his thumbs up and continued.

Gina thought about what Toby had said. He described the girl as falling. Was she trying to stay in the van and had she been flung out as it sped around a bend? Was she trying to escape from her captor? She knew it would take a lot for someone to voluntarily jump out of a moving van, especially in her physical state. Had she seized her only opportunity to escape? Questions sped through her mind. She also thought that the van driver must have realised his back door was open and decided not to stop and close it. The van driver had now become their main suspect and she needed to find out who he was.

CHAPTER SIX

'Great,' Gina muttered as she fought to open the jammed window in her office. It was over twenty degrees already and the room felt like a sauna. She slammed her palms into the glass. Another maintenance job to report.

At least the incident room was dry. Spring had been difficult with the mould and mildew spreading up the damp wall, leaving a nasty smell throughout the room and along the corridors. That problem still hadn't been attended to even though she'd reported it on numerous occasions, but the emergence of summer had disguised it, for now. She pushed at the window, but it was still going nowhere. Giving up, she snatched her paperwork and headed along the short corridor, into the main office.

As she grabbed a slice of Bakewell tart, she sat on the desk and placed her paperwork down before devouring what was a late breakfast.

'You're coming to the pub tonight, aren't you, guv?' Detective Constable Paula Wyre called.

'Pub?'

'Nag's Head, after work. A few of us are going. I did mention my birthday earlier in the week. Thought I'd buy you all a drink instead of bringing cake. Cake would be wasted on this place. Tesco can't compete with Mrs O.'

'Oh gosh, yes. Of course I'll be there,' she said.

She began speaking to the team between bites. 'Jacob and I have just this minute finished interviewing a young man called

Toby Biddle in relation to this morning's call. As we know, a young woman tumbled out of a van around seven thirty this morning and she is now in a critical state and in Cleevesford Hospital.' Jacob nodded and took a slice of cake as he listened. He held the plate towards Wyre who shook her head. That woman's willpower was enviable, Gina thought. As always, her perfectly fitted, black trouser suit complemented the poker straight black fringe she'd recently adorned. 'After speaking to Doctor Nowak at the hospital this morning, we've since found out that she may not make it. There is evidence of heavy drug use, track marks on her groin and arms. Her organs were in a failing state. She was also admitted with a bleeding abdomen. To be frank, we've seen some sights and wondered how people survive, well, times that by five and you have this girl. She looked so thin, I have no idea how she managed to stand. Is PC Smith back as yet?'

Smith took his hat off as he entered. 'Got relieved from sentry duty about an hour and half ago. I'm not up to much, I have a list of visits to make and minor incidents to attend to.'

Gina held out her hand, gesturing for him to sit in the empty chair beside Wyre. 'We won't keep you long. Any updates, Wyre?'

'I just checked with the hospital again. She has been placed on a ventilator so won't be good for any talking. Forensics turned up and took samples with Doctor Nowak present.'

'Great, they'll probably already be heading to the lab.' She continued addressing the room. 'The biggest complication we have at the moment is that we can't identify our victim. We have taken a DNA sample in the hope that her DNA may be on our database. If it isn't, we start with the basics. Research runaways, people reported missing, you know the drill.' She glanced at her phone to see if she'd received a missed call from Bernard, wanting to catch up on his preliminary findings at the hospital. She hadn't missed a thing. It was way past lunchtime and a call was imminent.

'What did the interview with Toby Biddle give us?' Wyre asked as she turned over a new page in her pad.

'Keith confirmed that Biddle's car had not touched the girl. She hadn't landed on it nor had she been hit by it. His car was so full of his own rubbish she can't have come from it either. Biddle stated that she fell from a white van as he went round a corner on Laurel Lane. The way he described the incident, I'd say one of the back doors was open, she lost her balance and flew out of the door, falling onto the ground. We don't know for definite whether she jumped on purpose to escape the van or she accidentally slipped out. We need to know how she got in the van, what she was doing in the van and why she was so emaciated. We need the van driver found. It was described as a white Transit size van with dark green signwriting.'

'What did the sign say?' O'Connor asked as he leaned back in his chair, chewing the cake in his mouth. Gina looked at the last bit of cake between her fingers and placed it on the table. The sound of O'Connor's chewing had ruined any enjoyment of the sugary treat. Of all the things that could have ruined her eating experience – it could have been the way the girl had looked, the thoughts that were running through Gina's mind on what the girl may have been through, or the look on her daughter's face when she passed Gracie over to her that morning, but no, it was O'Connor's mastication that had ruined her enjoyment of the Bakewell tart.

'Toby Biddle couldn't read any of the words on the van. I don't think he had the chance while he was performing an emergency stop. Everything happened too fast for him. He said the lettering was dark green. Unfortunately that's all we have to go on at the moment.'

'So, a large white van with dark green signwriting.' O'Connor wrote a few notes down. 'Shall I look into this, start to at least form a list of vans like this in the area?'

'Yes, please,' Gina replied.

'Toby said he thought he heard her saying, "help her", suggesting that there is another girl somewhere. This is a worry and it's why we need to get on to this with all we have.'

'Guv, I have to get going,' Smith said as he stood.

'Sorry. I know you're really busy and I didn't mean to hold you up. I want you to keep your eyes and ears open. The girl in the hospital is a very serious user and covered in syringe marks. She or her captor was getting the stuff from somewhere. It's important that we work closely with uniform on this one and I'd like you to report back to me on anything that might be relevant because, as yet, we haven't even identified her.'

'I will, guv. Catch you later.' He grabbed his hat and hurried away.

She spotted Briggs watching from the back of the room. He must have entered while she was speaking.

DCI Chris Briggs had kept a friendly distance since their break up. Remaining on good terms had started off easy, but an awkwardness had developed between them lately, or maybe it was just her. Being around him still led her mind back to their brief but passionate relationship.

Gina cleared her throat. 'We need to put out a press statement for anyone who saw a large white van with dark green signwriting travelling along Laurel Lane this morning. The incident occurred between seven fifteen and seven thirty.'

Briggs placed a hand on the door frame. 'I'll liaise with Annie in Corporate Communications to get that done ASAP. For this case, Harte, you'll be Senior Investigating Officer but make sure you report to me daily with progress reports. I want to know what's happening and when, and I'll also deal with the media. Keep me updated.'

'Will do, sir,' she replied. SIO again, she was relishing the thought. The pressure was immense but, once again, being in control of the investigation and the path it took, along with controlling the budgets, was everything she'd worked so hard for over the years. She smiled at him and he returned her smile. The other detectives began to speak to one another, comparing notes and talking about what happens next. Briggs turned and left the room, leaving her there with her thoughts.

Smith darted in, car keys in hand, ready to dash out. 'Is this cake for anyone? I'm starving.'

Gina nodded. 'Of course.'

'Great.' Crumbs flew from his mouth as he continued to speak and eat. 'Right, I'm off to Cleevesford Chippy.'

Gina scooped her paperwork up and stood. 'I don't know! Cake followed by fish and chips at lunchtime, and a pastry for breakfast. Sounds like a recipe for diabetes.'

'I'm not pigging out, guv.'

'It wouldn't be any of my business though and I'm a fine one to talk. I live on takeaways at the moment. Ignore me, I'm pulling your leg, Smith.'

He gave her a knowing look and let out a little laugh. 'I was actually responding to a call. Apparently, the owner and staff have seen what they believe to be drug deals going on in the bus stop opposite the chippy. We'll be keeping our eye on that.'

'Sounds like you have a lot on.'

'It makes the day go fast. See you later.'

'Remember, keep me updated,' she called, but he'd already left the room.

Gina's phone began to buzz in her pocket. She snatched it and placed it against her ear while Keith spoke. She hoped forensics had come up with something. When he finished she ended the call. The room went silent as everyone stopped what they were doing, to hear what Gina was bursting to say. 'You won't believe what Keith has discovered on the girl. Bernard is sending the reports through. We need to find the van driver and bring him in, now.'

CHAPTER SEVEN

Gina checked her messages as she walked back towards the incident room, mulling over the information Bernard had sent over.

Hannah hadn't tried to contact her at all during the day, she doubted she would after the words they'd had. The morning seemed like a lifetime ago but the disappointment etched on Hannah and Gracie's faces stayed with her. When she had handed the toddler over, the little girl's bottom lip had quivered.

She placed her phone in her pocket; there was no use stalling and delaying the inevitable. The morning's events couldn't be dwelled upon any longer. She felt a sense of relief that the case had ended any thoughts of leaving early to go to the pub to celebrate Paula Wyre's birthday. She hadn't really wanted to go and sit alongside Briggs in a social setting. He'd known things about her that the others didn't. She could have almost kicked herself for telling him what Terry had subjected her too, but he had been a good listener.

Over the past few weeks, the counselling she'd been attending had dragged so much up, muddying her thoughts. She was relieved the sessions had ended, that she had said all the right things at the end, convincing the counsellor she was fine. Her relationships and her fears over the attacks were all they'd concentrated on. She closed her eyes and thought back to one of the sessions.

She swallowed and began to tremble as the last case, in which she'd nearly been killed, played out in her mind. Her daughter was right. A man had tried to throttle her in her own home and she'd stared death in the face. Every time she sat working in that damn kitchen, she was transported back to that night. Then there was Terry, her abusive ex-husband. She'd revealed the depth of his violence towards her to Briggs, the counsellor and her daughter, but the deepest darkest secret remained within the confines of her mind. It didn't matter how violent he'd been. The only thing that truly mattered was that she'd delivered the death shove from the top of those stairs. That she hadn't called the ambulance until he had no pulse. There was a lot she had to be guilty about, but not now. She needed to find the van driver and act as though all was okay in her life.

She wished she had someone to confide in, someone to tell all her deepest secrets to, but people didn't keep secrets. Secrets never remained secrets forever. A shiver ran up her spine even though the corridor was stuffy.

As she entered the incident room, she straightened up her top and smiled. 'Happy birthday, Paula. I know this isn't the night you had planned—'

'Don't mention it, guv. This is what I signed up for.'

'Guv.' Jacob nodded. Briggs seemed to be laughing about something with O'Connor at the opposite side of the room. She remembered when they laughed in that way but they hadn't gone out much, always trying to hide their relationship. She remembered when he bought the suit he was wearing. He'd taken it out of the suit bag, stripped down to his underpants in his kitchen and tried it on, parading back and forth, asking what she thought. They'd laughed so much back then. But the past was the past.

Awkwardly, she stood in front of the incident board and cleared her throat. Briggs sat in the seat closest to her. A slight breeze travelled through the window, catching his hair, gently ruffling it. The smell of his aftershave entered her nostrils as she turned. Enjoying the moment, she inhaled further. She wondered if thoughts of her were going through his mind. If they were, he wasn't giving anything away. Then again, neither was she. Her heart skipped a beat. Maybe the memories she'd had of Briggs were nothing more than a leftover feeling she was simply meant to enjoy.

'Oh, happy twenty-first all over again,' O'Connor said to Wyre.

'Hey.' Wyre tapped O'Connor on the shoulder. 'I'm only a very young thirty-two. It's still spring in my world.' She stopped speaking for a moment and looked away. 'Down to business, I suppose?'

Gina nodded, poured a glass of water from the jug on the main table and took a sip. 'Right, we have the gorgeous little road that is Laurel Lane, lined with beautiful hedges and foxgloves.' She pointed to the location on the wall map. 'On an equally gorgeous day, a girl falls from the back of a van and she's almost dead. What's even odder is that Bernard has confirmed all her fingerprints have been burned off. Someone doesn't want us to identify her, but who?' Gina pondered over that thought. 'That's going to haunt me tonight. Or just maybe, she doesn't want to be identified.'

'Chris,' called a piercing voice from across the room.

Gina turned to see Annie waving at Briggs, her blonde locks shining like she'd just stepped out of a shampoo advert. Annie of Corporate Communications seemed quite fond of him lately and she wondered if Briggs thought as fondly of her.

'I thought Annie should be here. The press may want some information at some point and it's important we come up with a plan. Annie and I will be working through that one,' Briggs said as he pulled out a chair for Annie to sit next to him. He glanced up and smiled at Gina. Was he playing with her? Their break up was still recent and he seemed a little close to Annie.

'I won't keep you long.' Gina grabbed her phone and scrolled on Facebook. 'Just to update you all, the press have published a short article online and on their social media, releasing information about the van that we are looking for. A local community group called "What's Up Cleevesford" shared their post for all the Cleevesford community to see. People have been tagged in the post – people with white vans. Those who tagged made smutty comments about their friends, jokingly accusing them of all sorts. I've noted the names of the people that had been tagged so far. O'Connor, can you follow up on them?'

'Yes, guv.'

'You all have leads to follow up on. Are we all clear on what we're doing next?'

Everyone replied before beginning to discuss the missing fingerprints on the girl. Everyone pooling thoughts and ideas. Gina began to update the boards then glanced back, watching as Briggs and Annie spoke. They looked so cosy together.

Gina felt a flush of heat travelling through her body and a wash of nausea followed. She didn't want to be there, she wanted to go home. Her hands trembled as she gripped the pen and a palpitation ripped through her chest. *Find a reason to leave. Gracie is sick and Hannah needs to go to work. I forgot to feed the cat. I left my door unlocked.* The excuses sounded pathetic but she had to choose one and make it quick. She needed to get out before she embarrassed herself. 'I have to go. I think I left my door unlocked. I just wanted to go through what we have. Wyre, when you're finished up here, go forth and enjoy your birthday celebrations. I'm going to work from home. If you need me, just call.' She grabbed her bag, forced a smile and left.

'See you tomorrow, guv,' Jacob called.

She waved back as she walked away. At least her swift exit had got her out of going to the pub with everyone. She couldn't do it. She didn't want to be sociable, sitting in some pub watching Annie and Briggs flirt all evening. She wanted to go home, sit with her cat and watch reactions to the press release and that's exactly what she was going to do.

CHAPTER EIGHT

Sunday, 15 July 2018

The bed felt soft and Miley enjoyed the sinking feeling as she lay on her side, falling further and further into the mattress, and into the next phase of the most lucid dream she'd ever had. Was she at Stacey's house? She hoped so. Stacey's bed was lovely and she could never resist lying on it whenever they sat in her bedroom. Any minute now, she expected Stacey's dog, Jitterbug, to come and lick her face.

She giggled as she chose the next dream scenario. She and Stacey had skipped history, as it was so boring and they both hated Mondays. Mr Simpkin never failed to send them all to sleep with his droning voice and his talks of old stuff that would never be relevant to her life. She vaguely remembered something about some battle of roses. Something to do with Lancashire. He'd shown the class pictures of stuffy old kings dressed in silly clothes, similar to the clothes they'd used in their last pantomime at school. But instead of being there, being bored to tears, she was hiding out with Stacey in Stacey's bedroom, while her parents were at work.

Later that afternoon they had a careers talk to get through at school. Jobs and future career expectations, those subjects always started a row at home. Her mother had quizzed her about jobs and the future. The main thing she knew was, after the last exam, she was never going back to school. She didn't know what she wanted to do but she liked looking after animals. Her mum was no help though, wouldn't even let her have a cat. That was it, her dream had been realised. She wanted to care for animals. Biology was her subject and she was set to get a B. She'd try and scrape a C in maths and English too. That might just help her get an apprenticeship with a local veterinary surgery or pet shop.

She struggled with the sheet as she turned onto her side, dragging the material with her. The pillow was so soft and she badly wanted to enter a deep sleep phase, but her mind was racing. Giggling, she ran her fingers over the material, untangling the soft blankets. 'Stacey,' she called. They had to get back to class before English. If the school rang home, her mum would freak. Even worse than that, her mum's boyfriend would go on and on until she stormed out. The arguments only got uglier. Insults would be hurled back and forth, but she'd give as good as she got. Who was he to dictate anything? He was not her father and he'd moved into her mother's house – her house – coming between them and then always going on at her. Nothing she ever did was good enough for him and he made her know that. Her house felt like a strange place in which she did not belong. 'Can I stay at yours tonight, Stacey? Stacey, don't ignore me.' She laughed again. No doubt Stacey was standing above her pulling a ridiculous face. As soon as she opened her eyes, she'd see.

'Don't you stare at me, Stacey. I can feel your presence. I'm opening my eyes after three. One, two, three.'

She opened her eyes and there was no one around. It had felt like she was at Stacey's house. Her muscles tingled, so relaxed she couldn't move. It was almost as if she was ascending from the bed, so high and floaty, like she was going to fly out of the window and reach for the skies. The room was tinged with a fuzziness, almost making it look pretty as the morning light shone through the window. Golden rays blending with coppery shades caught her eye and bathed the back wall with their colour. She must have overslept. Stacey was nowhere to be seen. She must be at home. Maybe they hadn't bunked off history.

She rubbed her eyes, trying to shift the cloudiness. 'Mum.' Why hadn't her mum woken her up? She normally did. Maybe she was late for school, or was it Saturday? Who cares? She laughed as she turned on her pillow and laid her cheek on what felt like a wet patch. She'd been dribbling in bed again. That dream of skiving off school and hanging out with Stacey was just that, a dream.

Slowly, the power of small movement returned to her body, starting with a tingle in her wrists, reaching her arms and legs. Then the knowledge of where she was dawned on her. She had duties to fulfil. She rolled off the bed and fell to the floor. 'Take it slowly, Miley.' It would take a while for her muscles to work and her memory to defog. That dream had been the best ever and she wanted more. She missed Stacey but life goes on. One day she would go home, savings in hand, ready to rent a place of her own.

As she sat up, her head sunk and it felt like the room was gently rotating. Maybe she wouldn't get much work done yet. Flopping back down on the creaky bedframe, she stared at the brown patch on the ceiling and wiped a tear from the corner of her eye. The beauty in the coppery tones she saw only a few minutes ago was long gone. There was no use crying. She was now a grown-up in a grown-up world and she wouldn't go home until she'd proven herself.

She remembered back to the last time she saw her mother. The expression on her face had been furious when Miley had told her she was being a cow for not letting her go to Stacey's party. With her mother's boyfriend beside her drunken mother – the united front they called it – they blocked her entry to the door, trapping her at the bottom of the stairs. She didn't like him but everything she'd done to try and make him leave had backfired.

He'd had words with her, words he had no right to have. It was her house and he'd pushed her out. It wasn't like when she had her mum all to herself. With her mum, she'd always got what she wanted and that had ended when he came on the scene. That was the moment she promised herself, they were never taking her freedom. A tear slipped down her cheek as she yearned for the mother she once had and a relationship she grieved over. Her mother had stresses, maybe Miley should've been a bit more understanding. Her stomach began to turn as she rolled off the bed. Work beckoned.

Her heartbeat sped as she heard the boss enter the next room. She placed her ear against the wall and listened to his murmurings. She normally heard him coming up the stairs but this time, he must have crept up. 'I can't believe she's left you like this. I am so sorry. Will you ever forgive me? Please hold me, like this, like you used to hold me.' The room went silent and a few seconds passed. The man let out a pained scream as he slammed the door and roared. As he passed Miley's bedroom, he banged loudly. She crawled along the floor and placed her back against the wall in the corner of the room, hoping she'd sink into it and wake up in Stacey's bedroom finding that this was all a dream. 'I hate you, I hate you so much!' He slammed into her door. She held her breath and placed her hands over her ears, hoping that he'd leave her alone.

'Please don't hurt me,' she whispered as tears began to slide down her face. 'I'm doing my best, it's just… it's not easy. I'll try harder.' Soon she'd be out. Just a little while longer. Get the money and leave. Save enough to put a deposit on a room, that's all she needed.

CHAPTER NINE

Gina arrived at the station as the sun was breaking. Silence echoed through the corridor leading to the incident room. After waking every hour during the night and lying awake, overthinking everything that had occurred with Hannah and then with Briggs, she needed work and it needed her.

'Morning, guv,' Smith said as he walked through, heading in the direction of the main desk.

'Morning.' Gina began to pin one of the photos that Bernard had emailed through on the board. She gazed at the girl's face still remembering her shocking state. She stuck the photo of her burned off fingerprints underneath and continued sticking the others around it, showing the marks on her body, the wound on her side.

'You dashed off quickly last night,' Wyre said as she placed her bag on a desk.

'As I said, I forgot to feed my cat.'

'I thought you said you forgot to lock your door.' Wyre pulled a few longer strands of her fringe aside and tucked them behind her ears. She leaned forward, almost holding her hand in Gina's direction.

'Ooh, did I say that?' Gina turned back to the board.

Wyre nodded. 'It's okay. You don't have to explain yourself.'

'I feel rotten now. I'm really sorry, with it being your birthday and all. I'd had a bit of an argument with my daughter.' Last time Gina had really let her hair down with the team she'd ended up drinking too much and sleeping with Briggs. That wasn't going to happen again, ever. Not that it would have happened last night with Annie sniffing around him.

Wyre removed her jacket and placed it over the back of the chair. 'Don't worry about it. I know how these things can play on the mind. One row with my dad and I'm fit for sod all for the rest of the day. We left soon after and popped to the Nag's Head for one. Briggs and Annie stayed on. I think she has a bit of a thing for him, it's quite sweet really.' Gina scratched her brow, hoping to hide her expression. 'Jacob had to meet Amber, so I called it a night. It wasn't going to be a long one anyway as I had to get home. George had a surprise waiting for me.' Wyre placed her hand on the table face down as Gina turned again, continuing to make brief notes on the board. Wyre sighed. 'For a senior detective, you do miss a lot.'

Gina turned, gave Wyre a puzzled look and then stared back at the board. 'Can you see something I can't?'

Wyre held her left hand up and Gina smiled. How had she missed the shiny diamond that fit her slim finger so perfectly? 'You and George?'

'No, me and the dog.'

'You've got a dog?'

'No, I was just… It doesn't matter. George asked me to marry him and I said yes! I know it hasn't been too long but we're having a really long engagement. I really love him and that's not something I thought I'd ever say about anyone.'

'I'm so happy for you both.' Gina smiled as her phone buzzed. It was a message from Briggs.

Can you pop through to my office?

'If anyone wants me, I'm in Briggs's office. You can tell me all about it in a bit.'

Wyre took the rest of the photos and continued where Gina had left off.

She hurried along the corridor until she reached Briggs's office. The door was closed. After gently tapping, she stepped back and waited.

'Come in.' As she opened the door, he finished typing. 'Right, that's that done. Any updates on the new appeal?' he asked.

'Not as yet. There has been a high volume of calls, mostly everyone and anyone who knows someone with a large white van.' She felt the familiar prickling climbing across her chest. It wouldn't be long before Briggs would catch her reddening.

'The call team have emailed me the first list. Just printing it now.' She heard his printer chugging into action. 'It's a shame you didn't come for that drink last night. Annie and I headed off to Stratford to get some food. How are you holding up, with things?'

'Good… really, everything's fine. I just had to get back. I thought I'd left my back door unlocked.' That lie again. Was he going to catch her out this time?

'I thought you had that all dancing and singing security system installed since the last incident?'

He was correct. She could have just looked on her phone to see the camera images of her house at any time that evening, but she had chosen to leave. Then again, it was a lie.

'I'm worried about you, Harte. You seem a bit distant.'

'I'm fine, sir. Really.'

'It's not what happened with us, I mean, it's all in the past. I get that, totally. We're friends, have been for years and I'm moving on. You'd tell me if something was bothering you? We're still friends.'

Nothing was bothering her. She had a past like everyone else. Why could everyone see a version of her that she could not herself see? She was fine. It had been a bad few months. She'd had counselling. She'd opened up about her fears and her past.

'I'm sorry if I gave you that impression, I really am fine, and I wish you'd stop asking.'

'Sorry. I'm always here, remember that,' he said as he stood and walked over to her. She took a step back, placing some distance between them. She knew his game, getting close to Annie, flaunting it, all to make her jealous.

'I can look after myself.'

He reached over, grabbed the reports and passed them to her. 'Here you go. I hope you find the answer in there.' He returned to his chair and scrolled on his computer mouse. 'Any news back from the lab yet?'

'No, sir. Nothing. As it stands, this is all we have. This and any potential CCTV. O'Connor is following up on all the van leads and Wyre will continue looking for any CCTV showing a white van in the area.'

He began typing again. 'I best let you get on with it then.'

She closed his door as she left, thinking about what Briggs had just said. She'd gripped the reports so hard they were screwed up in her hands. She flinched. O'Connor's voice bellowed through the corridor as she entered the incident room. 'Wow, congratulations,' he said to Wyre.

Gina flattened out the reports as well as she could and passed him the huge list of white vans to follow up on. She then pulled her own list from her bag. She'd written down as many details as she could of anyone commenting on the Facebook post about the van. Dropping them on a desk, she looked up and smiled. 'Sorry. I know this isn't exciting but you're so good at it. Wyre, keep looking for CCTV within the area. Someone must have something. Maybe some of the residents along Laurel Lane have CCTV.' Wyre nodded. Gina pulled out her phone and called Bernard. She needed to buck up and get on with all her tasks. 'Any news?'

CHAPTER TEN

Julia snatched the poster from the lamp post. It had only been up a week and already someone had defaced the picture of her little girl. 'Bastards,' she yelled as she pulled a fresh poster from her satchel and taped it around the post. She almost lost her balance as the breeze dropped, making the afternoon heat overpowering. The rain mac she'd chosen to wear was her biggest regret, making her sweat profusely, but then again, had it poured down like the weather forecasters had promised, she'd have been happy to have it. She dropped the satchel to the floor and peeled the plastic from her sticky arms before folding the mac and placing it in her bag. She continued to the next post.

Roy's words ran through her mind. 'She'll be back. It's just a teenage protest thing but you were right to not let her walk all over you. She'll come home when she's finished sulking.' She didn't believe him though. Her daughter hadn't even made contact once and three months went way beyond a sulk. She dropped the pile of posters from her trembling hands. A light breeze began to whip through her hair. As she gathered them up, a few of them landed in the river before being carried away downstream, alongside a couple of swans and several cygnets.

'No.' She kicked the bench before almost stumbling on it. All it would take was a phone call. Why hadn't Christina called? Maybe she was in trouble or was she administering the cruellest punishment ever? Wiping the sweat from her forehead she checked her phone. Another day would pass without so much of a word from her daughter.

It was obvious Christina had left voluntarily and they had been arguing a lot. Her suitcase was gone. Her toiletries had been taken. All that was left were gaps in her drawers where all her favourite jeans and tops had been. Her saver account at the post office had been emptied, evident by the paying in book showing the withdrawal in the bedside table drawer. She'd tried to call her daughter but the calls had been rejected. With only three hundred pounds to her name, her daughter can't have got far. She trembled. How far could she have got? She could get the train to anywhere in the UK with that much money. But then what if she'd run out of money and hitchhiked? Some drug-dealing pimp could have got his filthy hands on her. Every possible scenario seemed to run through Julia's mind.

The posters wouldn't distribute themselves. She began walking back towards the city centre. The cathedral stood tall to her right as she continued checking that all the posters she'd put up were still there and easy to see. They were. Taking a right, she spotted Roy sitting on a wall reading a newspaper while drinking a takeaway coffee. 'Have you put all those posters up, already?' She still had loads to do. She planned to hang posters by the river, he was meant to be doing the streets through the city centre.

'I was taking a break.'

She grabbed his bag and pulled out the posters. 'You haven't done any, have you?'

'Look, I just wanted a coffee. When I finish, I'll go and do the posters.'

'You don't care if she comes back, do you?'

He placed his coffee on the paper to weigh it down and stood. 'Of course I do, darling.' He put his sunglasses on and went to kiss her.

'Don't you darling me. If you cared, you'd be sticking posters to boards, walls and lamp posts. Instead, you sit here, reading crap and drinking coffee.' She glanced down. He'd been reading the sports pages, some news about the World Cup over the past few weeks. 'You never did care when she left.'

'That's not true.'

'Isn't it?' She watched as his thin reddish hair blew in the warm breeze. She couldn't see his reaction with his sunglasses covering his eyes. As she waited for him to answer, only the tangled hair covering her face reflected back at her in his mirror-finished glasses.

Her once chestnut-brown glossy hair that she'd always tied up was left free around her face. She hadn't washed it for days. She'd tried to act normally but it hadn't been easy when all she could think about was Christina.

'We need to move on because doing this, every weekend, is driving you mad. She'll come back when she's ready. She was pissed off when she left, you saw her the day before. Give her time.'

'Give her time! You've never been a parent. If you had, you wouldn't be standing there like a prick telling me to give her time. My daughter has been missing for months and I will not, just, give it time. I'm looking for her and I'll find her.' A woman with three young children crossed the road to get away from her raised voice. 'Hey.' The woman glanced back at Julia. 'If one of your three little girls ran away from home, would you sit back, do nothing and give it time? That's what this idiot here is telling me to do. You'd do everything you could. You'd be out there day and night, looking for her, wouldn't you?' The youngest girl, who can't have been more than seven, began to cry.

'It's okay, sweetie. The lady's just upset.' The woman gave the little girl a hug. Julia almost wanted to cry as the youngest girl stared at her. She looked so much like Christina when she'd been that age. She even had a similar lemon-coloured dress and chubby knees.

'You'd be out there every day…' Julia felt a tear slip down her cheek.

'I'm sorry. You're upsetting my children,' the woman called back as she grabbed the child's hand and hurried away.

'Now look what you've done. That poor woman was trying to cross the road in peace. This obsession has to stop. Christina chose to leave. She will come back when she's ready.'

'She wouldn't punish me like this.'

'Wouldn't she? You saw the way she changed, the way she was with both of us.'

He was wrong. The more she looked at him, the more she could see he had his own agenda. He never liked Christina and he was probably glad she'd gone. 'Christina was angry but she wouldn't go anywhere for this long. None of her friends have heard from her. The police are doing sod all. Appeals have come up with nothing. All she has is me. I don't care if you want to sit here, wasting time drinking coffee and reading your shit. I will never stop looking for my daughter. That's what being a mother means.' She snatched the rest of the posters and continued into the town.

'Julia? Bloody hell.' As she turned she noticed him, paper in hand, striding towards the car park. She'd get the bus home at her leisure, when she'd finished putting posters up.

A car horn buzzed as she stepped out. 'Get out the road,' a man shouted. Her heart pounded. If she'd been walking a little bit quicker, she'd have been knocked over. Holding her hand up, she continued crossing and headed towards the library.

The new building stood out like a honey themed beacon. The Hive was built with golden coloured tiles, making it look like a large beehive. That's where she'd start. With the city centre posters in her firm grip, she jogged towards the main entrance. She would find Christina. As she swallowed, she almost choked. The possibility that Christina would never come home hadn't crossed her mind. For a second it did, sending her legs into a wobble and almost collapsing beneath her. Tears began to flood her face. Never seeing her daughter again was too much to handle. She fell to the floor, gripping the posters as people passed with their shopping bags, not one of them stopping to ask if she was all right. Now she knew what true loneliness felt like.

CHAPTER ELEVEN

Heading back to the living room, Gina closed her curtains and sat on the floor in front of her computer as she finished eating a small wedge of cheese. It had been a long day. Ebony, her little black cat, meowed for attention. 'Not now. Some of us have work to do.' She pushed the cat from her lap and continued looking over the case notes and photos. The young girl's sunken closed eyes stared back at her, taking her back to a moment she'd rather forget. Hannah's fourteenth birthday which had been a chilly October evening. She ran her fingers through her matted hair as she ruminated over her argument with Hannah.

Back then, Hannah had said she was only going to the cinema with friends. When she hadn't returned by ten in the evening and wouldn't answer her phone, Gina had been pacing the floor, calling all her friends' parents to no avail. She'd spent the next two hours searching the streets in Birmingham City Centre, around by the Electric Cinema and along Station Street. She'd frantically run back and forth, taking in the faces of all who passed by. People shouted noisily as they headed towards clubs and fell out of pubs. Little pockets of homeless people gathered in doorways, begging for spare change. Gina pulled her attention back to the computer screen and zoomed in on a photo of the girl's face. Her eyes were drawn to her teeth. Yellow and furred, like they hadn't been brushed in a long time. A few strands of straggly hair stuck to her cheek. She flinched. Some mother out there had a daughter who sadly wasn't coming home.

Hannah had eventually came home that night. Her teenage girl had looked childlike as she tried to creep through the door, smelling of cider.

'I've pounded the streets tonight, looking for you. Do you know how scared and worried I was?'

Hannah giggled as she tripped up the first step, trying to escape to her room. 'Mum, just chill out. I've been enjoying myself with friends. It's my birthday,' she slurred.

'It may be your birthday but what you put me through, I've been beside myself all night. Anything could've happened—'

'But it didn't. I'm all good. I bet Dad wouldn't have moaned so much if he were here—'

'How dare you!' Everything Gina had been through and protected Hannah from had now been thrown in her face, and not for the first time. Gina had been doing her best to make sure that her daughter didn't end up with a man like her dad.

'Whatever, I bet he would've been a cool dad. He might have even had a birthday drink with me, not like you.'

'Ouch,' Gina whispered. She was certain that Terry would have had a birthday drink with his child daughter; that was the problem. 'Time for bed.' Gina kept close behind her, slowly steering her up the stairs until they finally reached the landing. 'Come on. We'll talk about this in the morning.'

'I want to talk about it now,' Hannah said as she held onto the handrail at the top of the stairs, swaying. As she lost her footing, images of Terry's body falling backwards from the top step flashed through Gina's mind. Her heart began to pound as she gasped for air and gripped her daughter's arm. There were things that Hannah would never know.

'I won't let you go,' she yelled as she gripped the girl. 'I would never let you go.'

As Hannah found her footing, Gina realised she was still gripping her arm. 'Fuck off, that hurts. Let me go.'

'What did you say to me?'

Hannah hiccupped and the colour drained from her face. Gina pushed her daughter towards the bathroom and listened as she retched. 'Happy birthday,' she whispered as the bathroom door slammed with a force that almost shook the top floor.

The computer screen had gone black but the picture of the girl in the hospital was still etched in her mind. Gina shifted the mouse, bringing the image back up. The girl was a little older than Hannah had been but not by much. Had she left home to be with friends and not returned that night? Maybe her mother had been pacing the floor, then the streets, looking for her missing daughter. Maybe she'd run away from something or she may have met someone she knew, someone she trusted. What had happened after?

She checked her phone. There was a message from Wyre.

We have the van on CCTV. White Transit with green lettering.

Gina finished the last of the cheese as she powered her laptop down. At last they had a lead.

CHAPTER TWELVE

Monday 16 July 2018

Her bones ached, especially her legs. Miley grabbed the bucket of soapy water and lugged it from the bathroom to Jackie's room. Where Jackie would be was always a mystery. On the floor, in bed, facing the wall, trying to clumsily pace until she tripped over, remaining on the floor, waiting to be helped up. Miley was meant to change the bed sheets but Jackie hadn't stepped out of the bed at all the day before and lifting the woman when she didn't want to be lifted was near impossible. She unlocked the door by sliding the lock, then she pushed it open, dragging the bucket behind her, water slopping over the edges.

'Morning, Jackie. How did you sleep?' The woman repeated the same incoherent words over and over while sitting on the edge of the bed. Miley opened the orange and yellow drapes, allowing some sunshine into the room. She held her arm across her face to shield the odour from entering her nostrils, being careful as she stepped across the uneven wooden floor. The room was in a state, no wonder her boss had been angry the previous night. 'Right, let's get you washed and dressed.'

Sweat beads began to form across Miley's brow as she lifted the woman's soiled nightdress over her head and pulled down her padded underwear. While trying to control her own light tremor, she bathed the woman with the warm soapy water, making sure she worked through the creases around the woman's stomach area. Her lower abdomen lay like a deflated balloon over her thighs, like she had once been a lot larger, but had lost the weight. Now, she was simply bones with a lot of skin.

The world seemed to tilt and Miley's mouth felt dry. She stopped and stared out of the window ahead, leaving the woman naked and damp, covered in soap, muttering to herself.

Caring for people hadn't been Miley's first option when it came to a career but it was money in the savings pot. By her calculations, soon she would have enough to start the life she really wanted to live. She leaned on the wall and closed her eyes. Where was her medicine? She held her hand to her brow. She needed her medicine and she needed it now. Her underarms were damp. Clammy and hot. Well, it was summer. Maybe it was because it was a scorching day and the windows were closed. Waves of nausea passed through her and blood began to pump around her body, filling her ears with a drumming noise. The beating quickened. *Take a deep breath.*

She inhaled and counted to three and filled her mind with pleasant thoughts of her past. In her mind, she was with one of her best friends, Stacey, outside the newsagent's. Stacey asked her to go in and buy twenty Bensons for them to smoke in the park. She smiled as she remembered their joy when she'd been served. Wearing one of her mum's jumpers over her school shirt had done the trick. They ran all the way to the park, hiding under the little wooden house that had been built under the slide. That was their mischief den. Miley had written in Sharpie that she loved Freddie. At the time she thought she and Freddie would be together forever. Writing it in a permanent marker seemed like the best thing to do. When they were old and married, they'd bring their grandchildren to see the graffiti. Stacey giggled when she wrote that she'd only ever love Jitterbug, her Labradoodle. They'd both been in stitches as they lit up.

But that was then. She began to weep as she thought back to all those uncomplicated times.

Deep breath in, slow breath out, back to the present. The nausea had subsided. Her stomach groaned and grumbled as she grabbed a towel and began to dry Jackie. As she lifted the woman's breast, she almost heaved with the smell. The flesh looked infected. She'd report her findings later when the boss came home. Jackie clamped her breast down as she continued to murmur nothings. 'Jackie, just let me help you. I need to clean the wound.'

The woman brought her stick thin arm down and caught Miley across the face, catching one of her spots. She felt a wet trickle fall down her cheek and wiped it away, leaving a red streak across the back of her hand. Caring was hard, one of the hardest things she'd ever done in her life, but it was a grown-up thing to do, and she was a grown-up. She'd prove it. 'I know you didn't mean to hurt me, Jackie.' She tried again. This time the woman allowed her to wipe away the pus. Miley almost gagged as she lowered her breast, grabbed a fresh nightdress from her top drawer and began redressing her.

'That's better. We'll do your hair and make you all lovely,' Miley said as she brushed Jackie's thin greying strands behind her ears. For a moment, Jackie looked back, her eyes red as if she might cry. She slapped her liver-spotted hand over Miley's. Miley wasn't sure if she'd meant to do that as a gesture of affection or if it was another one of Jackie's random acts. She placed her hand over Jackie's. The woman went back to staring at the window, making her incoherent noise.

The woman kept murmuring as she gripped Miley. The bed dampened underneath them. Miley hadn't replaced her incontinence pants and now the bed was wet. She jumped up before the wetness soaked through her leggings.

'Jackie. Damn it!' The woman rocked back and forth and waved her arms about. Miley kneeled in front of her. 'I'm sorry.'

The woman looked away. Jackie didn't mean anything. The grip of her hand had just been random. She wished that, only for a minute, Jackie would acknowledge who she was. They could be friends. They were friends but they never had a conversation like friends did, not like her and Stacey. She missed Stacey, their slide and bunking off school.

As she stood, she almost toppled over. The shakes were getting the better of her. She needed some medicine soon. She needed a hug, some reassurance. Leaning over, she embraced Jackie. The woman didn't flinch, pull away or respond. 'Please can you hug me, Jackie?' The woman began to rock until Miley let go. Tears ran down her cheek. It was just a hug. She wanted a hug off the only friend she had left but that friend didn't even acknowledge her. She grabbed the knitted doll from the bedside table. The thing had seen better days with its faded colours and its one button eye. She threw it back on the table as she felt the room make a sideward shift, causing her to lose her balance and sway a little.

Her stomach kept turning. She needed air. Stumbling to the window, she opened the small catch at the top and the faintest of warm breezes came in through the inch that the window would open. She rattled the main window but, as usual, it was locked. Body crumpling at the middle, she slid down the glass and sat on the ledge. She couldn't do this job alone. Miley fiddled with the little friendship bracelet that a special friend had made for her and she twisted it around her skinny wrist.

She needed a lie-down. After she'd had a few minutes to ease her discomfort, she'd bring Jackie some food. The other boss always left their meals at the top of the stairs. Miley staggered across the landing with the filthy bucket of water and stopped. The porridge was on the top step, as it always was. Two bowls, one for her, one for Jackie. She placed the bucket down and slid the bowls out of the way.

Taking one shaky step at a time, she eventually made it to the door at the bottom of the stairs. As she reached out to turn the handle, her trembling knuckles scraped the coarse wooden door, missing the handle completely. 'Try again, idiot.'

After a few attempts, her hand finally made contact with the handle. She turned and pushed, but it too was locked. It was always locked. The boss said it was to keep Jackie safe. Miley wanted to go for a walk in the fields outside, to smell the grass, just for an hour. That wasn't going to happen today. It didn't happen any day, despite her asking.

She gazed back up the stairs and closed her eyes. Through blurred vision, the stairs looked as though they were moving, like an escalator. Maybe it was the hideous brown swirly carpet, the pattern was confusing her eyes. She bent down and felt the stairs. They were still. It was definitely her mind playing tricks on her again. She crawled back up, using her hands until she reached the top. Porridge. Jackie needed her breakfast.

CHAPTER THIRTEEN

'How are we doing on the van front?' Gina asked as she grabbed a biscuit from the central table. 'These cookies are the best so far. Tell Mrs O that she's a genius.'

O'Connor looked up and Jacob glanced at him. 'I bought them from the bakery on the way in,' Jacob said as he placed his down next to his computer.

That was the second time in so many days she'd dropped herself in it. First with the lie she'd told when leaving the station the other evening. 'I can taste it now. Definitely shop bought – totally inferior. Look, I'm sorry.'

O'Connor's serious stare turned into a fit of laughter. 'Give over, guv. It's no big deal. I won't tell my lovely wife, who works hard for hours on end to try and make us all happy with her really special cookies. I won't ever tell her you preferred the mass-produced version.'

At least he wasn't about to hold it against her. Any more guilt loaded on the guilt pile would probably drive her insane. She shook her head. She had to learn to let these things drop and move on. Hannah would get over their argument, eventually. Wyre didn't really care that she didn't go to the pub for her birthday drink and O'Connor couldn't give a stuff that she really liked the cookies his wife didn't bake. Time to take charge and stop dwelling on things she couldn't change. 'Right. Where's Wyre? We have CCTV I hear. I want to see it.'

'Morning, guv.' Wyre entered with a coffee. 'I'll just get it up on my screen and we can have another look. Unfortunately it's too blurry to see much. We do know from the shape etcetera, that we're definitely looking for a Transit van. That narrows the search down quite a bit. The camera was too far back to see the lettering. It looks like three strips of green on the side panel so that matches the description that Toby Biddle gave.' She leaned forward and clicked into the system, selecting the CCTV file.

The clip lasted all of six seconds. The van passed the house. The doors at the back were closed at the time and there was no way they'd have any hope of getting a registration number. The resolution was so poor they'd only be able to confirm what they already knew.

'O'Connor, any luck with the list of van owners that Briggs passed to us? We can now narrow that down to just Transit vans. Start within a five-mile radius of the incident.'

'That's exactly what I did, guv. I have thirty-seven left to contact.'

'If we don't get any further, we'll start moving outwards until we find the driver.'

O'Connor rubbed his head. 'Then there's all the people who have phoned in. There are absolutely stacks.'

'Can we get Smith to help?'

O'Connor shook his head. 'Already tried that one. They're busy with other cases.'

'I suppose you'd best get cracking then. Any news on the girl?' If only they could ask her what had happened, they'd get all the answers they needed.

'No. Doctor Nowak called. She's still in a medically-induced coma. He described her condition as highly critical.'

'Not good.'

'It's not,' O'Connor replied. 'Like you said, all we have is the van lead.'

'Unless forensics come up with something. Anything back from Bernard yet?' She could hope. She knew they had been busy with people taking holiday and other things they were working on. Also, budgets had been tightened again. Gina could mark everything a priority but they still took time. As it stood, they had a girl who seemed to be a drug user, possibly climb into a van and jump out. That was the very least. At the worst, they had an escaped abductee who was now in Cleevesford intensive care unit and could possibly die. As the girl's last words were 'help her', Gina suspected the latter.

'Not a jot.' O'Connor continued making notes on his list.

'Any further CCTV footage from the area?'

'Most of the ones we checked were used for personal security on some of the bigger houses. The footage hadn't tracked the roads and many of the cameras were only there to deter, so were not working.'

'Have you and Wyre been looking into missing persons? The girl wanted us to help someone. Missing persons is the best place to start looking.'

'Started to, guv.' His phone went and he placed it to his ear. 'Thank goodness for that.' He shuffled the dismantled report into a thick pile and smiled. 'That's great. Thank you.'

'Well?' Gina asked.

'A lead. It's the van driver. Someone has called in and emailed the CCTV footage that overlooks their gate and a bit of the road. We have the van in full clear view. I'll call the company now.' He scoffed the rest of his cookie and snapped his fingers.

CHAPTER FOURTEEN

'I gather you're not making breakfast. Shall I grab a couple of bacon sandwiches from the buttie van?' Roy asked as he pushed Christina's bedroom door open. The buttie van had been one of their regular treats before Christina had left.

Julia looked up from her daughter's pillow. 'Do what you like. I don't want anything.' She wanted him to hurry up and leave for work, like he did every morning, especially after their argument in Worcester over the posters. She wanted him to leave her alone with her thoughts. Instead, he walked over and sat on the bed.

'Shall I call in sick? Maybe we could go out for breakfast.'

The last thing she wanted to do was go out and waste money they didn't have on something that was no good for them with a man who had given up on her daughter. Since she left her job, they only had his income coming in. She shook her head and stared at the wall.

'I'm sorry about yesterday,' he said. 'It just all got too much for me. I don't want to lose you.'

He was trying to make it up to her but his efforts weren't enough. He'd left her alone in Worcester to catch the bus home. He hadn't cared about how she'd felt. No one did.

Everyone shared his views on her daughter, even her parents. Yes, the girl had been hard work, yes, she was plain rude most of the time and, yes, she could be hurtful when she didn't get what she wanted. But Julia knew the little girl she'd brought up, mostly alone, was still there somewhere, underneath the shower of hormones and anger. The neighbours had been fed up with the door slamming and the sound of her music blaring out of the window, which led to reports of noise pollution to environmental health. The school were never happy with her. She never tried hard enough, bunked off, had been cheeky to the teachers and didn't care if they gave her detentions. Roy fell into the category of not caring. She'd seen that for herself. While he was whistling around the house looking like he'd won the EuroMillions, she'd been sinking into a depression. 'I want you to go to work. I need to be alone.'

He leaned over and kissed her on the head. For the first time, she felt nothing. 'If you need anything, just call.'

She needed his help yesterday while she was breaking down in Worcester. She needed someone to tell her everything would be okay. He could stick his empty promises. She listened as he thundered down the stairs in his heavy work boots and slammed the front door. Rolling off the bed, she watched as he got into the car and drove off.

Christina's room was exactly as she left it. Her clothes were still strewn all over the floor. The towels she'd last used to dry herself on were still hanging over her desk chair and a half-eaten packet of cherry drops had spilled onto her bedside table. Julia had been through everything, carefully placing each item back after searching through it. There were no clues as to where she might be.

Her mobile lit up. It was one of Christina's school friends.

'Mrs Dawson—'

'Have you heard from Christina?' Blood rushed through Julia's head as she listened to the girl shouting at her younger brother to get out of her room.

'No, it's just something I was thinking about the other day.'

Julia's fingers began to tremble as she gripped the phone. 'What do you know?'

The girl paused. 'It's not much. She made me promise not to say but I thought I should call. I thought she'd come home by now. She hasn't even called me back. I'm so worried.'

'Look, you did the right thing. Tell me what you know.'

'She called me a week after she left…'

Julia waited, open-mouthed as her heart began to pound. What had Christina been hiding?

CHAPTER FIFTEEN

'The van driver's waiting in the interview room,' Jacob said as he grabbed his notebook. 'He confirms that he was the one driving the van that morning but says he knows nothing about a girl being in his van.'

'Darren Mason, aged nineteen?' Gina glanced at her notes.

'That's the one.'

They hurried to the interview room and saw the young man sitting there, almost disappearing under the desk. Gina cast her eyes over him, he looked about fifteen. Fresh acne covered his already scarred forehead and chin. She watched as he began picking at what looked like yesterday's half dried spot. Although quite short and boyish, Gina noticed how stocky he looked, like he did weight training.

'Mr Mason, Darren. What do you prefer to be called?' Gina asked as she and Jacob sat opposite him.

He moved his hands away from his face and linked his fingers on the table. 'Darren. My friends call me Daz.'

'The interview will be taped so that we can refer to it at a later date.'

'Am I in any trouble? I didn't know she was in the van.'

'At the moment we just need to establish what happened. We have a witness who saw a girl falling out of your van. That girl is in a critical state in hospital. We need you to tell us in as much detail as you can, all that you can remember and what happened on the morning of Saturday the fourteenth of July.'

Jacob nodded and started the recording device.

'Interview with Darren Steven Mason, aged nineteen years old. DI Harte and DS Driscoll present. Date is Monday the sixteenth of July, 2018,' Jacob confirmed.

Gina leaned forward. 'Please tell me, in your own words, what happened last Saturday morning.'

Darren unlocked his hands and placed them out of sight, under the table. 'At the weekends I help with the family business. My dad lets me use the van all the time even in the week. I go to university in Birmingham and work weekends. Mechanical Engineering.' He paused as if he was waiting for praise before realising nothing was going to be said and continuing. 'My dad owns Mason and Sons Tree Surgery, a company based in Warwick. I live at home with him and I was heading into Cleevesford on a job.'

'What job was that?'

'A domestic. Someone's tree was overgrown. It was a straight-forward trimming job, which is why I was doing it. My dad doesn't trust me with anything more demanding yet, which is disappointing. It was an older lady, about fifty, lives on Brindle Lane, the number is on an email.'

Gina wondered if he was purposely being antagonistic or if referring to fifty as old was merely youthful innocence. She was in her mid-forties. Admittedly, some days she felt older but fifty and older lady, in the same sentence? Her feelings towards him had cooled even more.

Gina glanced at her notes and almost wanted to smile. Something didn't add up and the detail was in his route. 'Why were you driving down Laurel Lane if you were coming from Warwick?'

'I err… I hadn't come from Warwick that morning. I'd come from Redditch. I stayed at a friend's flat. He lives in Winyates, in a flat in the centre.'

Gina glanced at Jacob. 'What is your friend called?'

'Callum, Callum Besford.'

'So you stayed with your friend Callum. Tell me what happened from then.'

Sweat beads lined up along the young man's forehead, mingling with his floppy fringe. His black oily hair shone like it was almost white on top as the light caught it. 'We got up about six… I mean, I got up about seven and left. I can't really remember the exact time. All I knew was I wanted to get the job done before it got hot. The woman said she was up early and she didn't have any neighbours close by so I thought I'd get over there, get the job done and have the rest of the day to chill with… I mean, go home.'

Gina sensed some hesitation as he spoke. He got up at seven or was it six? Did both of them get up or just the one? He closed his eyes at the mention of Callum's name.

'I was meant to be trimming the Brindle Lane lady's trees, in Cleevesford, for seven thirty. I remember stopping at the garage on Crump Lane to grab a coffee. This had to be about ten past seven. I drank most of it in the car park, so spent about five minutes there and carried on towards Cleevesford.'

He said he'd been hired to trim a tree, now it was trees. Maybe he was nervous, maybe he was trying hard to remember what he'd said a minute ago. A bead of sweat escaped down his forehead and slid past his eye. She could tell he wanted to wipe it away but he was resisting. His left eye half closed as it settled in on the edge of his eye. Trying to be in control, he left it and stopped flinching.

'Did you hear or see anything that aroused your suspicion?'

'No. Nothing. I noticed that as I was pulling into Cleevesford my van door was open. Luckily the tools were all strapped in, something my father never stops going on about.'

'Was the back door locked when you began your journey?'

He stared at the wall, over her shoulder. 'I thought it was, but it can't have been. There was no sign of anyone breaking in. I must have left it unlocked. My dad will kill me. He won't find out that I left it unlocked, will he? You don't have to tell him that?' He wiped the sweat with his sleeve. He was losing control.

'Darren, a girl was witnessed falling out of the back of your van on that Saturday morning. That girl is now in intensive care, fighting for her life. The van door being unlocked is the last thing to worry about. Do you know how she came to be in your van?'

'No.' The gentle tone he'd begun speaking in was replaced by a sharp response.

'Did you hear her getting in or falling out of your van?'

'I didn't hear anything. I had music on.'

'What were you listening to?'

'What? I don't know. Loud music.'

'All the way from Laurel Lane to your job in Cleevesford, you didn't hear the van door flapping open and closed as you weaved in and out of the country lanes?'

'No.'

'We will need to examine your van. Can we please have your keys?'

'No. I'm not under arrest and I've answered all your questions. You're not having the van. My dad will kill me and I need it. I'm done here.' He went to stand.

'Mr Mason, please sit.'

'No. I've finished here.' Again, he began weaving his fingers together as he stared at the wall. 'I want a solicitor.'

'Okay. Darren Steven Mason. I'm arresting you on suspicion of kidnap. You do not have to say anything, but it may harm your defence if you do not mention when questioned, something you later rely on in court. Anything you do say may be given in evidence.'

Before anything could be tampered with she needed to see his van and get hold of his phone. She needed Bernard and Keith to check it out as a potential crime scene. Under section eighteen, she needed his house searched and the clothing he was wearing on that Saturday morning seized.

'Have the van keys been booked in?'

Jacob nodded.

The company had been called in advance so that they could identify who was driving the van that day and that had led them to Darren, son of the company owner. The man had quickly given his son's name and then started ranting about how badly his son always drove the van and that he'd pay any fines. Gina wondered if his father had known something and had been overcompensating or if he simply knew nothing. Had he warned his son and had he – or they – already dumped potential evidence? More than likely. Her mind flashed back to the list of names she'd got from Facebook that she'd forwarded to O'Connor. Dazza Mason was on that list. His friends had tagged him in the post. He'd already been on O'Connor's list. They'd have got to him eventually.

'What? You can't take my keys. I haven't done anything. I told you. I don't know anything about anyone getting in my van or falling out.'

'Mr Mason. My colleague, DS Driscoll, will explain what happens next. This is a very serious charge and you've refused to cooperate with our investigation. We will keep you updated and a duty solicitor will be provided at your request. You also have the right to make a phone call.'

Jacob completed the interview with the time and stopped the recording. Gina pushed her chair back and left, leaving Jacob to continue booking Darren Mason into custody.

Briggs came out of the viewing room. 'There's something he's holding back.'

'I could tell. Right, the clock is ticking and we need to present something good to the CPS,' Gina replied. The Crown Prosecution Service would need more than they currently had. She sincerely hoped that what they'd find in his van or home would give them what they needed and provide closure to the case.

Jacob left the interview room with the van keys and Darren's mobile phone, both in a clear evidence bag. Gina took the bag. 'I need to see his van. Oh, and Crump Lane. Get Wyre to call the petrol station and tell them we are coming for the CCTV. I want to know what he's hiding.'

CHAPTER SIXTEEN

As Gina and O'Connor walked along the station car park, she spotted Darren's large white van. It was exactly as Toby Biddle had described. He thought it was a Transit and it was. It also had dark green writing on the side, Mason and Sons Tree Surgery, and below it was a small logo of a tree with their office number printed underneath. With gloved hands she went to open the back door just as Keith from forensics pulled up in the staff spaces. As he approached, bag in one hand while the other hand adjusted his comb-over, he let out a small cry as he placed his bag on the floor. 'Back is killing me. Bernard's on his way so I'll make a start when he gets here.'

'I'm opening it up for a quick look, then it's all yours,' Gina said.

Keith passed her a hairnet to go with the gloves she was already wearing. She tucked her hair in and tried the handle. It was already open. She didn't need the van keys. Maybe Darren Mason did forget to lock it the other day. She passed O'Connor the keys to put back in the evidence bag. The smell of marijuana escaped out of the door. She spotted the tiny bag of weed, no more than enough for one or two smokes. 'Looks like we have him on possession.' She'd pass his information over to PC Smith for his investigations. He'd no doubt want a word with Darren too. 'Bloody hell that stuff stinks.'

'I know, it's rancid.'

She spotted a bag spilling over with ropes, harnesses, carabiners and a buckled waist belt. A petrol chainsaw had been strapped to a frame up against the one side of the van, along with a few other tools. 'Pass me a forensics suit and some boot covers. I'm stepping in,' she said to Keith.

He flinched as he bent over and passed her the items. As she zipped the suit up, she gazed at structure of the van. The cab section was divided by a large panel so she couldn't see the seats. Leaning in, she gently lifted a few items. Her gaze travelled into all the corners, under the tools and in the crevices. The glint of something caught her eye. Reaching down, she turned the metal disc and waited for Keith to open a clear evidence bag. He got out some tweezers and gripped the edge of the item before dropping it into the bag. She closed the van door and handed the scene over to Keith.

'To work it is then,' he said as he finished suiting up.

'If you find anything else, call me out. We have him in custody now and the clock is ticking.'

Back at the incident room, with O'Connor in tow, she entered, holding up their prize find. A small disc that looked like the type a dog might wear on a collar.

'Found something, guv?' Wyre asked.

'Yes, as well as a bag of weed, we found a small disc with…' She held the bagged item to the light and squinted at the grubby disc. 'It has the letters E Ho on the front. It also looks like the rest have worn off. You can just about make out the E Ho. It's been engraved in an amateurish way, almost scrawled on, with a small sharp object. There is a brownish smear to the back. This could be a spec of dried blood. Get a couple of photos taken and send it straight to the lab,' she said to O'Connor.

'Yes, guv.' He took the bag, then he and Jacob left to take the item to Keith and Bernard.

'E Ho. Ho, who is Ho?' Gina queried. 'Darren's surname is Mason. If this was from the Mason's dog, the contact name would be Mason, surely. He mentioned the friend, whose flat he came from on the Saturday, his name was Callum Besford. E Ho…'

'It could be a customer. Maybe a customer's dog jumped into the van while he was working,' Wyre added.

'Could have. We'll soon find out if any of the forensics that come back match those of our victim. Time to play the forensics waiting game. In the meantime, I need to see the CCTV at Crump Lane. Did you call them?'

'I did, guv. Told them we'd be there soon.'

'Let's go.' She grabbed her car keys from her bag and headed towards the door, with Wyre following. She checked her watch, there was still a bit of the morning left. Plenty of time to collect the CCTV footage and speak to Darren Mason again. As they headed out to the car park she spotted Jacob. 'Prepare for a search of Mason's house when we get back. We need also to speak to Callum Besford. Hope you haven't got any dinner dates planned for this evening. It's going to be a long one.'

'Just cancelling,' said Jacob as he pulled his phone out. Gina had nothing to cancel. She watched as Wyre typed out a message to George. No one was ever expecting her to come home and for that she was glad.

CHAPTER SEVENTEEN

Gina drove in the midday heat through the snaking country roads as Wyre enjoyed the sun-drenched views. She listened to the birdsong through the open windows as she slowed down on the gravelly road. The smell of farm hung in the air; a cross between manure and cut grass, with a distant hint of smokiness. She slowed down a little more as she twisted and turned the car, avoiding potholes along the remainder of the road.

Trees sprouting from each verge met above them in a grand-looking arch. Dandelion seeds floated through the air and in through the car window. As they reached the main road, coming out of the short cut, she could see Crump Lane Petrol Station in the distance. The small independent station was a rarity, offering only two grubby pumps and a couple of spaces to park in for customers using the small shop. Behind it were fields of rapeseed flowers, covering the landscape like a thick yellow blanket. Just beneath the brow of a hill a patch of woodland met the cloudless sky.

She turned in, parking in one of the two spaces. 'Let's go and see what they've got.'

Wyre smiled and nodded, grabbing her pad and pen.

Wasps buzzed around the overflowing bin that welcomed customers as they entered. Wyre batted them away with the back of her hand as they rushed through the door, then were instantly hit by the air conditioning.

The shop was small, offering a few sandwiches and cans of pop in a fridge, the usual essentials such as bread and milk and racks of chocolate bars and crisps. A coffee machine whirred away in the corner as the shop assistant grabbed her almost finished drink and headed back behind the counter. She spotted the woman's name badge. Beryl Day – Manager.

'DI Harte and DC Wyre. We called earlier today. We've come to see the CCTV footage of Saturday morning, between six thirty and seven thirty.'

'Oh, of course.' She placed her coffee down. 'Come through.' The woman lifted a hatch and guided them into the small serving area. From the counter Gina could see the large split screen showing four active cameras and just under the counter sat a hard drive that was gently whirring away. The air con blasted onto the woman's grey bun, almost unravelling a few of her loosely pinned hairs. 'Sorry about the chill. I get far too hot in this weather.'

She needn't have apologised. It was a relief to be cool. The humidity was getting worse as the hours in the day passed. Twenty-eight degrees, the morning weather report had warned. Wyre began to mark out a CCTV viewing log, ready to document times and movement. 'What is your write-over period?'

'Thirty days. Everything will still be on there for last Saturday. Here we go.'

'Start at six in the morning.'

The woman pressed play and they watched until the front end of Darren's van came into view.

'Do you have any CCTV footage that covers the back of the van?'

'Sorry, this is as good as it gets.'

The man got out of the van and slammed the driver's door. Although not the clearest of images, she could definitely tell it was Darren. She watched as Wyre noted the time.

Six fifty-one in the morning.

They watched as he stood next to his van, grabbed his phone and pressed a button. Holding the phone to his ear, he began to pace. He placed the phone in his pocket and walked to the shop. At six fifty-six he left, holding a cup of coffee. With his spare hand, he made a one-handed call, pressing a button with his thumb and scrunching the phone between his ear and shoulder. He kicked the front of the van and placed the coffee on the ground before attending to the call properly. It looked like he was shouting but he turned his back to the camera as he spoke. He placed his phone back into the pocket of his long khaki-coloured shorts and turned around. They had a tear in them like a fashion tear at the knee. Gina made a note too. He was wearing a company T-shirt. He swigged his coffee and poured the rest on the road before wheel-spinning off in the direction of Laurel Lane. That was all they had.

'I've put the footage on a disc for you.' Beryl handed a box to Wyre who logged the item on her form. 'It also contains the footage of him coming into the shop. All he did was come in, go to the coffee machine and leave.'

'Did you see anyone else around that time or earlier?' If she had seen someone around, a young girl maybe, her information might back up Darren's story, showing that he didn't know she was in his van.

'No. It was a quiet morning being early and a weekend. I think he was the first. I didn't see a soul around before he turned up.'

'Well, thanks for the footage.'

'Always happy to help. Is he in some kind of trouble? I heard on the news, about the girl and something about an accident.'

'We're just following up on all enquiries at the moment.' Gina headed back through the hatch and grabbed a bar of chocolate. 'Do you want one?'

'Me, chocolate? I'd need to do an hour and half on the cross trainer to undo that damage, guv,' Wyre replied with a smile.

Gina placed her lunch on the desk and fished through all the rubbish in her trouser pocket to find some change. As the woman rang up the transaction she couldn't help thinking about what they'd seen. Darren had looked agitated while on the phone, like he'd been arguing with someone. He hadn't mentioned stopping to chat on the phone during his interview and he'd made two separate calls, one that looked to connect with the caller and another that appeared to ring out. Were they to the same person? He'd been so angry, he'd kicked his van. Were things not going to plan? They had his phone, soon all would be revealed when it came to his call activity.

'There is something about that lad, that I think I should mention, you know, if he's a suspect.'

'Anything you can help us with would be most appreciated, Ms Day.'

The woman came to the other side of the counter and led them to the door. 'I quite often come out for a gander, you know how things are. I sit here all day, sometimes with very few customers. They tend to come mostly in the mornings before work, or during lunchtimes. I have a chair.' The woman pointed to the side of the building and Gina spotted the plastic garden chair. 'When it's quiet, I sit there, with a book. Anyway, he'd gone. I watched his van chugging up the hill towards Cleevesford. See that layby there?' Gina shaded her eyes from the sun as she gazed into the distance. She could just about make out a large gated field with a small space in front of it. 'He pulled in there and started talking on his phone again. He saw me watching so I went inside. I was watching and I suppose I was being nosey, but he wasn't exactly hiding.'

'Did you see anyone else come or go when he stopped on the hill?'

'Not while I was out there. I did come in though, when he saw me. I wasn't out there watching all the time.'

'Thank you again, Ms Day. If you remember anything else, give me a call.' Gina passed the woman a card and headed over to the car. 'Can you give the station a call, find out when the search of Mason's house is taking place?' Wyre nodded. Gina gazed across at the hill as they stepped into the car. 'Only a few seconds before, he'd stopped at the petrol station to speak on his phone. Why had he travelled up the road and stopped again so soon?'

It was her mission to find out.

CHAPTER EIGHTEEN

As they returned to the station, Gina headed straight to the kitchen. Briggs leaned against a wall and Annie was laughing at something he'd said. As soon as she spotted Gina, she stopped. 'Don't mind me. Oh, Chris, I'll fill you in with the rest of what happened in despatch later,' Annie said with a giggle as she grabbed a paper cup and filled it with cold water. It was rare to hear anyone around the station refer to DCI Chris Briggs as just Chris – it was normally, sir. They'd been intimate and Gina wouldn't ever call him Chris while working. He grinned at her, not commenting on the informality that had slipped from Annie's tongue.

The heat had been draining and chocolate on a stuffy day hadn't been the most fulfilling meal. She could feel the last of the cocoa paste sticking to the roof of her mouth.

'How did it go?' Briggs asked.

'I'll leave you to it,' Annie said as she left with her cup of water. 'Call me later.'

'Gossiping again? I don't know,' Gina said as she also filled a paper cup with water and sipped the cold liquid.

Briggs let out a small laugh. 'Not about you, Harte, just everyone else. Okay it was about you a little. It looked odd, you leaving the station the way you did the other night and not coming out for Wyre's birthday drink. Gossip is still rife after the last case and everything you went through with the attacks. We're all concerned, like family. You know how things are. If it were any one of us, you'd be concerned too.'

'Well, thank you for not lying when I asked you. At least I know what I'm up against.'

'We're not your enemy, you know,' Briggs replied as he placed a hand on her shoulder.

She took his hand and removed it. 'I know. But seriously, all of you need to drop it. I'm not some delicate little flower you need to look out for—'

'We all need looking out for in this job.'

'Okay, but start planting some gossip that lets people know that I don't need anyone fussing. That case was ages ago—'

'Four months and you've only just finished the counselling sessions.'

'Finished, that's the important word here. I finished, I'm stronger for everything that's happened to me and I have what is turning out to be a meaty case to get my teeth stuck into. I know I opened up to you about my past, in those moments where my safety was compromised, but I'm fine now. That was a long time ago. I'm not vulnerable, sir.'

'We're all vulnerable, Harte, and we all need friends. Just remember you have friends. I'm here to talk should you need me.'

She smiled and finished her water. He had Annie now. She wasn't about to be confiding in him any time soon. 'About the case then, sir. We're planning to search Darren Mason's parents' house this afternoon. We have the team prepped. Keith is finished with the van. He and Bernard are just repacking what they need and we'll be heading over.'

'What are your thoughts?' Briggs asked.

'Same as yours. He was hiding something, I'm just not sure what. I think his reluctance to let us search the van on a voluntary basis could have been because of the weed we found. After speaking to Beryl Day, the owner of the Crump Lane Garage, I think there's a lot more to him and he's definitely hiding something. He was angry in the footage when he was speaking on the phone.

He even kicked his van at one point. Beryl also said that when he drove off, he then pulled over on the brow of the hill to talk on his phone again. Was he panicking about something?' Gina frowned as she thought.

'We're no closer to finding out exactly when the girl got into or was loaded onto the van. The fact that she had been using drugs and weed was found in his van provides somewhat of a connection.' Briggs began to undo his cuffs and roll his shirt up.

'Not quite in the same league though. I'm really hoping that the search turns something up otherwise it's back to questioning.'

'What about his friend?'

'I'll go there on the way back from the search. Obviously, we have no right to search his home but Darren Mason had come from there. I'll drop by with one of the team and get a witness statement. We'll play it from there. I have a feeling they're lovers.'

'Lovers?'

'Yes, listen to the recording of his interview. He mentions getting up and chilling with Callum Besford, but then he breaks off during the sentence.' Gina stepped back and looked around. Neither of them wanted anyone else to ever guess that they once may have been lovers. She threw the cup in the bin. 'Right, I best get prepped for this search.'

CHAPTER NINETEEN

Elisa checked her watch; it was three thirty, only an hour and a half to go. She stepped over to the window and stared out at where the silver car had been parked a couple of days ago. Maybe Mrs Hanley was right. Whoever it was probably just pulled over for a break. She hugged herself as she recalled him watching her, at least she thought the person was a man. She couldn't be sure, but he or whoever had really freaked her out. Whenever a car pulled up, she ran out to check it, gripping her phone just in case she needed to call for help. She wanted her phone now, it would make her feel safe, but she'd been told not to use it by Mrs Hanley.

Her bag lay under the counter and she could see her phone sticking out. Using it would be risky. She reached under the counter and grabbed a cola cube, popping it into her mouth.

Smiling, she thought of her friends, most now preparing for sixth form. She hadn't decided what to do after the holidays; it would depend on how well she'd done in her exams. Her father wanted her to do A levels like he did, but her mother was more supportive of her love of cooking. She'd decided that an apprenticeship was for her. This job was merely a fill-in until the right position came along and she'd passed her driving test.

Her jam was much better than the cheap muck they sold here. She lifted a bit up on a broken cracker and sniffed it, before dropping it back in the cracker bowl. Her recipe had been passed from her grandparents to her mother and then to her. All they'd done at the shop was repackage a value range in fancy jars with frilly tops. She could tell. There was nothing better than helping her mother to pick damsons and make the jam, it was an experience they'd shared for as long as she could remember. They'd also regularly baked from scratch, her mum also teaching her how to decorate her creations. It was all about the sugar work and chocolate tempering. Temperature was the key to getting it perfect.

This morning her mum had dropped her off in silence. Elisa had overslept again and had to be dragged out of bed. She knew she'd pushed her mother to her limits but getting up had been hard after meeting Ethan and cruising in his car until the early hours. Her mum wasn't happy about that either. She looked at her watch, only a few minutes had passed since she last checked the time. Her hair was looking a bit lank. She stared into the window's reflection and fluffed it up a little. The mousy brown colour did nothing for her. Maybe going blonde was worth trying.

She heard muffled shouting coming from the office upstairs. 'Are you okay, Mrs Hanley?' she called. The woman was probably whining that not enough customers had come through the door again. It wouldn't be the first time. Even she'd have expected more customers, despite it being a Monday. In fact, she'd have welcomed more customers to pass the time. She noticed how rubbish the shop was on social media, maybe she could offer to set them a Facebook page up. Even their website was one of the free versions that was barely updated. They needed offers, reasons to bring people in. She smiled as she headed out the back, towards the stairs to the office. She would offer to set up their social media accounts right now. Maybe, if it worked, her employers would give her a bonus or a small pay rise. A good online presence would spread the word. It wouldn't make the produce any better but it may tempt a few customers through the door. She had almost three thousand people liking her Facebook page and all she did was post food and cake photos, snapped and edited on her phone.

As she reached the halfway mark of the staircase, she heard a thud followed by silence. What if the creepy man had come back? Heart hammering, she crept up the final few stairs and the door blew open as a breeze filled the building. Mrs Hanley was bending down, her underwear showing as she lifted the cash box off the floor.

'Can you please knock before entering?' Mrs Hanley said as she stood and pulled her skirt down.

'I'm sorry,' Elisa muttered as she closed the door and rushed down the stairs. She really thought something had happened. She should've stayed downstairs. They'd sack her for sure now. They didn't know the breeze had caused the door to open. 'Stupid, stupid, stupid,' she repeated.

She listened as the footsteps above came from the far end of the building to just above her. She needed to think of something different, take her mind off being scolded. She wanted to go home and shower, maybe watch a film or play some music so she didn't have to face Mrs Hanley.

The pacing and shouting ended and she heard heels clicking down the stairs. Great!

Mrs Hanley entered, carrying a pile of paperwork. 'Do you know to knock at closed doors before you enter?'

Elisa nodded. She didn't want to contradict her and explain that the wind had blown the door open.

'Well, why did you enter without knocking?'

Elisa shrugged as she crunched on the last of the cola cubes. She wished it was home time and her mother was outside in the car but there was still ages left. Maybe she should quit. Her fingers brushed the bottom of the tabard. She could just pull it over her head, leave it on the side and never come back.

'Look. It doesn't matter. Okay?' The woman's crow's feet framed eyes stared at her, waiting for a response.

What she was saying was good. *It doesn't matter,* she could live with that. She let go of the tabard and nodded. 'I'm sorry, Mrs Hanley. It won't happen again.'

'Good. The honey looks like it needs stacking better. That's our best seller. Make sure people can see it when they come through the door.' The woman flicked her hair and wiggled out of the room in her stupid undersized dress. She hadn't sold any honey since she'd started; their best seller was sweets and onion chutney.

Exhaling, she listened as Mrs Hanley went back up the stairs. Elisa would stay put for the next hour and be ready to go as soon as five o'clock came. As she headed back over to the counter she spotted a piece of paper on the floor. Mrs Hanley must have dropped it on her way out. She picked it up and began to read. It was a notice of court action from one of the suppliers along with a demand for two thousand pounds. They were in debt. If only Mrs Hanley had been a bit nicer, she would have mentioned the shop on her social media accounts for all her foodie followers to see. She may have set them up with a spanking new Facebook page. Not now. She would stand here all day, bored, until it was time to go home.

CHAPTER TWENTY

The Masons lived in the type of house you see printed on the top of a biscuit tin. Gina could imagine living somewhere that quaint. They had neighbours but a high shrub wall divided the gap between them. The double-fronted detached cottage wasn't overly huge but it had a quaint look about it. Hanging baskets provided a colourful greeting to guests of the family. The double garage to the side of the house was topped with a little roof so that it blended in with the house. She looked at her notes. Mr Dennis Mason, owner of a tree surgery business. Mrs Mason, architect for a Stratford-based firm.

The curtains twitched as Gina led the rest of the detectives and officers to the door. As she went to knock, a tall woman opened the door. Her pale pink lipstick almost made her lips blend into the skin on her face. Her icy blue eyes and white blonde hair gave her a Nordic look.

'Mrs Mason, DI Harte. We have a section eighteen notice to search your house,' Gina said as the woman opened the door. Mrs Mason's brow furrowed as she dropped the hand that was holding the can opener.

'I see you didn't bring my son with you?'

'Sorry.' Gina shook her head. The woman stepped aside as she nervously scratched her hair. 'We'll make this as quick as we can.'

Mr Mason stomped through, blocking the way. The tubby man stood about two inches shorter than his wife but he looked strong and muscular with shovel-like hands, which were covered in calluses. 'Get out. My son was just in the wrong place at the wrong time and you've arrested him! Yes, he called *me* with his one call and I've sent him the best legal representation. Duty solicitor, my arse. He'll be home for supper unless you find something with which to keep him, but you won't as he's done nought wrong.'

'Mr Mason, could you please step out of the way? A girl is seriously injured and she'll be lucky to survive. She happened to fall from the van your son was driving. If he's done nothing wrong, then you don't have anything to worry about but we need to search the house.'

'But this is my house. Not his. He lives here but—'

'Mr Mason, he lives here. That makes it his home too. We'll be as quick as possible but you need to step back. PC Smith will sit with you, tell you what is happening and explain the process to you.'

He went to speak but his wife interrupted. 'Just leave it out, Den. The sooner they get on with it, the sooner they leave and Darren can come home.'

The man shoved his hands in his work trouser pockets, huffed and reluctantly followed his wife to the kitchen.

'Half of you upstairs, half down, Jacob, come with me. Seize any computers, phones or tablets that Darren Mason may have access too. Wyre, O'Connor, are you okay starting with the communal rooms? Make sure you go through the garage and the sheds. Bernard, follow us to Darren's room. Keith, go with the others.' If there was any trace evidence that the girl has been in the house, Keith and Bernard would find it.

Gina made her way to the bedrooms. The first door she opened had to be Darren's. There were clothes everywhere and an unmade double bed. Used cups dotted the room. It was kitted out with the best tech, including the largest television that Gina had seen in a bedroom. The stale smell of over-filled ashtray and damp towels filled her nostrils. 'Bag those up,' she said to Jacob as he followed.

'The shorts?'

Bernard nodded and opened his bag.

'And the T-shirt. They're the clothes he was wearing in the CCTV footage and it must be our lucky day. It looks and smells like he hasn't washed them.' Gina looked out of his bedroom window. Not a bad view of the garden. She spotted Wyre heading towards the shed.

Jacob and Bernard began retrieving the clothes, and Gina opened his bedside drawers. Jacob continued searching through the wardrobe. The first two bedside drawers contained a mix of boxer shorts and socks. The bottom drawer contained a roll up cigarette. With gloved hands, Gina picked it up and sniffed. 'More weed.' Jacob came over with a bag and they sealed it away. She reached towards the back of the drawer and pulled out an old Nokia mobile phone. One that didn't take photos or access the internet. She tried to turn it on but the battery was probably flat. She passed it to Jacob to bag. As soon as they got back to the station, she wanted it analysed.

Footsteps thundered up the stairs. 'That bitch has taken my laptop. I need it for work. How the hell am I meant to do my invoicing and access my diary? I run my whole business on that thing.'

'Mr Mason, you will get it back.' Gina felt a bead of sweat running down the side of her face. How dare he refer to one of her team in that manner? He was angry, she got that. Her hands trembled as she resisted the urge to argue with the man.

'You're not taking it.' He ran down the stairs, the pictures jangling on their hooks as his hefty footsteps passed. Shouting and commotion followed.

'Mr Mason, you will be arrested if you take another step towards me in that manner,' she heard Smith saying. She ran down the stairs to see what was happening. Mr Mason's side-parted, dark hair was now sodden with sweat. Backing down, he let out a roar as his wife guided him into the garden to calm down. Gina watched as they bickered behind the closed patio doors. He went to walk away but she dragged him back by the arm.

'I want that laptop checked first. Maybe he just uses it for work or maybe he has something to hide.' The man stared through the window and caught her gaze. He broke his stare and pulled a packet of cigarettes from his pocket, turning away from them as he lit up.

Officers left the house with evidence bags. If there was nothing amiss, everything would be returned in the same condition that it was taken. But Darren was holding something back and she wanted to know what that was. She wanted to know who he was arguing with at the petrol station. His dad looked hot-headed. Maybe Darren had been arguing with him that morning. If he had, Gina wanted to know what they'd argued about.

Wyre returned from the garden. 'Anything?' Gina asked.

She shook her head. 'Nothing out of the ordinary. There are no signs that anyone has been kept on these premises against their will.'

'Guv, I've found a syringe in Darren's room,' Jacob said as he ran down the stairs with the item in a clear bag. Gina thought back to the needle marks all over the girl's body.

'Nice work. We need to get out of here soon.'

'Why, guv?'

'We're popping in to see Callum Besford on the way home. Darren's friend, the one he stayed with. See if we can get a voluntary statement out of him. With any luck, he'll let us take a look around if we ask nicely. Darren was arguing with someone that morning. I want to see where he was staying.'

'I'll just drop Amber a message.' Gina could see he was disappointed. It had been a long day for them all. Gina's phone rang. It was forensics.

'Hello. The girl. Have you identified her from the DNA sample?' She paused as she listened to the rest of the information. 'Thank you.' She smiled as she ended the call.

'What was that about?'

'I'll tell you later.'

Mr Mason gazed at her through the window once more. He was nervous about something. People always had something to hide, most of the time the things they hid were maybe just shameful or personal to them, but not illegal. What was on the Mason family laptop that he didn't want her to see? Whatever it was, his wife didn't know. In comparison to her husband, she looked calm. Gina smiled and placed the phone in her pocket before continuing with the search.

CHAPTER TWENTY-ONE

Jacob leaned against the car window as they headed towards Winyates in Redditch. Gina steered into the shopping centre car park and spotted the flats that surrounded the small shopping area.

'How are things going with Amber?' she asked.

'Really good, I think. We get on so well and the biggie, she still hasn't dumped me. It's been three months now. Apart from Beth, she's the longest. Any good-looking men on your horizon?'

She let out a comedy laugh as they stepped out of the car, heading up the ramp towards the flats above the shops. An old bike was secured to the railing. Gina doubted anyone would pinch it, given its rusty condition and flat tyres. A large spider dangled from a cobweb that reached all the way from the handlebars to the saddle.

As they waited for an answer at Callum Besford's flat, a group of six youths kicked a ball and supped energy drinks below, shouting obscenities. She knocked on the door again and inhaled the smell of fresh paint.

'Hello,' the young man said as he opened it. He was wearing a T-shirt with a designer tear on the shoulder. He removed his glasses and pulled his jeans further up his super skinny waist. There was someone he reminded her of. His facial features matched that of a young Clark Kent in the original *Superman* films. He looked to be in his early twenties.

'DI Harte and DS Driscoll. May we come in and speak with you?'

'Of course. Is it about what the kids did the other week? I had to repaint the door.'

'No. We need to speak to you about Darren Mason.'

'Oh. He told me the police had contacted his dad about his van being in the area where that girl was found.' He led them in through the hall of a small flat. They passed a basic kitchen, one worktop and an old-fashioned cupboard with sliding wooden doors. Washing-up filled the sink and there was a smell of fried food in the air. The sitting room was tiny and overlooked a chip shop. That was where the smell was coming from. Gina's stomach rumbled as she and Jacob sat on the old brown settee.

Callum pulled a wooden chair from against the wall and sat opposite them. 'About the other incident. I know the kids were cautioned but things are becoming unbearable here. I'm gay, my neighbour is from Pakistan and he is lovely. The kids never leave us alone. It's not all the kids, most are okay. It's just the one group. They run up and down the ramp at all hours with their spray cans screaming homophobic and racist slurs. I'm trying to get out of here. Just need to save a bit more money. We were going to wait until Darren finished his degree before we officially move in together.'

'That was one of my questions. Are you and Darren in a relationship?'

'Yes. Look, I haven't heard from him all day. I'm worried, especially with the way things are around here. I went for a walk around the car park, looking for his van. I was relieved when I couldn't see it. I thought he'd been attacked or something, not that he can't look after himself, he can… I just worry. He never ignores my calls and his phone is turned off.'

'We have Darren at the station while we conduct our enquiries. He's perfectly safe and you can rest assured, he's all in one piece. I'm sure he'll call you as soon as he's able.'

'Phew.' The man leaned forward, clasped his arms around his legs as if hugging them.

'Can you tell us how Darren was on the morning of Saturday the fourteenth of July? He said he stayed here.'

'That's right. He stays a lot and even goes to uni from here. He left really early, said something about trimming a tree in Cleevesford. Said he'd be back in the afternoon and he was. We hung out here until evening and someone tagged him in a news post on Facebook, something about the van. I didn't take much notice but Darren kept going on about it, but we soon forgot.'

Jacob began making notes and Gina leaned forward, partly so that she didn't have to sit on the sticky patch behind her. She sniffed her hand hoping it wasn't anything sinister, and was relived to discover it was golden syrup. 'Let's go back to that morning. What time did Darren get up?'

'It was early, I know that much. He wanted to make a start before it got too hot. I think it was before six. He threw his clothes on and left.'

'Did you speak?'

Callum sat up and looked away. 'A bit.'

'What about?'

'Him and his family, well, his dad.'

'Could you tell us more?'

He looked at both of them in turn and nodded. 'We started arguing the night before and I barely slept.' She could tell he was nervous as he was scratching his neck. 'His dad doesn't know about us. We've been together for two years and I haven't met any of his friends. I kept telling Darren, if I meet them I'll be on my best behaviour and I won't embarrass him. I'm not a bad person and I'd love to be a bigger part of his life and not feel like some dirty secret. I know it's hard though. He's not ready to come out.'

'I see. Did these *words* carry on after he left?'

'I was really upset when he left and things got a bit heated. I suppose I hoped he'd call me to apologise. A while later, probably just before seven, he tried to call. I didn't answer. I wasn't playing games, it was just that I was still wound up and upset. I didn't want him to know that I was crying. Anyway, he tried again and I answered. Things went from bad to worse. He told me that I'd never meet his parents and that's how it had to be if I loved him. I hung up and that pissed him off because he tried to call me a few more times before finally giving up. Of course, when he got home, I forgave him as I always do. I know how hard he's having it because I've been where he is now. But people accept these things once they know. Family do, friends don't care; at least mine don't. Darren cares though. I don't pretend to know it all.'

'You've been really helpful. Would we be able to see the call log on your phone for that morning?' Callum handed his mobile to Jacob. He took a few photos and made a few notes. 'I know this is a big ask but it will really help Darren and us. Does Darren share your room?'

'Yes. He even has his own wardrobe.'

'May we take a look?' Gina held her breath as she waited for his answer, hoping that he'd consent to them conducting an informal search.

Callum nodded and led them to the dark bedroom. The black curtains looked like they'd been drawn all day. There were no clothes on the floor like there had been in Darren's room at his parents' house. Gina placed a pair of gloves over her hands and opened the wardrobe. Darren's clothes were neatly hung and his shoes were lined up along the bottom. She felt between the clothing, in pockets, and inside the shoes before heading to the bedside tables. She slid the drawers open and found nothing of interest. There was a copy of *The Lord of the Rings* and a box of tissues. She flicked through the book, nothing fell out. She kneeled and looked under the bed. Again, it was as tidy as the wardrobe and the carpet was clean.

'There really isn't much to see in here. I keep it tidy, can't bear clothes everywhere.'

He was right, there was nothing out of place. She spotted an old greyish stain on the pale green carpet and moved her hand away from it. Tidy but grubby, she concluded. After a quick glance behind the furniture, she gave Jacob the nod. 'Thank you so much for your cooperation. I'll call Redditch Police to follow up on the incident you reported.'

'Thank you. Will I be able to see Darren soon?'

'I'm sure he'll call you when we've finished our enquiries. He's perfectly safe though so you don't have to worry about his welfare.' Gina smiled. 'May I use your bathroom?'

He nodded and held his hand out, pointing to the next door. He and Jacob headed back to the lounge. The damp room still smelled of what was probably his morning shower. Black mildew covered the whole back wall and the light looked like the wiring had become slightly exposed. She wondered how landlords had the nerve to charge for properties in this state. She made a note to let the council know. Maybe they'd conduct an inspection and force the landlord to improve the flat. She opened the bathroom cabinet. Again nothing out of the ordinary. She checked her watch. It was almost seven in the evening.

'Right, we'll leave you to it. Once again, thank you,' she said when she returned to the lounge.

They left and Callum closed the door.

'So, Darren had been arguing with Callum, that's why he was on his phone a lot. There was nothing in that flat. Callum was totally cooperative and he seemed like a nice lad.'

'He did,' Jacob said as he opened the car door. 'Briefing first thing, I suppose?'

'Yes. I'll check that the system's updated with the forensic results that came back on the girl in the hospital. We have so much to talk about. In the meantime, we can only hope that the technical team get back to us before Darren Mason's twenty-four hours is up. There's no way we'll get an extension on what we have so far. We need to know what was on the phone and the laptop and what had been in that syringe. Bernard will be attending to go over any updates on what he and Keith found.'

CHAPTER TWENTY-TWO

Miley curled up in the corner of her room at the back of the house, shaking and hoping that the boss would bring her some medicine soon. Her stomach had been playing up something rotten. Jackie had been calling out until about half an hour before, but her room was now silent. There was no way Miley could go and check on her. She had to stay near the bathroom, like she'd been doing for the last two hours. She heaved again but there was no use going to the bathroom, there was nothing left to come out of her. 'Stop,' she screamed as a pain shot through her body. The heat was the worst. Sweating – she dripped like a tap; her misshaped T-shirt had soaked through. All she had wanted was to walk on the grass but no one had come to let her out. She wanted to feel what it was like to breathe in fresh air, to walk barefoot on the ground, to listen to the birds chirping. 'Let me out!' Tears mingled with sweat and ran down her cheeks. No one ever heard. She didn't really care about going out for a walk any more. She only wanted her medicine.

Reaching down, she scratched her leg until she drew blood. The flaring red stripes going down her shin were now allowing little droplets of blood to escape. She scratched again. It was like there were insects burrowing under her skin, trying to find an escape. She'd let them out so they could be free. She clawed and clawed until finally she'd sliced a piece of skin with her nails.

An armoured black insect with a visible exoskeleton emerged from the wound, having pushed through muscle and flesh until its large head poked out, peering at her with its compound eyes, each receptor an eye in itself. Her mind turned to how the creepy crawly must see. How many of her could it see? One, five, a thousand. She screamed as the creature pushed the final part of its body out, the abdomen. As it did, the wound stretched further and blood began to drip down her leg. 'Get off me,' she cried as she went to hit it. The insect pushed its wings from its thorax, dodging her hand as it flew away, buzzing around the window. It wasn't like any fly she'd ever seen. 'It's not real, it's not real,' she kept repeating. 'You're not real.'

'There, this should make things better. You know I always make sure you're well looked after. I don't know why.' Her skewed vision caught sight of him as he leaned over her.

'Thank you,' she whimpered as she lay flat on the floor. He could administer her medicine wherever he liked.

'Not that you deserve it. I can't believe how little care you've been taking of her. She's precious to me, you know. Have you ever loved someone immensely?'

As the medicine coursed through her body, a wash of calmness began to replace the anxiety. She was on the floor, in her room, with her boss leaning over her. Such an understanding boss. No other boss would ever give her another chance after what had just happened. She reached down and brushed her fingers over her shins and legs. There were a few raised lines but no wetness. The insect had gone and she was fine. *There was no insect. There is no insect,* she kept repeating in her head.

'I love Jitterbug.' A smile spread across her face as she remembered Stacey telling her how much she loved Jitterbug. 'And my mother.'

'You need to remember why you left home and focus on that. That woman in the next room is my world and unless you treat her like she's your world, you will be punished. You know what that means.' He held up an empty syringe. 'Imagine if there were no more of these. How would that make you feel?'

Her face scrunched up as she burst into tears, laughing and crying at the same time.

'That pain you feel, before you have your medicine; it's a killer, isn't it?'

She nodded and sobbed as she dragged her fingernails along the floor. The very thought of not having the next fix lined up was shaking her to the core.

'So you will look after my darling Jaqueline?'

'I will, I promise. I love Jaqueline.' She lay back and wiped her tears away.

'You need time to think, remember how lucky you are. Remember, I saved you. Remember that.'

She sobbed and reached out for his hand, just wanting some close human contact, just a hug. 'Get off me, you filthy cow. Don't ever touch me, you hear? I never touch you, do I?'

She let out a half giggle as the drug continued to work its way through her veins. 'I hear you, loud and well. I need to go out for a walk. I want to go out,' she murmured with a smile as she wiped a string of snot from her face. 'Please let me go in the garden.'

'You will one day. Work hard, and when you deserve a treat, you will get one,' he whispered in a soothing voice.

She closed her eyes as she listened to the call of the crows coming from outside. Within moments she'd nodded off, entering a world of most welcomed dreams.

It was dark, maybe the middle of the night. She flinched as she reached down to pull the blanket from her sticky body. She shrieked in pain as she tried to touch the lamp to turn it on. Pressing the switch with her knuckle, she stared at her stinging fingertips. Each one had been burned, leaving a seeping, blistered mess where they should have been. Was that the punishment he'd promised her? It pained her to cry as she rolled on her back. They throbbed from tip to wrist. What had happened? She remembered needing her medicine and then one of the bosses had returned. She must have had her medicine as she'd felt so calm and sleepy. The insect had vanished and she'd had the most perfect dream. She'd dreamed of Freddie, her school crush. He'd never shown much interest in her but when she finally finished with this job, she'd look him up, find out what he was doing and maybe they'd date for a while, go to the cinema. That dream had ended and she was here, all alone, working hard to make something of herself. She sobbed as she bent her fingers.

Her gaze stopped at the opened bottle of unbranded vodka on the floor. There was at least half left and the top had been removed. She struggled to open the cap, careful to lift the bottle between her two palms and took a swig, before pouring a little over her wounds, letting out a yelp as she held the bottle. A creature flapped past her head. Freezing mid swig, she let the bottle slip from her quaking hands and took a few sharp breaths. The insect was back. As it flapped in front of her, following the light, she exhaled. It was just a moth, a plain old moth, searching for light in the darkness – a bit like her at this moment.

She flinched as a screech filled the air. Jackie had woken. It was her duty to attend to her. The woman constantly yelled repetitive sounds and this was followed by a bang. She held her breath, fighting against the need to gasp for air. Jackie had stopped babbling. Something had happened. She was going to be punished again.

CHAPTER TWENTY-THREE

Tuesday, 17 July 2018

All eyes were focused on Gina as she stood at the head of the main table in the incident room. 'Thank you for all being here on time,' she said as Jacob entered, looking flustered. Briggs removed his jacket and fanned a pile of paperwork in front of his face.

It was only seven thirty in the morning but the heat was already stifling. O'Connor gave the window a shove and it finally opened, letting in no breeze at all. In fact, all it let in were the midges and drunk-looking wasps that had been buzzing around outside. He pulled the cord, dragging the blind across to block out the intense sun.

Gina walked over to the front of the room with a pen, ready to update the board as they spoke. 'Thank you. Right, I have updated the system and some of you might have seen that we received the forensics results from the girl's clothing. Traces of blood have been identified that do not belong to the girl. She is A negative, the blood found on her clothing is group O. The results from her fingernail clipping show a trace of human faeces present under the fingernails, again, not her own. The question is, whose? Her state is worsening. I called the hospital for an update before this briefing and she is on almost constant monitoring.'

'So we might never get to speak to her and find out what went on?' Wyre asked as she rolled her crisp white shirtsleeves up.

'I hold out hope. She's still fighting. Have we managed to find out what was on the old Nokia phone we found in Darren Mason's room?'

Keith scratched his nose as he turned a page in his notebook. 'The battery was indeed dead. We recharged the phone and managed to turn it on. There were old messages on it, but they were messages between kids, a nine-year-old Darren and his old school friends. It looks like the parents gave him this basic phone years ago to keep tabs on him when he was playing out. I passed these over to O'Connor.'

'Yes, I followed up on the numbers. Some haven't been in use for a few years. The ones that were still in use belonged to his mother and father. Again, I read through the transcripts of the answerphone messages and his texts and there was nothing that relates to the case. All the messages date back to around 2008. I really thought we were on to something, finding that phone, but nothing. Sorry, guv.'

It wasn't what she hoped it would be, O'Connor was right. 'Damn it, anything back on the family laptop?'

O'Connor annoyingly tapped his fingers on the table as he read his notes. 'Yes. This was interesting. I know why Mr Mason didn't want us to take his computer.' He paused and smiled. Gina shrugged her shoulders. 'He was downloading porn, of the legal adult variety. The account was in his name anyway.'

'So nothing again? We can't have him on his father's legal porn downloads. What about the syringe in Darren Mason's room?'

Keith swigged his drink and sat back. 'We analysed traces of the substance in the syringe. It had been used to inject anabolic steroids. They are injected into the muscle, where the steroid is released slowly. He was probably hoping to increase muscle mass. Also, as part of the testing that we did, the results from the girl's blood shows us that she'd been using heroin.'

'So we can't even link the contents of his syringe to her?'

'That's right, guv.' Keith closed his pad.

'The orders for the steroid injections were also showing on the laptop. Didn't even try to hide it. He was still logged in. Darren Mason had made the order via an online supplier. Looking into the supplier is just another job to add to the ever increasing list,' O'Connor said.

'I suppose we have to release him on bail, for now. Nothing linking him to the girl in his house, nothing at Callum's Besford's flat and no further evidence. Given that he's in a relationship with Callum Besford, we need to make sure he's safe when we release him if he's heading back there and not home. Callum told us that some local youths were harassing them, homophobic harassment. I've contacted Redditch Police and the council, they are following up on these incidents.' Gina slammed a fist on the table. 'Looks like we're back at the beginning and I really thought we were getting somewhere. We need to make sure we've plotted every stop that Darren made that morning and work on the theory that she got into the van during one of these stops. Although the girl could have been in his van since leaving Callum's flat. Maybe she got in when he was parked up in Winyates, Redditch. O'Connor, can you follow this one up? Arrange a door to door of the area. Find out if anyone saw her getting into his van on that morning or the night before. Wyre, can you go over the plot points on the map, where Darren said he'd stopped to talk to Callum on the phone. Find out what's around, anywhere she could have come from. Any CCTV, private or commercial? I know you've been working on this, but spread the net a little wider.'

Wyre nodded.

Gina's phone went. She recognised the number. The call was coming from Cleevesford Hospital. 'Excuse me,' she said as she stepped towards the window to get a clearer signal. The room filled with chatter as the rest of the team discussed their next moves.

'DI Harte.'

'Doctor Nowak,' he replied with a faint accent.

'Any updates? Has she been brought around?'

'Quite the opposite, I'm afraid there was nothing more we could do for her.'

Gina placed the flat of her hand on the window and stared out at the car park. That wasn't what she wanted to hear.

CHAPTER TWENTY-FOUR

Jacob entered Gina's office and sat opposite her. She scrolled down her messages. 'I've just forwarded some information to corporate communications detailing the girl's description, hopefully this will be on their websites as soon as they receive it, and on the radio and local news for mid-morning or lunchtime. Someone must have seen her getting into the van. Winyates is a highly populated estate. If she ended up in the van there, someone must have seen something. Maybe the youths did.'

She made a note to task Wyre and O'Connor to follow that up. 'What about CCTV? The back of the businesses lead out to this car park too. Some of them have probably got CCTV. The buses run on the road just behind the car park. People would be coming and going at most hours, and after the pub closed. It's a busy little estate centre. Maybe someone saw the girl hanging around. We need the CCTV from all the shops and the pub.'

'Then the question is, did she get in of her own free will?'

Gina began picking at the end of her biro where the plastic had broken off. She tried to imagine Winyates centre on a Friday night. Maybe the pub had been full or the chip shop had been busy. People may have been visiting one of the later hours convenience stores. Maybe someone had seen the girl; she may have been high and wandering around. Did she find the van open and decide to sleep there until morning then awoke to find the van moving? Gina shook her head. 'Why was she splattered with someone else's blood?' Gina paused for thought. 'She had a cut to her side. Had she been attacked and defended herself? Maybe she'd run away from something, using the van as a hiding place. Maybe it was the blood of another girl. Toby Biddle's words keep coming back to me. He said she whispered, "help her" to him as she lost consciousness. We have to find out if she was there first and that starts with asking questions and gathering CCTV.'

Jacob leaned back in the chair. 'Definitely. Can I nick a biscuit, guv?' She slid the almost empty pack of chocolate digestives across the table.

'No breakfast this morning?'

'No, Amber didn't stay over so I didn't bother making any just for me. She seemed a little miserable last night and left. She's just realising what it's like to date a detective. It took longer than I thought it would. They all say they don't mind the hours and the call-outs, but eventually they get fed up. It's been a passionate few months,' he said with a smirk.

'I gather it's not love then?'

'I did wonder. I suppose I had high hopes, but nah. I'll survive. I might be wrong, she said she was coming over tonight but what will be will be.' He took the last whole biscuit and crunched down on it.

'Wyre is working on all the stops that Darren Mason took. I can see this is going to take up a lot of our resources and I can't see us getting any extra officers to do all the groundwork. What a luxury that would be. We are going to need Smith's assistance. I know he's battling the drug issues in Cleevesford so do be nice.'

'Aren't I always? We both know Smith loves assisting us on the juicier cases.'

'Get some of his team over to all the places Wyre pinpoints. Ask at the houses and businesses. See if anyone knows anything. We also have the appeal, as soon as that airs, I'm sure we'll be inundated.'

'Full day ahead then, guv?'

Gina finally snapped off a piece of the pen's casing and dropped it onto the desk. 'Isn't it always? The singed off fingerprints bug me a lot. Either she or someone else was trying to conceal her identity. Why? After the conversation with Doctor Nowak, he also said they spotted a very small amateur tattoo on one of her buttocks – *live the dream*. I suppose we'll learn far more from the post-mortem. We need to check missing persons too. Someone out there must be missing a daughter, a sister, a friend.'

'I'll get on to missing persons before the influx of calls come through.' Jacob pulled her door closed as he left.

Gina grabbed the last bit of broken biscuit and began crunching on it as she opened the case files, her mind wandering into her own life as she caught up on the case. *That girl could be anyone's daughter, it could have been Hannah.* As the biscuit mulched in her mouth, she shivered as her stomach clenched and her heart rate increased. She tried to swallow but her throat wasn't obeying her wishes. She grabbed the paper bin and spat the biscuit out as she gasped for breaths.

She tried to block out the difficulties she and Hannah were having, hoping that the silent treatment would end at some point. Closing her eyes, she tried to think about happier times.

She remembered taking Hannah to the park when she was about six. They'd laughed so much as Gina had gone down the big slide, head first, following six-year-old Hannah. She'd got wedged in the middle. Hannah ran back around and went down the slide behind her, placing her little feet over Gina's, slowly pushing her to the bottom, both of them in fits of laughter. 'I'll rescue you, Mummy,' Hannah had said. 'I'll rescue you.' She had rescued her, in more ways than one. Her little girl had kept her sane over the years as she processed what she'd been through with Terry. Without Hannah in her life, who knows where she may have ended up? Only, it was a shame things had to change. Hannah changed as her teen years took over and their relationship had never recovered.

Gina flinched as the office phone went. Briggs.

'Harte, the press release is out. It's online but it will be hitting the radio soon and the local news on TV at noon. Be ready.'

CHAPTER TWENTY-FIVE

Julia threw her backpack onto the kitchen table, flicked the switch on the kettle and placed a cup on the worktop. Her daughter was still out there somewhere, mixed up in who knows what and here she was, making a cup of tea. She grabbed the cup and screamed as she threw it at the patio doors, making a slight chink in the glass. With white knuckles, she gripped the spoon and allowed her pent up tears to fall down her cheeks. If Christina's friend had said something sooner, she might have found her daughter. After this long, the trail was weak and she could be anywhere. And who was the lad she'd taken off with? The girl had told her all about Christina's crush on a boy at school. If only that boy had accepted her proposition of a date rather than humiliated her in front of everyone, telling the whole school that Christina was a mini stalker because she swooned over him when he walked by. Isn't that what a lot of teenagers do? Swoon over boys and girls they liked.

Their conversation had been useful. She was looking for someone called Westley, no surname as yet. Apparently, he was known for hanging around by the river in Worcester, exactly where she'd hung the posters up. Christina must have been hanging around there with him and not one person had called with information, not one person had anything whatsoever to say. She opened the fridge and grabbed a half-opened bottle of wine and poured a glass. Coffee wasn't going to cut it today.

Christina had only spoken about him to her friend once or twice, saying that she'd met him in Worcester and that he was good fun to be around. A bit older, she'd said. What was a bit? Was he seventeen or was he in his twenties? She had said Christina mentioned that he wanted to try living in Birmingham at some point, thought there might be some work for him. Had he groomed her little girl and taken her to Birmingham? Or had they run away together? Christina certainly had a wild and rebellious streak but she was so naïve in many ways, always thinking she knew it all.

The police needed to know. She ran away, yes, but had she gone off with someone dangerous and was she still with him? Maybe they'd received reports about someone called Westley in Worcester or even Birmingham. It might provide a link at least. Her mind conjured up images, from homeless young people sitting in the doorways of Birmingham Centre shops to sleazy houses offering massages, where runaway kids were being pimped out.

'Roy,' she said as she turned. 'I didn't hear you come home. You're meant to be at work.'

He took the wine from her hand and poured it down the sink. 'This has to stop. I know you blame me for the other day, but every weekend since she left I've been out there with you, haven't I?'

'Reluctantly.'

'You never shut up, do you? I'm trying my best here.'

She nodded, holding back any further tears. Things were already tense between them. He'd said a lot he probably regretted and so had she. 'Whatever.'

'I want to help, I really do. But every weekend we replace posters that don't need replacing. It's not getting us anywhere. I can't keep doing this. I get really pissed off when you throw it in my face that I've never had kids of my own and I can't possibly understand. I've been there for you both, haven't I? Yes, things have been difficult. Yes, she doesn't really like me living here and threw that in my face more than once when having one of her outbursts. I've let all that ride because I can see it from her point of view. She has you all to herself and suddenly it's you and me all the time. Anyway, I'm here now. So, what next? I am not going to just replace posters on lamp posts. Now what was it you wanted to tell me?'

He was right. She'd thrown so many insults at him and pushed him away. 'This morning, you wondered where I had been.'

'Yes?'

'I met Christina's friend. She told me Christina went off with someone she'd been hanging around with along the river in Worcester, someone called Westley.'

'She what? Why didn't that girl say something earlier? What else did she say?'

'She wasn't much help, she seemed really upset that she hadn't told me earlier.'

'No wonder. Had she said something back then, we could've been looking for this Westley all along.'

'She promised Christina she wouldn't say anything.'

'Not good enough.' Roy slammed his fist on the kitchen table and his face began to redden. 'All this time she knew something and she didn't say a word, not to us, not to the police. Did you ask the other kids about this Westley?'

Julia wiped a tear from her cheek. 'I did, but no one had ever heard of him. What if someone has been grooming my girl and taken her? All the arguments we had, both of us… we drove her away. If she was happy, she wouldn't have gone with him.' Julia burst into tears and gripped Roy.

'All the arguments were about her and it wasn't just me moaning. The neighbours complained every five minutes, the school were always on at us. Are you really saying this is my fault?'

'I never said that. You know I never said that.'

'I'm sorry.' He pulled her close to him and hugged her. 'We will find her, I promise. We'll call the police, tell them what you've found out. They may have heard of him. We'll call the local papers, ask if anyone knows of a Westley who hangs around by the river. Here. Come on.' He led her into the lounge and put the television on. 'I'm going to make you a cup of tea, we'll call the police and you can tell them what you know. If Christina's friend does know more that she's not telling, the police will get it out of her.'

Julia slumped into the armchair and stared blankly at the television screen as Roy went out to make a drink. A report came on the local news, something about an appeal, an unidentified girl being found in the Cleevesford area, between the age of fourteen and seventeen years old. The girl was now dead. 'No!' she yelled, hands shaking, heart hammering.

Roy ran in holding a teaspoon. His gaze followed hers until they were both staring at the screen. He kneeled down and hugged her closely. 'It's not her. It can't be her.'

'She's dead. My little girl is dead,' the woman cried as she broke down.

CHAPTER TWENTY-SIX

Gina rewatched the appeal that had aired on the lunchtime local news. Someone had to come forward. Tapping her fingers on her desk, she scanned the files in front of her, catching sight of the girl's photo. The one of her lying in the hospital bed. She'd been too weak to pull through. She turned the photo over, not wanting to look at it any longer. Someone tapped at her office door. 'Come in.'

Wyre sat opposite her and brushed her trousers with her hands, in her usual neat way. 'The lines are going mad from the appeal. Nothing serious to follow up on as yet and everyone's on it.'

'How's it going, pin-pointing all the possible places Darren Mason may have stopped?'

'He's been fairly cooperative since we've released him on bail. He remembers several places he stopped but he says he can't remember all of them. I've been going through his whole route and he agrees the route we marked on the map was the route he took. There are so many little passing places and pull in areas, there could be a few more. I've made a list of places to check, businesses, houses etcetera, and I'm hoping to be able to head out this afternoon to do the legwork. I asked Smith. He looks stressed, to be fair, but he said he'll assist us for a couple of hours and there are a few members of his team that can come along too.'

'Sounds like all is organised for the door to doors. Such a large area to cover.'

'How are things with you, guv? Found out much else?'

'Only what we discussed in the briefing. I was speaking to Jacob earlier and went back for a look at the information that has come back from forensics so far. The full pathologist's report isn't complete as yet.' She paused and turned the photo back over. 'I can't stop thinking about the burned off fingerprints. I reread the report. It mentioned that there was a circular shape in the burning. It made me think of car lighters, the ones you press in that heat up. It's not confirmed as yet, but it seems like a possibility.'

Wyre picked a piece of lint from the shoulder of her crisp white shirt. 'Ouch. That sounds horrible.'

Gina picked the only nail she'd successfully managed to grow. 'It would hurt so much, there's no way someone could do that to themselves.'

'What if the drugs masked the pain?'

'They'd probably also affect her coordination. Look at this.' Gina turned the screen around so that Wyre could see it.

'They're all perfectly centred.'

'Too perfect for someone who is writhing in agony or has just shot up. It didn't even look like she'd put up a struggle. There's no evidence to show that whoever did this missed the target at any point. If someone was singeing my skin I'd be wriggling around, frantically trying to get away. There's not one burn mark that looks like it's gone over the outer circle.'

'Maybe she was sedated.'

'That's what I was thinking. It's looking even more sinister now.' Gina turned her screen back and flicked to the photo of the disc with the letters E Ho scrawled across the front. 'Then we have the dog tag with the letters E Ho. Had she stolen or found it? Are those initials hers or did the disc end up in Darren Mason's van by some other means? I go with the thought that the girl had it on her. The report mentioned that traces of her blood were found on the disc, probably from the abdominal wound.

Whether she found it in the van, who knows? Maybe she isn't E Ho, maybe she is. The appeal needs to come up with something and it needs to be quick.'

Her phone rang. Wyre sat back as Gina took the call. 'DI Harte.'

'I think…' the woman began to sob. 'The girl you found, she might be my daughter.'

CHAPTER TWENTY-SEVEN

Bryn Tilly pulled his vest over his head and threw it down by the old house. He'd never suffered with the heat as a young builder but since his fifties had crept up on him, the weight had become harder to shift and played havoc with his joints.

The biggest investment he'd ever made was standing beside him. The bricks and mortar had been solid, which is why they'd bid so high for it at the auction, knowing that the work would be mostly cosmetic. One hundred and eighty-four thousand pounds had been a bargain for this rundown house with land to the one side and dense woodland that backed onto the garden. It would make him and the investors a tidy profit. He almost wanted to run around the garden, singing with glee as he imagined his soon to be bank balance. Cleevesford was a sought-after area. Good links to the motorways to get to London or Birmingham made it even more appealing.

His phone flashed as an email pinged up. Stan and Elizabeth North wanted the full breakdown of what had been spent to date. As investors they deserved to know but he'd been a bit disorganised. He hadn't told them that he'd skimped on the country kitchen to have a summerhouse erected at the bottom of the garden. People want more, they want outbuildings, little escapes from everyday stresses – hobby rooms, and he was going to provide that to hike the price up. When Stan and Elizabeth came to see the progress, he knew he'd win them around. At the very least, they'd stop nagging him for not having it done on time. It had only been eight weeks and he had no idea why they were going on at him so much. He had another month and, he guessed, about eleven thousand pounds to reach completion.

The sun was beginning to burn his head. He used his vest to mop the sweat away. Slapping the belly that hung over his shorts, he leaned down and pulled a sausage roll from his cool bag, and began chomping on the buttery pastry. The old lady who had died in the house wouldn't recognise it if she came back from the dead. She'd died without leaving a will and had no living relatives to leave the house to. The estate had finally been passed to the Crown before being auctioned off.

Finishing the sausage roll, he checked the time. He could go and tackle the shrubs at the back of the garden. Shaking his head, he sat down. He would wait for the mini digger to arrive before tackling the overgrown shrubs and levelling off the back area, ready for the summerhouse to be erected next week. He'd booked his mate Jack and would use him to the full when he got here and that meant not doing sweaty work alone.

In the distance, he heard Jack's van trundling up the bumpy drive. Right on time.

'Jack,' he called, beckoning his old friend over. Sixty-two and still operating diggers for a living. Their paths had crossed on many projects and they quite often met at the Angel Arms for a few bevvies after a hard day's work. Maybe today he'd treat Jack, but only if they got all the work done.

'You need to put the T-shirt back on, you fat old sod,' Jack called back as he pulled the trailer up.

'You're a fine one to use the word old!' Bryn grinned and stuck his middle finger up at his friend. 'I didn't start on the garden, thought I'd wait for you.'

Jack backed the mini digger off the trailer as he shouted out the window. 'Charming. Like you say, I'm old. Now I have to start digging up shrubs before we can start digging the excess earth out.'

'You love it really.'

Bryn followed Jack to the end of the garden. Jack turned and looked at the house. 'You know I always take the piss but this… I mean, you've done a grand job in such a short time. This house is something. Wish me and Maisie could live somewhere like this. It's so peaceful around here, no bloody noisy neighbours to ruin the atmosphere with the stink of their weed and loud parties.'

Smiling, Bryn put on some gardening gloves and started to wade through the wild rosebushes, long grass and stinging nettles, until his eye caught on something entangled in the grass. Off white, covered in what looked like gnaw marks. It was probably an animal bone. Curiosity drew him closer.

'What you fixed on?' Jack asked as he stepped towards him.

'Nothing, I think it's just an animal bone.'

'Let me see.' Jack nudged Bryn out of the way and bent over for a closer look. He placed a glove on it and brushed the dry earth aside. 'It's not an animal bone. Look!'

'It could be anything.'

As Jack brushed more earth away, Bryn could see more of it appearing before him as more earth was shifted. Bryn straightened up. Sweat glistened, sliding over his forehead, into his eyes. He wiped it away and refocused. His normal jovial expression now a wash of seriousness. 'Bloody hell, that's a human hand.'

CHAPTER TWENTY-EIGHT

Prising her sticky eyes open, Miley stared at the skirting board, watching the insects crawling through the carpet. The beetles had been breeding, laying their young in the fibres. One of the larvae wriggled towards her nose. Heart pounding, she jolted up, fighting the sway of the room. She shuffled away and nudged the caterpillar with her big toe. It still kept coming at her. She leaned forward, flinching as she poked the creature with her index finger.

A burning pain shot from her fingertip to her hand, the burns now starting to blister. Tears spilled from the corners of her eyes as she shook her hands, trying to shake away the stinging sensation. As she struggled for breath, she cried out. The pain wasn't easing at all.

The caterpillar remained still. She'd killed it. Maybe it wasn't a moth caterpillar, maybe it had come from her. 'It was a dream,' she yelled as she closed her eyes, willing the wriggly creature to be gone. *Imagine that it will be a beautiful butterfly soon.*

There was another bang on the bedroom wall, coming from Jackie's room. She remembered the bang in the night that had filled her with fear. She hadn't heard anything of Jackie since. Holding her breath, she listened. Her heart began to pound.

She had work to do. No work, no medicine. No medicine, she would be forced to live in a perpetual state of horror. She gazed around the room, an empty bottle of vodka sat on the bedside table and the lamp was still on. She lifted her hands up and stared at her seeping fingertips. Besides the vodka bottle was a pack of unopened bandages. Tears fell down her cheeks as she pulled the packet open with her teeth and struggled to wrap, tie and tape down the thin bandage over some of her fingertips. 'What have you done to me?' she yelled, her voice weak and breaking as she sobbed. 'What have you done to Jackie?'

Again, someone banged on the wall and Miley's heart sunk. Someone was there, listening to her every move. Her heartbeat throbbed through her head, affecting her hearing. Jaqueline began to make the only noises she could now manage, repeating the same pattern over and over. She exhaled and smiled. Jackie was still there.

'Just keep still,' the other boss's voice called out. She heard a slap. Jackie began to shout uncontrollably and there was a crash to the floor. 'You're nothing now, look at you. Nothing!' the other boss yelled, slapping Jackie once again. 'Look at me. Who ever thought things would turn out this way. I told you then, what's yours is mine, and I meant it, every word. You little bitch. This is what happens to little snitches.'

'Jackie,' Miley called, tears streaming down her face. Caring for Jackie was her job and she'd failed her – she couldn't protect her friend. He wouldn't be happy with her now. She shivered, wondering what punishment he'd dish out.

Whatever happened in the night was a blur. Maybe she'd had too much vodka and stumbled out after taking her medicine. It's possible she could have gone downstairs and somehow reached the kitchen. Maybe she touched the cooker with all ten fingers. She shook her head and hit it with the flat of her hand. 'Stupid brain, remember!' However hard she tried to recall what had happened, nothing was coming back. She had no recollection of how the burns had appeared on her fingertips. She remembered waking in the night and pouring vodka on the wounds. How did the vodka get there? She'd drunk the last of it to try and numb the pain and somehow she had woken on the floor.

A large spindly-legged spider dangled from the ceiling. She batted it away with her wrist. Heart pounding, she hoped it wouldn't come back. She needed to clean her room. A vacuum would be most welcome but she'd never been given a vacuum. Crumbs littered the carpet and dustballs collected all along the edge of the room. Everything was dirty and every inch of space was slowly being taken over by insects or spiders. At first, she'd freaked out when they'd invaded her space, but now they just startled her when they came close. Now she could cope. It was an old house after all. She staggered over to the door. It was locked. She kneeled and tried to focus through the keyhole. The top of the stairs was void of any activity. No breakfast had been left. With jittery hands, she leaned on the door as she willed the dizziness to subside. Water, she needed water and her stomach was rumbling. She didn't know if it was screaming for food or screaming with upset. It had become hard to tell. She looked down at her ankles and winced. Her legs had become so thin, almost looking like they might snap. They were scratched and blotchy from the spots and her habit of tearing shreds out of them.

Jackie's screaming got louder and she heard a muffled shout, followed by a whacking noise. She flinched. Jackie was such a poorly woman with no one to love her. She could be difficult but it wasn't her fault. Huntington's disease they'd called it. She had a disease and Miley was her carer. The person in there with her didn't care. Without Miley, Jackie would probably die. She banged on the wall. 'Please leave her alone. Let me out. I'll look after her. Please. She needs me.'

She listened as footsteps crossed the room and continued out of the bedroom door. The other boss unlocked the bedroom door, grabbed her scrawny arm and dragged her across the landing, flinging her into Jackie's bedroom. Without thinking, Miley protected her face with her hands and landed on her side, elbow first onto a threadbare rug, narrowly missing a clump of spilled porridge. Yelling in pain, she listened as the other boss yelled and stomped down the stairs, locking the door at the bottom.

It was just her and Jackie, like it always was and how it should be. She couldn't afford to be wasted that badly again. If she was wasted and the other boss came to care for her, Jackie paid. It was her fault Jackie had been hurt. Crying out, she held her burning fingers up. Jackie was sitting on the bed, wetness pooling underneath her. Angry red welts covered Jackie's face and her swollen left eyelid began to cover her eye. Miley wanted to sit on the floor and cry all day but that wasn't an option. She needed to tend to her friend's sores before her face inflamed even more.

The bottom door unlocked once again and her oppressor stomped back up the stairs. 'Do what you're paid to do or else you'll be out, and not out for a walk either.'

Out, as in out of work? Maybe she could go home and tell social services that Jackie wasn't getting the care she needed. Her money had been saved for her. She must have earned a few hundred pounds by now, maybe a thousand. She could take the money and leave. 'How much money have I got saved?' she muttered.

'Young lady, you owe me. You know full well that I have to deduct the cost of your medicine from what we pay you. You'll be working it off for a long time. When you've paid your debt, you're welcome to walk. You don't deserve what you do get. You're useless.'

She scraped her arm across her eyes, trying to catch the tears. All this work and she had ended up in debt. Going without her medicine was not an option. She needed it to function. She was sure she'd die without it. She'd only had it once to ease her nerves and now, she couldn't live without it. Her boss had joked about it to begin with, telling her it made the job more bearable, that it was a beautiful thing that would ease the loneliness. Apparently, it was just a mild anti-anxiety solution that was injected once every day or two. She had been assured it was safe. And it had been beautiful. So beautiful, she'd wanted more until she developed a need for it. 'How much debt am I in?'

'Just two months' worth. Work hard and you could be out of here before you know it. Work. Hard. Those are the key words. She needs you. You are her carer and you signed a contract of employment, so do your job.'

Two months. She could put a little more effort in for a couple of months. 'Can I just go in the garden one day, please?'

'No. Your work is here. We agreed and you knew what you were agreeing to.'

Her boss was right. She'd agreed to give her all to the job. 'What happened to my fingers?'

The other boss grinned and headed back down the stairs, once again locking the door. 'Why do you always lock me in?' she yelled.

The answer had always been that Jackie was being locked in for her own safety. She couldn't understand it. Jackie wasn't going anywhere quick. In fact, it would be good for Jackie to be able to sit in the garden, air a little in the sunshine rather than spending the whole day in a dingy room that stunk of urine.

Using the flat of her hand to avoid aggravating her half-bandaged fingertips, she struggled to stand. Jackie needed her. She needed to be cleaned and fed the rest of her food. Maybe they could share the rest of the porridge that was left, after all, she'd missed breakfast again. It was her fault, she'd been asleep. She only had herself to blame.

She leaned forward and hugged Jackie. It didn't matter that she didn't recognise her or show any emotion, she was human and Miley really needed a hug. 'Come on, my lovely friend, let's clean you up and I'll think of a story to tell you. We can pick up where we left off. The girl trapped in a bad place managed to escape and find the most amazing friend ever. Her name was Jackie. She and Jackie told each other everything. It's a happy ending, I promise.'

The woman began to rock and murmur incoherently. Miley cried into her thin hair, wishing Jackie would hug her back. The woman placed a hand on her back and she cried more.

'I know you care, Jackie. I know you love me and I'm your best friend in the whole world,' she said as she sobbed. 'We are going to get out of here together, I promise.'

CHAPTER TWENTY-NINE

'We could do without this, with all that's happening lately,' Jacob said as he and Gina passed the large, flustered looking man in the garden.

'The man said it was a hand,' Gina replied.

Bernard's lanky frame blocked the sunlight as he approached. He pulled down his mask, allowing some of his long grey beard to escape. 'We beat you to it. The bad news is, the hand has been dried out, due to being exposed to the sun. We found gnaw marks on the bones from the wildlife. The good news is, if you can call any of this good, we have found the rest of the body and it wasn't too far away. More bad news though, it is in a shallow grave, resulting in some of the limbs being missing. As you know, this happens quite a lot. The wildlife gets a whiff of death and comes looking for a meal. We have crime scene investigators searching for the rest along with the officers that arrived first.'

She gazed into the woodland and watched the CSIs in their white suits erecting a tent. 'Is that where the grave is?'

'Yes. The tent is to preserve the body as much as we can. It's not a pretty sight. Both of the left limbs were taken and have since dried out as has the rest of the body. The animals in question probably caught the scent of the cadaver, dug a little, exposing the body, leaving it out for the elements and heat, and it has been hot for a while now.'

'Can I see?'

'Yes, suit and boot, then head over. I'll come with you.'

'Thanks.' Gina grabbed a forensics suit, boot and hair covers, and gloves. 'Jacob, will you go and take statements from Bryn Tilly and Jack Dunn? Find out what they were doing here and who owns this house. Find out who's keeping a scene log and make sure they have Bryn and Jack's shoe sizes and prints etcetera.'

Jacob nodded. 'Will do, guv.'

As she zipped the forensics suit up, she began the walk over to the tent, being careful to step on the plates that had been laid down.

Bernard beckoned her over. As the investigators were finishing off with the tent, Gina stood back. She could see the grave and the body. One CSI walked around with a camera, taking photos of the exhibits they'd discovered. 'The left femur is over there, exhibit two. The radius is over there.' He pointed into the distance. 'They weren't scattered too far.'

'Thankfully not,' Bernard replied.

'Right, talk me through your initial observations.'

'I've had a chance to see the body close up. The hip formation shows that of a girl, I'm estimating fifteen at the youngest, possibly up to adulthood. It's hard to tell and I'll know more when we've taken her away from here and examined her properly. As you can see, she is lying on a blanket, which will also be taken away and analysed for forensic evidence once we've carefully removed her bones. Look at what's left of her hair.'

Gina leaned to the side as the crime scene photographer walked in front of her. 'The hair looks red.'

'Yes, pheomelanin adds the orange colour to the hair and this doesn't break down with oxidisation. The red pigmentation has been left behind. She had shades of red in her hair.'

'Height?'

'Again, a good estimate. As you can see, she's been scrunched up into that position, almost like a very compressed foetal position. She would have been buried very soon after death otherwise she'd have been too stiff to bend. Between five foot four and five foot seven.

As you can see, what was once a white nightdress was pulled over her body. She is also wearing underwear. Stating the obvious, but this will also be sent to the lab for analysis. I don't know what we'll get from it. At least three months have passed for the body to be at this stage, could be as many as six. Given the weather patterns, extreme wintery conditions to heatwave, and the geographical location, the soil etcetera, I would say it's more likely to be about four months. Further testing is needed, so don't take that as exact.'

Gina nodded as she made further notes. Her gaze locked onto the grave. The girl looked as though she'd been carefully placed, dressed in a decorative white nightdress with broderie anglaise around the neckline, cuffs and hem. She had been dressed in underwear. There had been a certain amount of dignity applied in her burial suggesting that the victim may have been cared for.

'Jennifer over there is just taking samples of the soil.' She focused on the CSI kneeling down and placing the sample in a tube, before filling out the evidence bag and placing it in her box. 'We will be looking at the soil concentration as this will help in pinpointing the time of death. The soil's make up varies with how decomposed the body is. There is a little muscle attached to the bone, which we will also be testing. There are also nails to swab. There may be traces of something telling underneath. Teeth may identify her through dental records but you know all that already. Her bones will be examined, giving us an even better indication of her age,' Bernard said.

'Thanks for that and don't let me keep you. The quicker this is all done, the better.'

Bernard nodded and waved at one of his assistants. 'I'll be back in a moment. Just going to have a close look at the limbs. Do you need anything else from me?'

'Like I said, only for all these tests to be done immediately. We need to identify her. Someone out there is missing a daughter.'

He laughed. 'I'll do my best. I know you always need things *now* but we'll work as quickly as we can. We have a lot of staff booked out on holiday, trying to get it in before the kids break up. The samples will be taken to the lab in a short while. This is a big job though.'

'Do your very best. I'll see you at the next briefing with at least some results to share? I'll call you later.'

He nodded and left her in front of the tent. The canvas was now pulled completely over the grave, shading what was left of the body from the sun. The general public weren't a worry as the woodland was far out from the town. She listened as a tractor chugged in the distance. About thirty yards from the main road, there was a small pull in place on the single-track country road. That particular road provided a barely used cut through, just on the outskirts of Cleevesford. One person could just about manage to drag a body alone for that distance.

Not many people would know the cut through existed and whoever brought the body would probably know that they wouldn't be disturbed. Someone with local knowledge had to have buried her there. They chose this location for that very reason.

Another girl. The girl who had died in hospital had been found only three miles from the body in the shallow grave. Could they be linked? Both estimated to be in their mid-teens. Maybe the lab results might throw up a connection. Maybe both were taken at the same time and one died or was killed. The other girl could have escaped. From what and who? Gina's brain was alight with all the possibilities. Maybe they weren't even connected. Two girls of a similar age was a coincidence though.

'All right, guv?' Jacob called.

She turned and walked back. An officer walked past her with a roll of cordon tape. 'What did we get from the two men working on the house?'

Jacob removed his jacket then wiped the beads of sweat from his brow. The midday heat was at its hottest and the heatwave was set to continue. 'Bloody hell, it's boiling. Updates. I've just spoken with them. They're heading to the station now to make a formal statement. I've called Wyre and prepped her for their arrival.' She glanced over at the younger man of the two, probably in his mid-fifties, and watched him pulling his sweat drenched vest over his head before heading towards his car with the older man. 'The older man, the one on the right, he is Jack Dunn. Friends with Bryn Tilly. He was hired today to come along with a mini digger to help level this land off. They were just about to start clearing the shrubbery when they spotted the bones. The hand to be more precise.'

'Bryn Tilly, he had access to this property before?'

'Only since mid-April, the twentieth to be precise. He bought this property at auction with another two investors, a couple called Stan and Elizabeth North. Their aim was to do it up as quickly as possible and make a quick quid.'

'I suppose he could have come at any time before now, for a look. Entering from the road by foot through the woodland. Who owned it before?'

'From what he says an elderly lady died in the property about a year ago, of natural causes. From what he heard, she was ninety-six and lived downstairs as she had mobility problems. The place had stank when he started work and it was fairly rundown. He was told that the estate passed to the Crown and was subsequently auctioned.'

'The Crown?'

'Yes. She had no surviving relatives and hadn't left a will. She had no one to leave it to.'

'I see. Can you call the team and ask someone to verify that? So, the only person who had access to the property was an elderly woman in her nineties, with no family. Maybe the council can help us find out if she had help from carers or if social services had ever been involved.'

Had Bryn Tilly and the Norths had their eye on the property before and had they chosen this property for a reason? She struggled with her thoughts. If they had any involvement, why would Tilly call the police?

'Oh and, guv, Tilly looked well fed up about us being here, saying we were going to set the work on the house back and they wouldn't be able to sell it. Jack Dunn kept going on, saying that reporting it was the right thing to do.'

Now her mind was ticking. Maybe Tilly hadn't wanted Dunn to look too closely. Dunn had spotted the hand and wanted to report it. 'Where does Bryn Tilly live?'

'In Cleevesford, near the centre. He has done most of his life. Born and bred, he said.'

'So he'd know the area well.'

'What are you thinking?'

Gina turned and headed towards the car. 'Lots of things, lots. Is that the time? We need to get over to Worcester to speak with Mrs Dawson. Our girl who fell from the van may just have a name.'

CHAPTER THIRTY

Gina drove past Ronkswood Hill Meadows in Worcester. The smell of cattle and cut grass filled the car. She remembered bringing fifteen-year-old Hannah for a walk over the meadows in an attempt to reconnect with her. By the end of the walk, she realised it was too late. The girl spent most of their time together texting on her phone, asking when they were going home and moaning that she was missing out on what her friends were doing.

Back then she was working hard in the police to give them a better life. That day had changed things. Gina realised that she had to do things for herself. People told her the teen years were difficult and that she'd see the funny side of it one day. They also said that as Hannah aged a few more years, they'd become really close. She was still waiting. Maybe Gina had been selfish and put her work first – she still did and she knew it riled Hannah, especially as Gina was her only parent.

'You just missed the turning into Mrs Dawson's road,' Jacob said.

'Sorry, I was miles away just then.' Now was not the time to dwell on her past and present problems with Hannah. She continued down the road and pulled up outside Mrs Dawson's small end of terrace house.

'Take a seat in the living room,' Mrs Dawson said. Roy sat beside his partner on the small sofa. Jacob perched on the edge of the tiny footstool, leaving Gina with the only other chair. The rims of the woman's eyes were a flaming red colour. Several mascara dabbed tissues were strewn on the floor. The man placed a protective hand around her shoulder. Her gaze moved over to Roy Fisher and his light red hair. The girl they had found in the shallow grave had red hair. 'This is her, well how I want to remember her.'

Gina took the photo as she flicked her pad over and checked the brief notes she'd taken that related to the case of missing Christina Dawson. Roy Fisher was not her father. Maybe the red hair was a coincidence or maybe there was more to Christina's disappearance than appeared on the surface. She cast her gaze across the photo. Christina had brown, shoulder-length hair but there was a definite reddish-chestnut tone to it. She could see the tones as the sun shone through the frizzier strands that gathered in a curl by her ears. The girl had her mother's features and hair colour, a perfectly symmetrical nose and a thinner top lip. 'Are you related to Christina, Mr Fisher?'

'No. We, Julia and I, have been together a couple of years and I moved in last summer.'

Jacob made a note. She had to stop and think. Julia thought her daughter was the girl that had passed away in the hospital and here she was, considering that she might be the girl they found in the shallow grave. She glanced at her notes again. The girl in the shallow grave could not be Christina as she'd been there longer, or had she been? Weather conditions all play a part in decomposition and Bernard wasn't one hundred per cent sure how long she'd been there. It had been dry, especially over the past several weeks. The girl she'd seen in the hospital also had red toned chestnut hair. She felt her skin prickle. There was a very real possibility that the girl in the hospital could be Mrs Dawson's daughter. She glanced at the photo again. The girl that was looking back at her looked healthy, slightly round in the face, smiling with a set of white teeth. The girl in the hospital had looked like she was dying. Thin, sunken. Is that what Christina looked like after being on drugs for a few months?

'Is the girl on the news my daughter?' The woman pulled a tissue from her sleeve and began dabbing her nose.

'I can't be sure, Mrs Dawson. I really am sorry for all that you've been through. We would need a DNA sample from yourself.' The woman said nothing, then her bottom lip began to quiver before she began to weep.

'I want to see her!'

'You don't have to——'

'I do.'

'Of course. I can arrange that.' Gina knew the formal identification would be useful and would be quicker than waiting for test results to come back. Maybe seeing the girl would be best for both of them.

'When?'

'Hopefully, later today. I'll need to call you in a while to confirm arrangements.'

'Thank you. I need to see if it is Christina. You do understand, don't you?' The woman wiped her cheeks and the damp tissue began to break up, leaving specs of white on her eyelashes. Roy gripped her hand.

'Did Christina have any tattoos?'

She shook her head. 'Not when she left. But she didn't tell me everything, she never did.'

Jacob scribbled more notes.

'Do the initials E Ho, mean anything to you? Maybe they are initials or short for something?'

'Her middle name begins with an E.' The woman blew her nose. 'The Ho means nothing at all.'

'I see from the case that the last time you saw Christina was on Wednesday the fourth of April. You say you have some new information relating to her disappearance?'

Julia leaned forward. 'Westley. I think she left with him, I don't know how old he is. Her friend said Christina told her to keep it a secret.'

'Do we have the friend's details?'

'Her details were logged when I called. She's gone on holiday with her parents for a couple of nights, camping. She'll be home late Thursday night.'

'We'll make sure we speak to her as soon as she's back. So, what do you know about Westley?'

'Christina met him in Worcester and they hung around by the river. She must have gone with him. I don't know what he did to my Christina after that,' she cried as she flopped back. Roy pulled her head towards his shoulder and began stroking her hair as she wept. Gina made a note of the name, Westley.

'I'm so sorry. I know this is difficult for you.'

'This person might be a paedophile and he's probably looking for his next victim as we speak,' Roy spat as he held Julia. 'She went off with him. We have no idea who he is, how old he is, where he's from or if he targeted her.'

The room was intensely hot with the four of them crammed in. Had Christina felt this crammed in? Maybe she'd felt like an outsider in her own home, the home she and her mum had lived in before Roy invaded their tiny space. 'Mrs Dawson, where does Christina's father live?' That was a piece of information that seemed to be vague in the notes. He was noted as living in a bed and breakfast establishment after being evicted from a flat in Penzance.

She pulled away from Roy. 'Cornwall, at the moment. She has nothing to do with him. I have checked and, because of what's happened, I have to keep in touch with him. He left us when she was four. Got a young woman pregnant, one he'd been seeing while working away. He was a salesman, a bad one at that. She even saw sense and threw him out. He lives in a room in a converted barn now after being of no fixed abode for months.'

'Did Christina keep in touch with him?'

'She tried but he wouldn't always call her back. She gave up in the end. It's funny how he calls all the time now, asking if I've heard from her. Some people just don't know what they've got until they lose it. He's one of those people. Me, I've always been there for her.'

'I can see that.' Gina looked at all the photos on the bookcase against the far wall. They were full of framed photos, documenting Christina's whole life. They started at the top with a baby photo, followed by a little girl in a pink tutu. A whole shelf was dedicated to school photos and there were a few of mother and daughter. They had once been so close. 'We'll arrange a time and I'll give you a call in a short while. Is there anything we can do for you in the meantime?'

'Tell me it's not her.' Roy pulled her closer to him and began stroking her hair.

Gina wished she could. She hoped their girl wasn't Christina but if she wasn't, she was somebody's daughter. Someone will feel like their world has come to an end when they eventually get the news. She didn't want Mrs Dawson's world to come to an end though.

'Was anything said before she left? Arguments?'

'No,' Roy said as he held Julia and gazed in her direction.

Something didn't ring true. Teenagers were epicentres for volatility. She would have expected a fair amount of conflict within any family. She'd also scanned over the reports on her case. Christina had been in trouble at school on numerous occasions and the neighbours had opened a case with the council about the noise coming from the Dawson's home.

'Everything was fine when she left,' Roy said as he pulled away from Julia. 'Thank you for asking though.'

*

'That was tough,' Jacob said as they buckled up and pulled away.

'I'd be devastated if that were me. I don't know why, I don't quite trust Roy. No one has no arguments when there's a teenager in the house, especially one with Christina's record. The family had the council on to them about her noise and the school was always calling about her playing truant.'

'You think he might have something to do with it?'

'I'm keeping that thought in my mind. He has a guilty look about him but I can't arrest him for that.' The times she'd only temporarily lost Hannah, those nights when she'd come home in the early hours, when she hadn't answered her phone – on many of those occasions, Gina had thought something bad had happened. For Mrs Dawson, that had been a reality. She had lived the devastation and anguish that came after that. 'Two dead girls and there's a chance that one of them is Christina. I can't wait for today to be over.'

CHAPTER THIRTY-ONE

Gina grabbed a pen and headed over to the board. The photos of the girl in the shallow grave had been pinned up on a separate board to the girl who fell from the van. Gina threw Wyre a pen, knowing her handwriting would be more legible. 'As you all know, we have two major cases on the go involving two dead girls. We've talked at length about the girl who fell from the van. Any updates?'

'No further updates, guv,' O'Connor replied as he swivelled back and forth in his chair, in a half-circle motion.

She grimaced as he spun. 'Can you stop spinning? I'm struggling to think.'

'Sorry, guv.' He stopped and concentrated on what she was saying.

'Updates?'

Jacob leaned in. 'Only the blood traces that didn't belong to the girl in the van, but we already know this. The full report hasn't come back yet. I chased this up and forensics said it would definitely be tomorrow. As always, they are understaffed and have a backlog on the go.'

'Nothing new there, then. Jacob and I have just got back from interviewing a Mrs Dawson. Her daughter, Christina, went missing on Wednesday the fourth of April this year. From their photos, both she and her mother have a natural auburn tone in their chestnut brown hair. It was confirmed at the scene that our shallow grave girl had red tones in her hair. Just to confuse matters, the girl who fell from Darren Mason's van had dyed red hair.' Her mind ticked over. Their cases didn't feel so separate any more but she had to keep in mind that the hair colour of the girls may be purely coincidental. 'We need to keep going through missing persons. We have two teenage girls and only one possible identification, which is unconfirmed at the moment. If the forensics report isn't in until tomorrow, we work with what we've got.' She leaned across and pushed the two boards closer together. 'I want you all to consider that these two cases may be related. Two girls dead, both with red tones to their hair, both in their mid to late teens. Both of them turned up in Cleevesford. What are the chances of that over a few days?'

'Anything back on the girl found in the shallow grave?' Wyre asked as she finished updating the board with the hair colour connection.

'There's still a lot of ground to cover. Bernard and Keith are there with the team and I don't think they'll be finished today. We've extended the cordon and they're searching everything. As you all know, this is a painstakingly slow process but as always, we hope they'll find something that will either lead to the girl's or the perpetrator's identity. Her clothing and the blanket she was lying on have been sent to the lab.'

Briggs entered from the back with Annie and took a seat. Gina's heart rate began to pick up as they both cosied up to each other.

'We've been preparing the press release,' she continued. 'We need the public coming forward on this one. After discussing it with Annie, we agreed that issuing a holding statement would be the best course of action. No details. We'll keep it simple, give nothing about the scene away and make an appeal for witnesses.'

Annie flashed a smile at Briggs as she made notes. He looked up at Gina with a grin on his face. She could tell he was loving the attention and he was loving the fact that she was noticing.

Gina cleared her throat and looked away. 'Thank you. Let's hope someone knows something and calls in, at the very least, someone else who is missing a teenage daughter might contact us. Problem is, we still don't have the time of death. We don't know if she was killed in the woods and buried close by or if she was transported to the woods to be buried. If so, where had she come from?'

'What do we know?' Briggs asked.

'We know that a potential killer could have managed alone if they'd pulled up on the road nearby. The distance from the pull in area off the small country lane wasn't too far from where she was buried. The grave wasn't deep or long enough, maybe her killer didn't have much in the way of physical strength or maybe they were just sloppy. She was found half-wrapped in a blanket, wearing a white nightdress that had been pulled down. Some care had been taken with her burial but not enough to make sure the local wildlife couldn't get to her.'

'Right, good job all,' Briggs said. 'Get moving on this one. We'll let the press know and offer up a formal appeal tomorrow. Cleevesford is going to go mad when it hears we have a second dead girl in the same week. Parents will be worried and so they should be.' Briggs stood and Annie followed him out.

Gina gazed around the room. Everyone was deadly quiet, waiting for her to speak. 'O'Connor, would you call all the local schools, put out an alert. I know this will cause a bit of panic but we need our teenage girls to be a little more vigilant until we get to the bottom of what is happening. I'd love to stay longer but Mrs Dawson wants to see the body of the girl who fell from the van. At least we'll know either way if the girl is her daughter. My only fear is, if she isn't Mrs Dawson's daughter, we need to consider that the girl in the shallow grave may be. The timings don't quite fit but it has been exceptionally hot, and decomposition could have happened a lot faster than expected. We'll know more when the pathologist's report comes through. Wyre, look into the Norths and Bryn Tilly. Dig a little deeper and anything you find, update the system immediately as I'll be working from home tonight. They bought the property at auction on…' she checked the date she'd noted down earlier, 'Friday the twentieth of April. Had they visited the property alone beforehand? Both the Norths and Bryn Tilly live in Cleevesford. They have local knowledge and know the roads. The road that led to that part of the woods isn't well used by people who aren't local. Check with the auction house too. See if anyone else was unusually interested in the property.

Look at the time, I have to get going.' Gina scooped up her things. She wasn't relishing the idea of meeting Mrs Dawson to view a girl who may be her daughter, but it had to be done. She had to be there.

CHAPTER THIRTY-TWO

Gina led Julia Dawson and Roy Fisher down the white corridor, passing the Coroner's office. She knocked on the secure door and made eye contact with a woman of similar age to herself, through the tiny window. She finished her sandwich as she buzzed them in, wiping crumbs from her white coat. 'Sorry, I'm on my own at the moment,' she said as she walked over to the stainless-steel work surface. Gina knew that the girl would be ready to present to Mrs Dawson, behind the heavy door.

'DI Harte. I called earlier.'

The woman gave her a sympathetic smile and led them in.

Roy held Julia's trembling hand. Since leaving Mrs Dawson earlier that day, the woman had deteriorated. Her lips had bite marks on them. Gina watched as Julia snatched her hand from Roy's and began scratching, leaving angry red stripes behind. 'I'm scared,' she said as she took a step forward.

'I'll be here,' Roy said as he took her hand again, preventing her from scratching any more. Gina wondered if Roy really was there for her or was just going through the motions. She watched as he fidgeted on the spot, his gaze fixed on the side of the room.

The assistant finished with her paperwork. 'I'll be with you in a moment.' She headed down the far end, then through the door, leaving them waiting. The strip light above began to buzz and flickered slightly before finally going off.

Julia's gaze darted up towards the ceiling. 'It's a sign. It's going to be her, I know it is. She wouldn't have gone all this time without as much as a call to me. Even though we hadn't been getting on, she knew I'd worry. She wouldn't do this to me. She wouldn't!' The woman couldn't hold back the stream of tears any longer.

'Look, love. That wasn't a sign. The light is just faulty. It's just a light.' Roy placed a protective arm around her.

'How do you know? You know nothing. You always do think I'm a bit stupid but I know these things, I feel it. It's her.'

Roy went to hold her but she pushed him back.

'You want it to be her, don't you?'

'Why would you say that? You're really being silly now. I know we've had a bad time of it but I would never think that. Never.'

'You didn't like her much, nobody liked her. She was always a nuisance, always too noisy, didn't concentrate in class. No one knew her like I did. No one else saw the sweet five-year-old I use to watch doing ballet. No one saw how her eyes used to light up when I read to her before bedtime. I know she became argumentative, but teenagers do. You couldn't see it, Roy, but underneath all that anger, I could still see the little girl she always was. My daughter, my little girl. I just want to go back in time,' she yelled as she broke down. 'You must have said something to her, done something. She wouldn't have left like that.'

'What the hell are you accusing me of?'

'I know you had words.'

'We always had words. Her running away had nothing to do with me.'

She wiped her nose and looked him in the eye. 'What did you say to her? Something happened and I want to know what.'

Gina continued to watch as their little spat played out. Julia Dawson was convinced that Roy had some hand in Christina running away. She made a mental note to check him out, look a little further into his past.

'You're being stupid. Come here.' He went to place a protective arm over her shoulders but she shrugged him off again.

The assistant beckoned them over. 'You can come through now. Is there anything I can get you all? Water? Coffee?'

Gina shook her head and placed a gentle hand on Julia's shoulder. 'Are you still okay to do this, Mrs Dawson?'

She nodded as she wiped her puffy eyes. 'Let's do this,' she said as she blew her nose and led the way. Roy followed closely, one hand on the small of her back.

The viewing room had been decorated to offer the relatives the calmest experience possible when visiting. The walls were a warm cream and the light was low. A sheet had been pulled right up to the girl's chin. Julia closed her eyes and swallowed hard. Roy's gaze searched all corners of the room, everywhere but on the girl. Julia opened her eyes. Slowly, her mouth opened and she fell into a heap on the floor, frantic sobbing turning into laughter. 'It's not her, it's not Christina. Christina is still alive.'

'Can you please pop down to the station and give a DNA sample? This would really help us in our search for Christina. It is voluntary, of course.'

Julia nodded. 'We'll go on our way home, won't we, Roy?' The man nodded as he snatched her hand, almost pulling her out of the room. His light, freckly complexion had paled even more.

'Do we have to? After what we've just been through.'

'Of course we do,' Julia said. Roy looked away and sighed.

'Thank you,' Gina said to the assistant as they left. Little did Julia know that they'd already unearthed a body; another body that could possibly belong to her daughter. This body wouldn't be as easy to identify.

Gina took a final glance at the young girl that lay on the metal slab, covered in nothing more than a flimsy white sheet, and shivered. *Who are you?*

CHAPTER THIRTY-THREE

The white walls of the corridor swayed as she battled to stand upright. Each wall was so bright, Gina had to squint to see. The walk reminded her of the house of fun at one of the theme parks she'd taken Hannah to over the years. The further she walked, the more closed in the space became until she had to lie on the floor and wriggle like a worm along the shiny floor. Reaching a little door, she tried the handle. It was locked. The key, it was in the pocket of her nightdress. Sweat began to dampen her hairline as she struggled to reach her pocket. Hand touched metal. Struggling to bring the key around, she placed it in the lock and turned.

Through the door was another room. A room in darkness with a solitary spotlight pointing to a body under the sheet. Her heart pounded. It wasn't the first time she'd seen a body in a mortuary. Maybe she was at work and this was just another one of life's challenges. After all, as a department they were constantly being squeezed. She closed her eyes and shook her head. *Time to wake up.* She didn't wake up – it wasn't a dream. She wriggled a bit further, pushing her body out of the tiny gap. Hands first, she slid out of the opening and gently landed in a heap on the stone floor. 'Hello.' The sound of her call echoed, eerily filling the room.

Why was she wearing a white nightdress? She didn't even own one. Her gaze travelled down to her feet, which took on a blue hue from the light. Dirt had dried in-between her toes and mud had dried on the tops of her feet. There was no door. The only way out was the way she'd come in.

She flinched as the sheet twitched. She crept towards the gurney, her shaking hands resting on the corner of the sheet. Her heartbeat began to boom until it was all she could hear. Blood pumped through her body. She needed to escape, get outside, and breathe in some fresh air. But she couldn't. She had to face what was in front of her. More than anything, she needed to peel back the sheet. Holding her breath, she yanked it down and began to gasp. It couldn't be, no…

Hannah lay in front of her, decay spreading from her neck. Her pale face and closed eyes would stay with her forever. She was only fourteen. She had her whole life ahead of her.

Gina crashed onto the living room floor, catching Ebony's tail. The cat meowed and sprang out of the cat door. Sweat poured down her face as she tried to breathe in for a few seconds, hold, and then breathe out. She was safe. She was in her house and she was alone. *Breathe in and out.* Slowly, her heart rate returned to normal. She took a sip of the warm white wine that was still on the coffee table, knocking the computer mouse as she leaned across. The photos of the girl in the shallow grave flashed up. The girl in the white nightdress.

She hurried to her feet and checked the back door, it was locked. Then she ran back through the house and rattled the front door, which was locked, deadlocked and chained as well. She was safe. The alarm system hadn't been set. She quickly set the alarm and slumped back onto the settee. After the last case, no one was ever coming into her house again and attempting to kill her.

The heatwave was killing her, messing with her senses. She pulled her T-shirt over her head and leaned back, wearing only her bra and light trousers. Using the T-shirt to fan herself, she slowly got a grip of the situation. Hannah wasn't lying dead in a morgue and no one had broken into her house.

Her laptop screen told her it was two in the morning. Before she'd nodded off, she'd sat up, catching up with everyone's notes and updating her own. She'd finished off the sour wine that was in the fridge and had eaten crisps and toast for supper.

Hannah. The dream. Her daughter lying dead on a slab in a state of decay. She grabbed her phone, needing to speak to her to know she was all right. As she went to press the call button, she stopped. It was the middle of the night. The whole family would be fast asleep. Someone had to make the first move or their little spat would go on forever, but now wasn't the right time.

She wanted to cry and punch something, anything, or did she? She wanted someone to hug her, just a few minutes of security and closeness to another human being. She wished Gracie was with her. Gracie always hugged her back. She paused as she pressed another number. He always said he was there for her as a friend and she needed to talk, to hear a friendly voice, even though he had been annoying her by flaunting Annie in her face. Before she could change her mind, she selected Briggs's number and called.

'Briggs,' he said in a muffled voice as if he'd just been half woken from a deep sleep.

'It's like the middle of the night,' a woman said. Annie.

Gina hung up. She'd made a huge fool of herself. He'd wonder why she called and he'd wonder why she'd hung up. If it was work, she would have spoken. Her phone buzzed, she ignored it until voicemail picked up the call. She sent him a text.

So sorry. Wrong number. Sorry! See you at the station. Gina.

He didn't reply. She felt her sweaty face redden. Grabbing the wine glass, she poured the sour leftovers down the sink. Between the wine, the heat and her nightmare, she'd been turned into some anxiety-ridden mess. *Get a grip, Gina!*

CHAPTER THIRTY-FOUR

The first rays of morning sun were highlighting the back wall, resembling bony fingers reaching through gaps in the trees outside the window, trying to touch the darkest corners of the room. Miley turned over in her creaky bed, flinching as she pulled the thin sheet off her sticky body. She wished she had curtains. Maybe she'd ask again. The sun was making her head pound. She couldn't wait for the days to get shorter. She turned again, frustrated at being awake so early. Sitting up, she ran her fingers through her matted hair and flinched as she felt the pain of her burns, throbbing. She wiped the sleep from her eyes with the back of her hand and checked them. The blistering had simmered down a little and scabs had begun to form. Maybe a splash of water would help, she needed to keep her sores clean. She stepped towards the door and pushed. 'Great,' she said as she went back to bed. The door was locked.

She grabbed the bucket from the corner of the room and peed. She'd have to empty it out in a couple of hours, like she did most mornings. Slopping out! A friend on the streets had mentioned that term. He'd done a short spell in prison and he had to slop out. She felt like a prisoner. There was nothing dignified in peeing in a bucket and tipping it away. With the heat, the room would soon smell.

Fiddling with her friendship bracelet, she thought of her friend and remembered the evenings they shared together when they were on the streets. Her friend became sicker, more addicted, needing more medicine and getting worse, not like Miley.

Back then, on the streets, it had been chilly and wet. She hadn't thought how the weather would affect her when she ran away. Once damp, she'd stayed damp for days, in fact the dampness never left. There's only so long they could spend in public loos, trying to dry off under a cold hand dryer. She shivered at the thought of being back out there now, begging.

She hugged herself as she recalled a particular incident. She'd been curled up in a doorway and remembered her heart pounding as a man climbed under her blankets. His smell was something she remembered vividly – beer. Twirling the friendship bracelet her friend had given her, she shuddered as she thought back to how close she was to being attacked. She froze as he'd fiddled with her layers of clothing until he'd reached her underwear. She felt him try to feel her from behind. She struggled, tried to reach out and hit him, but he hit her harder. Through her screams she heard someone yelling at him to get off her. Trembling, she wiped the tears from her face.

It was the girl with the straggly hair, whom she'd seen walking up and down earlier that day. She dragged the man onto the path and kicked him. Angry, he'd slapped her as he zipped himself back up. Grabbing the pint he'd left on the step, he then poured it over Miley before swearing and continuing towards New Street Station. As she sat in that doorway crying her eyes out, the girl placed a warm arm around her shoulder, whispering that everything would be okay and that they would look out for each other. That's how their friendship had begun.

Miley wiped a tear from her cheek as she remembered her street friend. The following day, her new friend had become her protector and teacher at the same time. They stole food from the market, one of them snatching, the other distracting. For a short while, life had become a little more fun. 'Outside Symphony Hall is a prime spot,' her new best friend said as they begged for money and met up with another girl. She'd been right. They'd come away with forty pounds that evening. As a newly established friendship group, they had a slick operation on the go.

Things got tougher. Shop assistants began to remember their faces and started telling them to go away. And then there were the do-gooders. It was never, here's a sandwich, hope you enjoy. It was more, tell us about yourself and you might get a sandwich. Her friend had told her that one of the do-gooders, a man who had to be at least seventy, had asked her for sex in exchange for food. So much for doing good! She may have been sixteen but she wasn't a prostitute and her friend had described how betrayed she'd felt. 'Everyone has ulterior motives,' she would always say. Her mind wandered back to the present as she felt a little tetchy, her skin beginning to crawl. She needed medicine soon, just a little dose to be able to function.

Medicine. That was another subject that crossed her mind often. Their boss said that the job would be stressful and it was. The medicine was meant to help, and it did, for a while. Miley wasn't stupid, she knew what they were giving her was illegal drugs but she so wanted to try them, be a grown-up. Once she received a fix, nothing else in the world mattered. It was just her and euphoria. Medicine helped her get through the hard days and the long nights. Her hands began to tremble.

'I need some medicine soon?' she called as she banged on the door. She held her breath and listened. She couldn't hear any movement. 'I'm locked in again. Do you have to keep locking me in?' Tears streamed down her face. She knew she'd remain locked in until she paid her debts. It was nothing to do with Jackie. Her medicine was costing more than she was earning. She'd be forever indebted and she totally understood she had to pay her debts.

A few days ago, she had demanded to be let out. That time, she'd received another dose of medicine, a higher dose. It had felt like the first time all over again. 'Where did you go, leaving me here all on my own,' she began to sing, making up the lyrics and tune as she went along. Sliding down the door, she sat on the floor. That is where she'd wait until someone unlocked the door. 'You never said goodbye, you never said…' The tune tailed off. She wondered if she'd remember it. She'd like to remember it so she could work on it one day. She wished she had a phone or a tablet so that she could record these things, but she had nothing like that any more. All gone in the early days of being homeless, sold to make a little bit of money for food. Her stomach began to spasm and a hot sweat flashed through her body. 'I need my medicine,' she yelled, but no one was listening. Sweat dripped from her brow. It was starting again. Rocking back and forth, she clutched her stomach, hoping that the pain wouldn't make her sick.

Jackie began to murmur. All she wanted was to have her medicine and be let out. She wanted to sit with Jackie, sing her a new song and play with her hair. She listened as the floorboards creaked in the next room as Jackie staggered across the room. A new day had begun.

CHAPTER THIRTY-FIVE

Gina entered the incident room. 'The press statement has just gone out. Let's watch it back so we're all familiar with it, then we can talk about how we are going to handle the volume of calls that will follow. Our experience tells us this is going to be massive. Volume calls, mostly irrelevant as always. Then we'll get the confessors, we have a list of our regulars on file. They call every time, claiming it's them, whatever the crime.'

'It's started, guv,' Jacob replied as he straightened his tie.

Wyre grabbed the remote control. 'Here goes.'

'Go for it,' Gina replied.

Wyre fast forwarded to the local news and paused. Briggs came on, with Annie standing in the corner, her shiny locks flowing over her shoulders. Shame washed through Gina. She needed to never call him again, unless it was to do with work. Although he'd offered to be there, it wasn't right. He was clearly with Annie now. They'd been in a relationship, but crossing the work and friendship lines just confused things.

Briggs began to speak on screen. 'I'm issuing a brief statement today, any questions will be answered during the detailed press conference at a later date. An investigation is underway after a member of the public found human remains in the woodland, just off Senton Lane in Cleevesford. At present we are conducting enquiries and making an appeal for witnesses. Anyone who has any information is urged to contact us on the number that is on your screen now.' Wyre paused the news.

'Short but to the point.' Gina shielded her eyes from the sun.

Briggs almost made her jump as he stepped behind her. 'All it needed to be. I didn't want to reveal any information about the way our victim was found. As usual, this separates the crank callers from the genuine ones. Without the pathologist's report we don't have an accurate timeframe, telling us when the body was buried.'

'Right, back to it. Thanks for that, Paula. Monitor all incoming calls and just send the good ones through.' Gina turned and felt Briggs's warmth radiating from his torso in the hot room. 'I think we need a couple of fans in here. It's becoming unworkable.'

He beckoned her over to the corner of the room. A hum of voices began to fill the room, getting louder and louder. 'Did you try and call me in the night? I wondered if something had happened.'

She could feel her cheeks beginning to burn. 'It was an accident. I fell asleep with my phone and leaned on it. Sorry, sir.'

'No worries, Harte.' His gaze lingered on hers. 'If you need to talk, you know where I am. The welfare of this department is important to me and I know you've been through a lot this year—'

'I'm okay, sir, honestly. I really just rolled over onto my phone. Sorry to have disturbed you.'

'You don't look okay. When did you last eat a proper meal? I've never known weight drop off someone so quickly.'

'I've been working out.' He stared at her. 'Okay, you know me better than that. I've just been busy that's all. My clothes were getting too tight so I've cut down a bit.'

His serious expression broke into a smile. 'Well, don't lose too much more. Don't want you getting ill on us. Maybe you can have some of mine,' he said, laughing as he patted his belly. He wasn't too overweight. He's what she'd describe as just cuddly with a slight belly.

'If I need any, I know where to come.' *Please go now,* she kept thinking. Her weight, her health and her private life were none of his business. If she couldn't be bothered to cook and mostly ate crisps, then so what? Soon, she'd be back to normal. The counsellor said it would take a while. Almost being murdered in your own home wasn't a small thing, even to a police detective. It would take time that was all. 'Right, I'll leave you to it.'

'Thanks, sir. Please do.' She exhaled as he left and felt the prickling in her neck and cheeks subsiding.

'Guv?' Wyre came running over. 'Forensics have just called. They have all the results back from van girl's clothing.' Van girl. That's what she was being called.

'I'm on it. Pass the call through to my office.'

CHAPTER THIRTY-SIX

Wednesday was another day and Julia wasn't going to waste a minute of it when it came to searching for Christina. She passed the bakery on the corner of Redditch Town Centre, filling the air with the smell of fresh coffee. Her stomach turned as she thought back to the young girl at the morgue. She hadn't eaten breakfast and she still wasn't ready for any, fearing she'd bring it back up.

Before he'd left for work, Roy had left her one hundred pounds on the side with a little note.

> *Please go out for a couple of hours, get out of the house and treat yourself. We will find her, I promise. I know I haven't always been the best but I do love you. Xxx.*

Maybe that was his way of trying to make her forget that he was hiding something. It would take more than money. She'd settle for him being able to look her straight in the eye when he spoke of Christina.

He was right about one thing. That girl lying on the slab wasn't her daughter. Her daughter was still out there somewhere and she wasn't giving up on the idea that she was still alive. Regardless of what Roy said, she could feel it and she knew it. The flickering lights at the morgue had been a good sign, not the original bad sign she thought she'd felt in her gut. Tomorrow, she would go into Worcester again with her rucksack full of posters. She was going to spend this evening researching the homeless hotspots, where they were offered a meal or food, and she would speak with everyone she could. Someone had to have seen Christina. People don't simply vanish. Maybe someone out there knew who Westley was. A description would be a start. If someone had seen Christina, he might have been with her.

She passed another charity shop and saw a homeless man sitting on the step, giving his little dog some water. She pulled a fiver from the money that Roy had left her and dropped it by him, offering a smile.

His grubby hands took the money. 'Thank you. Bless you,' he said, revealing his almost toothless smile.

Her hands began to shake. She had to ask. Redditch wasn't too far from Cleevesford. She pulled the photo from her purse and kneeled in front of the man's sleeping bag. 'Have you seen this girl? She may be with a man, a man called Westley.'

The young man took the photo and concentrated. The little terrier nudged her arm, hoping to be petted. She stroked his nose and head. The tired dog lay down next to its owner, panting in the shade. 'I don't think I've seen her. Are you going shopping? If you leave it here, I can ask my mate when he comes by. Should be here in a few minutes, maybe half hour.'

She had many copies of that photo. It was the one she'd used when making the missing posters. 'Of course. Can I have it back though?' She didn't need it back, but the thought of a stranger keeping a photo of her daughter made her shiver.

'Of course. I'll show it to my mate and you can take it back. I'm not going anywhere for a bit. He might have seen her, he's a bit more switched on than me. Is she on the streets?'

Julia's face reddened. She now felt judged by all. Did people suspect that her daughter came from an abusive family and had run away? Would this man be reluctant to say anything if he had seen her? 'I love her. She's a teenager and went through a funny time. Had problems at school.' She hoped that explained things a little.

'We're all going through a funny time out here, except it's never funny.' He pulled a half drunk can of something she couldn't quite identify from his weathered old bag and took a swig.

'I meant, she wasn't hurt at home. I love her and want her back.' Why was she saying so much? Maybe she was judging herself. Had some of their arguments gone a little far with the name-calling? Maybe Christina had felt sidelined by Roy's presence. Why hadn't she seen the signs that Christina had been so unhappy? She hadn't meant to be so angry all the time. Her mind wandered back to Roy. He said the right things, made the right moves, but something wasn't gelling together well.

'Leave it with me for half hour, an hour, maybe. Come back then. If I can help, I will. Little girls should be at home, not out here, alone.'

'Thank you.' She stood and left him with the photo.

She entered the Kingfisher Centre and began browsing in the shops. She passed New Look, Christina's favourite shop. Whenever they came into Redditch, Christina had hassled her to go there before they did any real shopping. She spent ages looking through the teen section, trying on the new ranges, even checking out some of the more adult clothes in smaller sizes. That had been a sign of Christina saying goodbye to childhood. She'd smile and wonder if one day they'd share clothes or maybe she'd end up with Christina's hand-me-downs. She wondered if they'd always go clothes shopping together, followed by hot chocolate and cake at one of the many cafes. She passed the sale rack and began mooching through, trying not to knock all the tightly packed clothes off their hangers. She stopped when she reached the black jumpsuit. Earlier that year, Christina had begged her to buy it for one of her friend's birthday parties. It had looked so adult with its low-cut front but she wanted her daughter to be happy. She remembered looking and realising that the jumpsuit was a part of the adult range. She wouldn't normally have agreed to it but she wanted to put an end to their arguments. At the time she thought that buying the jumpsuit would end the tension, but it hadn't.

Her eyes began to fill as she gripped the piece of clothing against her chest. *Don't lose it in the middle of New Look.* She shoved the jumpsuit back on the rack and shook her head as she left. She checked her watch. It was a little early but she was heading back to see if the man's friend had turned up.

As she approached, another man was standing there, talking to the first man. He looked a lot older and walked with a stick. Limping as he moved.

'I'm done in town,' she said to the man she had left the photo with.

'This is John, he's not really called John, but he likes John, don't you, John?'

'Always John,' he replied in a raspy voice, sounding like he had tonsillitis. 'Here, no one cares what we're called. I could be called Beetroot, no one cares. What's your name?'

'Julia, I'm looking for my daughter. Have you seen her?'

'I was just getting to that. John gets around, spends some time in Birmingham and Coventry too,' the first man said as he passed his friend the photo.

The older man scrutinised the photo and walked into the sunshine. 'Sorry, I can't see that well. Need some glasses but as always, can't afford a thing.' He squinted with an open mouth as he concentrated on the photo. 'You know something. I never forget a face, not one as pretty as this anyway.' Her stomach turned slightly. Had he found her teen daughter attractive? 'I have a daughter. Haven't seen her for years and your girl reminds me of her. I love her but what can I say, her old man is nothing but an embarrassment. She doesn't want my drunken arse around the grandkids. The reddish brown hair and slightly thin top lip, that's what makes me remember her.'

Julia exhaled. His comment was likely an innocent one.

'You remember her?' Her heart rate began to ramp up.

'I saw her, if not someone who looks just like her, a few months ago. Probably in April. My diary keeping isn't that good though so don't take that as gospel.'

'Was she with a man?'

'No, she was with a girl. A little streetwise thing. There were three girls to begin with but after a while, I just saw the two of them hanging around. Other girl probably found her way off the street. I used to watch them thieving from shops. They were masters at it. I can't be totally sure, you know. She looked like the girl in this photo, but the streets, they roughen you up, you know. People get grubby and their clothes turn craggy, I mean, look at me. I haven't had a good wash since the snow in March. We were all brought in then by the do-gooding community, but people forget us at other times.'

'Can you describe the other girl, or where she was?'

'Well, I used to see them hanging around at the entrance of the Bullring. I used to hang out by the bull statue sometimes. I think they were mostly there trying to scrounge or shoplift, but then so was I.'

'And the girl?'

'The other girl. I'd say she was a bit older, sixteen to eighteen maybe. Always wore her hair in a cap. Quite a skinny thing and could pack a punch when someone harassed her. At night you see it all. We get harassed by the drunks, they like to abuse us. Don't get me wrong, some of them are generous and can give big when they're hammered but others, they can punch us, spit at us, piss on us. It ain't any fun being out at night in a busy city, which is why I come back here. Sick of it in the end. Sick to the back teeth. And I was missing my mate 'ere, weren't I?' The man sitting with his dog passed his friend the can from his bag. He grabbed the can of cider and took a long swig before passing it back.

'Were they based anywhere? Did they have a favourite spot or do you know where they slept?'

The older man shook his head. 'I wish I knew more, I really do. I hope you get your daughter back, miss. Take care of yourself out there.'

Julia smiled and nodded. She held out the rest of her cash, ninety-five pounds. 'Please, both of you buy some lunch and things you need and thank you so much.'

'Bless you, but I didn't say all that for the money. I really want you to find her. The streets are no place for a lovely girl like her and it looks like she has a family who love her. Don't give up. Find her and take your little girl home, where she belongs.'

She pressed the money into his chapped hands and gave him a smile as she left. Roy was wrong when he thought throwing money at her would make everything better. She didn't want it. For the first time in a while, she had hope. They had given her hope and that was worth everything she owned. As soon as Roy left for work the next morning, she was leaving for Birmingham in search of Christina.

CHAPTER THIRTY-SEVEN

'Okay, crowd, gather round. Try to stay with me. The girl from the van, we have further results back from her clothing. The girl in the shallow grave, we have the results back from her clothing and the blanket she was lying on and partially wrapped in. You can see how, from the photo.' Gina pointed to the board with her pen. 'The site is still being worked but the clothing and blanket were sent to the lab to be processed while the excavation is still going on. We have a link.'

The room was silent. O'Connor stopped tapping the desk. Jacob titled his head, anticipating what was going to be said and Wyre crossed her legs as she rolled forward on her chair, closer to the table.

'A link, guv?' Jacob said.

Gina smiled. 'I can see you're all excited. I'm not as good at explaining these things as Bernard or Keith but both of them are working flat out at the site and in the lab. I'll try to get this correct, excuse any mispronunciation. Latin is not my best subject. Cast skins of *Anthrenus verbasci* were found on both of the girls' clothing. To you and me, that is a carpet beetle. They typically grow to three millimetres long and to anyone who's had the misfortune of dealing with an infestation will know they are a nightmare pest. The larvae chew on textiles, carpets, clothing, and then tend to hatch in spring and summer, leaving these little casts behind. There is also a further link. The microfibres found on the casts both match. The creatures were living in the exact same carpet.' Gina reached into her files. 'Here's a lovely poster showing the lifecycle of a carpet beetle. O'Connor, could you Blu-Tack it to the wall?'

'Yes, guv.' O'Connor pulled a packet of Blu-Tack from a drawer and began fixing the poster to the wall.

'It's horrible, guv,' Wyre said as she began to scratch her arm.

Gina agreed as a shiver ran down her spine. She'd be horrified if she found those little grubs and beetles all over the place. That would be another thing for her to worry about. She was definitely going to check the dusty corners of her house, armed with a vacuum, when she got home.

'Agreed. Mini-freaks of nature. Before we all join in with your scratching, we best move on. The other thing they found in the clothing of the shallow grave girl is a hair and, get this, the follicle is attached. It has been run through the database and there isn't a match. There is, however, a DNA match to the blood that we found on the van girl's clothing. As you remember, it was confirmed that this blood did not belong to our victim. So, we have blood and hair belonging to another person, not either of our victims.'

'Wow, this is huge,' Jacob said.

'I know. What is happening to these girls, and on our doorstep? We are working on the theory that our perpetrator is local given that they knew about Senton Lane. Only locals really take this shortcut.'

'Any more on the hair?' Jacob asked.

Gina began adding to the board details as she spoke. 'The hair is brown, barely noticeable auburn tones so this hair might not mean anything, and about thirty centimetres long. The root is grey, which doesn't fit the pattern. Whoever this hair belonged to was certainly a lot older than the girls. Again, this adds slightly to the red hair connection. All different strengths of red but the connection is clear. Any more information, I'll feed it to you as I get it. Going back to Mrs Dawson and her missing daughter. Her DNA has been sent to the lab and she gave us full permission to keep it on the database. She wants her daughter found. We'll soon find out whether her daughter is the girl who was found in the shallow grave.' Again, Gina hoped the girl wasn't Julia's daughter but there was a chance. She was about the right age and matched Christina's height. 'The lab are going to run the shallow grave girl's DNA through the database and get back to me. This was a little harder to obtain but we have it, which is great news. Results should be in anytime now.' She checked her watch. Maybe they were running late. They all knew what time the briefing was and she'd fast-tracked the tests.

'Two girls and we have no idea who they are. We could really do with a break on identifying these girls,' Wyre said as she tightened her ponytail and neatened her fringe.

'Certainly could. We will find out what is happening but as it stands, again, working on the theory that there is evidence to link the two girls, we are looking at a murder and kidnap at the very most. No doubt, there could be another story behind what we see, but it isn't going to be a good one either way. We will need to know if there are any signs of trauma on our shallow grave victim but we know our van victim was in a right state. She could have escaped from somewhere, but where, and why? There are drugs involved, which is why we are liaising with Smith and his team. It's not our best lead but I'll go with anything at the moment. We need to make sure we're on top of what's happening. Link information. Share with them, them with us. Our van girl was on heroin. If we pull any dealers in, we can check the blend that they sell, this may provide a match for what was shown in the girl's toxicology report. I know I'm giving you all a lot of information and it's overwhelming, but bear it all in mind as you proceed. Always have one eye on the board, check the system for updates, as these will constantly be added. As soon as you have any information, *update, don't wait* – that is the motto.'

'I suppose we're all on free overtime? I'll call Mrs O and tell her not to wait until I get home to have dinner.'

'I'm really grateful for all that you do. The community is really grateful and, most of all, these girls deserve to rest in peace and to do that we need justice. Justice involves catching whoever is behind this. I have a daughter. My daughter was a prize pain in the arse as a teen but no one deserves this to happen to them. If I were the parent of these girls, I'd be so thankful for what you're all giving up to be here. I'm sorry the rewards aren't huge, I'm not getting any overtime either. I know you all put in more than you get out. We all do at times like this. I'll take whatever time you can spare.'

'I'm with you, guv,' Wyre replied.

'Count me in. Amber hasn't texted me all day. I now sense that I have all the time in the world. One day I'll meet someone who understands,' Jacob said, half-jokingly.

Gina smiled. She couldn't have chosen a better team to work with. 'Right, in that case, O'Connor and Wyre, you will both work closely on our shallow grave victim. Jacob and I will work on the van victim. We'll reconvene at the next briefing and discuss what we've found. I can't promise I won't interfere in the case of the grave girl though. In fact, scrub what I just said. I'm on both cases.'

PC Smith passed the room as he headed towards the toilets. 'Smith, can you come here a moment?'

He glanced at the toilet door, then back at Gina. 'Of course. How are things going with the case?'

'We need to be kept up to date at real time with any drug-related finds or investigations. I'll come and chat with you in a while, update you on where we're at and why it's so relevant.'

Smith began squirming on the spot. 'Okay, guv. I'm desperate for a leak. I'll catch up with you in a minute.' Jacob laughed as Smith hurried out of the room.

Gina stared at the board. The words 'help her', written under the girl from the van's photo stood out. She pointed to the words with her pen. 'Given that we have a definite link between the two girls, we need to seriously start thinking about a third girl. 'Help her' – who was our van girl referring to? We have no time to waste. I don't want a third girl to go through what these poor girls have been through.'

Gina's phone began to buzz. She took the call and hurried to the back of the room. A huge smile spread across her face.

'What is it?' Jacob asked.

'Our database has come up trumps. Our girl from the shallow grave has been identified as eighteen-year-old Simone Duxford. O'Connor, Wyre, call Bryn in on a voluntary basis, and ask him if he knows a Simone Duxford. Jacob, I think you and I should pop over to Big North Project Investments and talk to Stan and Elizabeth. If we hurry, we'll be back by lunchtime. Someone will have to inform her family. Paula, Harry, can I task you with this too?' O'Connor and Wyre nodded.

CHAPTER THIRTY-EIGHT

Big North Project Investments stood a little back from the main road and was located just on the way out of Cleevesford. Not a weed littered the block paving and the hanging baskets looked as though they were competing in the annual Cleevesford in Bloom competition. The simple detached modern office building looked tiny against the backdrop of meadows it was set within. Sheep grazed in the distance and a bird's nest topped a dried-out tree. The Norths had money; that was clear. A purpose-built business property set in all this land wouldn't be cheap. Gina had checked their records. They constantly invested in property projects, new-build estates, they had made huge sums from everything they'd been involved in and they had working office blocks throughout the country.

Gina pressed the buzzer as Jacob tried to look through the tinted windows.

'Big North, who's calling?' the voice asked though the intercom.

'DI Harte and DS Driscoll. We're here to see Mr and Mrs North.'

'Please wait in reception, I'll be down in a moment.' The door released and Gina led the way into a plush waiting area. Two grey couches faced each other, divided by a long, high-gloss coffee table. The mid-shade grey and mustard yellow colour scheme worked well with their logos and designs. A large and complicated looking coffee machine adorned one end of the room. Jacob took a few steps forward on the stone floor, each step echoing through the room.

'Hello, let me show you up.' The woman who she'd heard on the other end of the intercom and who looked to be in her mid-twenties with shoulder-length brown hair beckoned them over. They followed her up the stairs until they reached another wide corridor with several doors leading off. She opened one of them and did a slight bow to the Norths. 'Mr and Mrs North will see you now,' she said as she closed the door.

'What an unfortunate thing to happen. You know how much this is going to cost us?' Elizabeth North asked.

'It's already cost someone dearly. The bones we found on your land were that of a girl in her teens,' Gina snapped.

Mrs North cleared her throat and looked at the pad in front of her. Gina made a mental note that the work culture seemed a bit odd. She could see that Stan and Elizabeth North were firm bosses. There were professional photos of both of them adorning the walls. On each photo, Mrs North had a different hairstyle of varying colours. One collection of photos held Gina's attention for longer than the others. The Norths standing in front of a block of flats, then a housing estate, followed by a development in Canary Wharf. Not one of the pictures showed them with their team, their builders, and all the other people that did the ground work. Mrs North sat at the head of the table with Mr North to her left. Gina walked along the wall and took the seat beside Mrs North. Jacob slumped in the seat beside her.

'We're sorry to hear that, really we are, but we have work to get on with. Do you know how long you lot will be and can you try not to make too much of a mess?' Mrs North asked. She tapped her plum-coloured nails, which matched her perfectly applied lipstick, on the conference table. As the woman awaited her answer, she turned to the window, checking her reflection. She smoothed her blonde bob down.

'Mrs North, we are potentially investigating a murder. It will take as long as it takes. As soon as we have all we need from your land, we will let you know straight away. Right, when did you first go and see the property?'

Elizabeth North sighed as she placed her hands flat on the table and stared directly at Gina. She was asserting dominance. She sensed that Mrs North always got her own way. 'We drove by early April, just before the auction. Never been before.'

'I see from our records that you had access from the property after the auction on the twentieth of April. You're telling me you never went to the property before April.'

'That is what I said. Did you not hear me the first time?'

Gina watched as Mr North rolled his eyes and looked to the side. 'Elizabeth, not now. Sorry, detectives. My wife and I are upset by what has happened. I'm sure you can appreciate that.'

Gina was certain Mrs North was upset but only about potential profits lost. 'Mrs North. We have contacted the auction house in which the property was listed and sold by. Graham Danks, the person in charge of your property at the time, stated that he first took you both to the property on Wednesday the seventh of March so I'll ask again. Can you tell me when you first went to see the property?'

'Are we under caution?' Mrs North asked.

'No. We are just trying to establish what happened at your property. You are not under arrest or under caution. We just thought you might be able to give us information that will help with our investigation. We appreciate anything you can tell us. We would appreciate your cooperation or we may have to do this down at the station.'

Mr North dragged his chair closer to the table. 'Can we start again? My wife is very protective of our interests. This will hurt our investment, that is all. We don't mean to hamper your investigation.' He took his glasses off and placed them on the table. Mrs North folded her arms and leaned back. 'Let me check my diary.' Mr North selected his diary on the tablet in front of him and scrolled back to March. Gina could just about see the entry from her side of the table. 'Graham occasionally gives us a good tip on what's hot to go for. On this particular day, March the seventh, he gave us a call and we went to visit Foxglove Cottage. He didn't have the keys at that point so we just looked through the windows. I was able to make a rough assessment from the outside of how much it would cost us and what margins we needed to achieve. I'm sorry that this information escaped our minds but it was a while ago. You can see from the diary and how much we have booked in, this would be easy to do.' He held his tablet up. His diary was bursting with appointments.

'Thank you for confirming that for us,' Jacob said.

'Did you go back between seeing the property that day and purchasing the property?'

Mr North scanned all his diary entries. 'No, we didn't. I went into this investment with Bryn Tilly though. He may have gone back for a look.'

'May I ask? Why did you invest with Bryn Tilly when you clearly have enough capital to handle this property by yourself?'

'I lived near Bryn, growing up. He was a decent kid back then, worked hard after school on building sites. He came to me, begging for a chance in property development and showed me a portfolio of his past work and said he had a bit of money to invest. What can I say, I like the guy. He was prepared to do all of the day-to-day running of the project and most of the work. He was a bargain, really. I know him well, he wouldn't harm a fly. As for going to the property before we bought it, he probably did. He'd need to see the extent of work needed for himself.'

Gina nodded at Jacob. She only had one question left to ask. 'Do you know this girl?'

The couple looked at the photo for a moment. 'Never seen her,' Mrs North said.

Mr North put his glasses back on. Gina wished she had a better photo but Simone's mugshot was all they had on file. 'Is this the girl on our land?'

'It's just another enquiry we're following up on.' Gina hadn't even contacted Simone's family as yet but she needed to know. One of the team back at the station would be making the call right now.

'I don't recognise her at all,' Mr North said. His gaze lingered on the photo a little longer and he placed his hands in his lap, under the table. 'No, never seen her.' He removed his glasses and rubbed his eyes.

'Are you sure?'

He swallowed and took a swig from a glass of water. 'I'd know if I'd seen this girl and I'd tell you.'

'Is that all, detectives, as we have work to do?' Mrs North slammed her notebook shut and stood.

'I'm sure he recognised her,' Gina said as they headed towards the car and whacked the bonnet.

'Me too but hitting your car won't help,' replied Jacob as he opened the car door and slumped in the seat.

He was right. She took a deep breath and got into the car. She'd soon find out what he knew, somehow.

CHAPTER THIRTY-NINE

Wednesday was as boring as Tuesday, which was as boring as Monday. No one had checked on her at all for a couple of days. She pondered over the fact that she'd considered quitting her job after her telling off. On her ten pound per week allowance her parents gave her, before she started work, she couldn't even afford a proper trip to the cinema, which to her meant a ticket, some nachos and a large cola.

The door made a ping as a man entered. The tall man in the suit stopped at the counter and looked past her. He opened his mouth to speak then stopped. He reminded her of her father, all suited up with a tie. Receding hairline. Expensive-looking watch. Her dad had once owned a Rolex too. He was handsome in a way, for an older man, but she wasn't into that. He was probably in his fifties, like her dad. She preferred boys of her own age or just a little bit older, not like a couple of her friends. His gaze met hers. She glanced over his shoulder and spotted the silver car in the car park. It was the man who'd been watching her.

An icy shiver ran up her spine. She gulped as he stood in front of the door, blocking the exit. Her breathing quickened as she took a step back.

'Can I help you?' she asked as she fiddled with the corner of her tabard, trying to control the tremble that was working its way through her body.

'I'm just looking.' He walked over to the jam and honey and fiddled with the jars. He glanced back as she stared at him, open-mouthed, not knowing what to do or say next. 'Sorry, I'm just after something for my wife, are you okay?'

She nodded and dropped her shoulders. Maybe she'd got him all wrong. It might be like Mrs Hanley was saying. Perhaps he pulled in for a break occasionally and decided to come in the shop this time. *Stop being an idiot Elisa.* She took a deep breath and forced a smile. 'I'd recommend the honey if you're looking for something to go on toast.' Maybe if she shifted a bit of honey, Mrs Hanley would be pleased. She'd also spent ages making a honey pyramid by the entrance.

'Not the jam? My wife prefers jam on her toast.'

'The jam stinks,' she whispered, hoping that he'd act a little friendlier and put her at ease. 'The honey is local and is far superior.'

'Thank you for the warning.' He grabbed five jars, some set and some runny. She'd definitely formed the wrong opinion of him. Smiling, she took the jars from him and led him to the counter.

The man followed her and once again began looking over her shoulder into the staff area. 'Is there anything else I can get you?' She fiddled with her hair as the man's gaze slowly met hers, the shiver up her spine returning. She wanted him to hurry up and leave. If he took a step closer to her, she'd run as fast as she could up the stairs, straight into the office.

'Huh?'

'Sweets, chutneys, anything else?' Her voice cracked as she forced the words out.

'No, thanks. Who else works here with you?'

He was getting creepy. As he awaited her answer, a loud chugging noise came from above them. Someone was printing and the old printer made a racket. She smiled and pointed to the ceiling. 'There is always someone else on the premises.'

He nodded before leaving fifteen pounds on the counter and rushing out of the door. His transaction only added up to twelve pounds fifty. She rung up the transaction and placed the two pounds fifty change into her pocket. It was the least she deserved after almost being scared to death by the creepy customer. She ran to the door, checking that he wasn't coming back. His car turned onto the main road, heading to Cleevesford, as before.

Mrs Hanley came down the stairs. Elisa dashed back behind the counter and began cleaning the glass.

'How are things going?' she asked.

She smiled. 'Okay, but—'

'But?' She waited for her to continue. 'Look, about the other day when you came upstairs—'

'I've forgotten about that, I shouldn't have come up.' She gave her a goofy smile. 'It's a customer. He just came in and creeped me out. That's all.'

'I see. If anyone comes in and bothers you, just give us a shout. Did he bother you?'

'No, he just seemed a bit weird. It's probably just me. It's nothing. I'm being an idiot.'

Mrs Hanley responded with a broad smile. 'You're here on your own most of the time. I suppose you feel a little vulnerable. It's normal to feel like that. If you're ever worried, you just have to shout up the stairs.'

'Thanks, Mrs Hanley.'

Mrs Hanley grabbed her phone and held it to her ear as she headed back into the staff area before stomping back up the stairs.

Elisa's phone beeped. It was Ethan offering to pick her up from work. She listened to Mrs Hanley settling back in her creaky chair before she replied, accepting his offer straight away. They could go cruising and at least if the creepy man came back at closing time, Ethan would see him off if he came near her. She shivered at the thought.

CHAPTER FORTY

Gina threw her jacket over the filing cabinet in her office and wiped away the line of sweat that was forming at her brow. She wrestled with the creaky window, finally managing to fully open it. Hot breeze blew her hair over the front of her face, the light revealing her split ends. After this case, she was going to get a much-needed haircut but as always, her self-care was at the bottom of the list. *Hair is just hair,* she thought. *It can wait.* Solving the case or cases of their two dead girls was her priority and that started with familiarising herself with the one they'd identified, Simone Duxford.

She sat and shifted the mouse until the screen lit up. She put Roy's name into the search bar and waited. He wasn't on their system at all. Her mind wandered back to the morgue. There was definitely some tension between Roy and Julia.

She flicked back to the previous screen and Simone's file flashed up along with an email notification. There was an update from O'Connor. Simone's foster family, social worker and biological mother had been informed of her death. Bryn Tilly had been in to speak to them and had not shown any recognition of Simone Duxford, not of her name or photo.

Eighteen, nearly nineteen. Date of birth tenth of August 1999. Registered as living in foster care up until she was eighteen. There was a note on the file. The foster family had wanted her to stay with them, but Simone hadn't got on well with their children and had left after securing a hostel placement in Birmingham at the

end of August that same year. Another note told her that Simone
never checked into the hostel. Her foster family, the Smiths,
reported her missing at this point but she later called them to
say she was staying with friends. As she was an adult, they felt
the only thing they could do was leave her to it.

Gina scanned Simone's conviction file. There were three
cautions for shoplifting in Birmingham and finally a conviction
for theft of wallets in a nightclub in Birmingham. This resulted
in an eight-week suspended sentence. Gina continued scanning
Simone's arrest notes. Simone had become tearful, stating that
she had no choice as she'd needed money to fund her drug habit.

Gina scrolled down further. There was also a caution for
soliciting outside a bar in Birmingham in October 2017. So many
young people ended up like Simone. Out of the care system, into
hostels or on the streets, with nowhere to go. Maybe she'd tried
to reconnect with her blood relatives. Opening the family tab,
Gina stopped on the passage that described her mother's drug
problem. Simone was removed from her care after a drug bust
on her property revealed a dealing operation. Miss Duxford was
only twenty-eight when her daughter was removed from her care
and she'd never tried to maintain any relationship with her after
that. She scrolled down further, trying to find out who Simone's
father was. There was no one registered.

Gina tried to put herself into Miss Duxford's mindset. At
fifteen she becomes pregnant and gives birth to Simone when
she's sixteen. Had she been disowned by her parents? Had the
father given her empty promises at the time, then failed to live up
to them? Why hadn't she registered him as the father? Maybe she
didn't know who he was. Was she assaulted? So many questions
that maybe weren't relevant to the investigation, or were they?
Had Simone gone looking for her father? Who were the friends
she was meant to be staying with? There was only one way to find
out. She picked up her phone. 'Wyre, we need to speak to Simone

Duxford's foster family. I know I tasked you and O'Connor with investigating this further, but I need to be there. It's also important that one of you are with me to hear what is said and get straight onto follow ups when we get back. Despite what I said, I'll still also be actively working both cases and keeping in mind that they are looking certain to be one case. Do either you or O'Connor want to come with me now? Simone Duxford's foster family only live in Bromsgrove, so we won't be too long.' She heard Wyre relaying the message to O'Connor.

'O'Connor said he'd like to go. I'm snowed under going through the masses of calls we've had and all the information from the door to doors.'

'Any of it relevant?'

'Not as yet, but they keep coming in thick and fast.'

'Right. Let O'Connor know I'll be ready to leave in five.' Gina hung up, powered her computer down and grabbed her phone.

CHAPTER FORTY-ONE

Gina took the right-hand turn into the estate on Bromsgrove as O'Connor played with his phone. It was an area she'd passed only a couple of weeks ago when she'd visited the High Street. She'd brought Gracie and sat outside, enjoying a coffee in the sun while her granddaughter played with her milkshake before tipping half into her lap. Gina almost grimaced at seeing the look on Hannah's face when she returned the little girl. Her yellow-coloured dress had been splattered with chocolate milk and by the time she pulled up, given the heat, the milk had begun to take on a rancid smell that still lingered in her car. This time, though, she wasn't going over the brow of the hill and into the centre for a leisurely morning, she was visiting the Smiths. Foster family of Simone Duxford.

The closely set houses followed the neat windy road, until they got closer. Gina paused and pulled up outside the Smith residence. 'I hate these types of visit.'

'Me too, guv,' he said as he wiped the beads of sweat from his bald head with a crumpled tissue. 'I hope they have a fan. I'm melting.'

The grass on the garden had dried out and the frontage looked like it could do with a clean and de-weed – a bit like her own.

'This is where Simone was placed in 2011 and had been her home until she left.' She checked her notes. Mr Josh Smith, teacher of maths at a higher educational institute in Kidderminster. Mrs Angela Smith, currently working at Asda in Bromsgrove as a shop floor manager. They had two children of their own, twelve-year-old Chloe and fourteen-year-old Emily. The door opened as she went to knock.

'Come in.' Mr Smith stepped aside so that they could enter. 'Can we get you a drink?'

'Water would be lovely, thank you,' Gina replied. O'Connor politely refused. Mr Smith took a seat at the head of the kitchen table. Mrs Smith placed a jug of water with a few slices of lemon in it on the table and placed a glass in front of her husband and Gina, before pouring it out. As Mrs Smith settled, Gina noticed the slight tremor of her fingers that lay on the table. Her eyes looked puffy and her face was pale and blotchy.

'We're finding this hard to take in, as you can see,' Mrs Smith said.

Mr Smith looked into his lap and took a deep breath. 'I know she wasn't our biological daughter but we loved her like she was. Things had been far from easy but we never gave up on her, however hard she pushed us, and she did test us to our limits, didn't she?'

Mrs Smith rubbed her eyes.

Mr Smith nodded. 'I'd be lying if I said it was easy but that's what we signed up for. We knew about her background and we wanted to make a difference. I tried to help her with homework, with career direction, but the anger and upset that she carried, well it was hard to break through. It's not like she went without, living here, with us. I know I'm only a maths tutor and my wife works at the supermarket, but we work hard. We earn a decent enough living. We keep a nice roof over our heads and don't get into debt. We don't go out drinking, we don't smoke and we love our children.'

'We don't know what we did wrong with Simone and now we'll never be able to fix things.' Mrs Smith looked up as if trying to hold back tears of loss, guilt and confusion as to where it all went wrong.

Gina could see the painstaking thoughts that were going through both of their minds. Mrs Smith hugged her large frame, her scrunched up shoulders and arms providing a protective barrier between her and the feelings she was trying so hard to supress. Her shoulder-length brown hair, bronzed skin tone and dark eyes, gave her a Mediterranean look. Mr Smith cupped the one side of his stubbly chin with his hand, elbow on the table. He had a full head of grey hair, parted to one side.

'Can you tell us a little about the relationship you had with Simone?' Gina asked. She watched as O'Connor began searching in his pockets for a pen. She pulled hers from her bag and placed it on his notepad.

'When she first came to stay with us, she was a quiet kid, really underweight and not in the best of places. She'd been through so much, so many things a child should never have to go through.' Gina had read her files but she let Mr Smith continue as she wanted to hear what he had to say and get a fuller picture of their victim. 'They told us that her mother was an addict and had invited a string of men to be a part of their life. The last one was the worst. Our poor girl had endured a lot at his hand. She was found in a skinny, sorry state. She'd been abused sexually but we never knew the extent of how much. Simone would never say. She never told the social worker, the police or anyone else. We always told her she could talk to either of us at any time, day or night – that we were always here. We do know the last man her biological mother was with beat her. Poor girl was covered in bruises. She came to us in a state; battered, bruised, riddled with head lice and scabies.'

'We just can't believe this has happened to her. We knew she couldn't settle and she was an almighty handful but we were hopeful. I know the girls found it harder over the last year Simone was with us…' Mrs Smith paused.

'How did your girls find it harder? Gina asked.

'They were all clashing, especially when it comes to the bathroom. We have one family bathroom and had two teens and a preteen competing to use it, that's without adding us to the equation. They argued every morning. Things even got nasty a couple of times. Emily had purposely left the shower running and locked herself in the bathroom, using all the hot water. Simone had lost her rag and shouted at her. It had ended with Emily throwing the fact that they weren't real sisters at her, and because of that she deserved more bathroom time. It had been a bad spell and yet, despite their differences, Emily was so upset when Simone left, blamed herself for driving her away, said she didn't mean what she said.

'There was more to it though. Simone used to hang around with a load of losers from town, just kids but kids that smoked and drank a lot. I could sometimes smell weed on her and, of course, the confrontations over this just made everything worse. She started going into nightclubs and pubs, not coming home. As I said, we've always provided for our family. I don't know why she was the way she was. She basically told us where to go, said she'd had it with the girls and us trying to dictate rules to her when she was now eighteen. It wasn't like that. We just cared for her. She'd been offered a place at a hostel and she was determined to take it. I wanted to go with her to see it but she said it was something she had to do alone. She never checked in to the hostel.'

'What happened after that? Did you hear from her or see her?'

'She called us a couple of times, normally after she'd been drinking. She said she was doing fine and had found somewhere to live. Around then, the police turned up to tell us that she'd been arrested for stealing wallets in nightclubs. She'd given them our address.' Mrs Smith remained in thought. Gina spotted a tear welling up in the corner of her eye. She'd held it together well, Gina didn't quite know how, but the woman was now beginning to crack. 'That was the last time she called. I offered to go to court with her, help her, offered her bedroom back to her but she said she needed to do things on her own for a while. Said she'd call again soon and that she could handle it all. She then thanked me for being there. That was the last I, or indeed we, ever heard of her. I should have insisted. I should have turned up whether she wanted me there or not but I didn't. I thought I was respecting her wishes and I suppose I thought she'd come back to us in her own time, when she'd got everything out of her system. We failed her!' The woman wiped the trailing tear from her face. Her husband moved his chair closer to her and placed his arm around his wife.

'You didn't fail her, Mrs Smith. We are going to find out what happened to Simone. This is not your fault at all.' However much she told Mrs Smith she was in no way to blame, she knew she'd always still blame herself. She would never see Simone again and never be able to make things right. However, Gina could get justice for Mrs Smith. She could find out who put Simone in that shallow grave, hoping she would never be found. She could find out how she got there and what she'd been through. She felt her knuckles clench under the table as she thought of the system, the underfunding and how it was letting vulnerable youngsters like Simone down. The girl had left with barely any support in place.

'Can you please just find out what happened to her? We loved Simone and when her body is released, we are going to have a proper family funeral for her. Does her mother know?' Mr Smith asked.

Gina nodded. 'She has been informed. You may need to speak with her about any arrangements.'

'That bitch caused all of this. Had she been a good mother not a raving junkie, this would never have happened. That woman didn't deserve Simone. I wish she'd been our daughter from the start. She was ours.' The man hugged his wife as she sobbed into his shoulders.

Mrs Smith pulled away from her husband and rubbed her eyes. 'I still haven't told our daughter, Emily. I don't know how to tell her after all the bad feelings and arguing. She hated herself for what she'd said after Simone had left. This is going to destroy her.'

Gina was fully aware of how guilt could destroy a person. Ultimately, Emily would need help in forgiving herself. Families argued, that was normal. Families said hurtful things to each other. Hannah had hurt her on many occasions. If something had happened to Gina, would Hannah be that wracked with guilt? She'd hope not. As someone who loved her, she'd simply hope that Hannah would grieve and move on. That's what true love was, not controlling someone with guilt. Her mind flashed back to Terry and how he had always made her feel guilty at never loving him enough, controlling her as she constantly tried to prove him wrong. He'd left her with the ultimate guilt trip. She'd killed him and never paid the price. She was the real murderer in all this. If anyone should feel guilty, it should be her, and she did. Always guilty.

'It will be hard but you need to be there for her.' Gina said to the Smiths. 'People always say things in the heat of the moment. We can be mean to each other, we all can, but Simone's death was not Emily's fault. Someone did this to her and I'm going to find out who it was.' The only way she could help this family was to catch whoever did this and she would. They said their goodbyes. For now, she had what she needed.

The door closed behind them and Gina's phone beeped. A message came through from Jacob.

We have a partial print – van girl forensics!

'That's good news. We need to hurry back. Also, when we get back, can you make a note to contact Miss Duxford, Simone's biological mother? I know Wyre was unable to get hold of her after giving her the news. We need to speak to her.'

'Will do, guv.'

Her heartbeat sped up with excitement, a partial print was just what they needed.

CHAPTER FORTY-TWO

Miley began to weep as she thought of what she'd left behind. She wanted to be free again, free to walk out, free to go and see her mother and free from addiction. Her hands shook as she wiped her face. She lay shivering on her bedroom floor, thinking back to how it all began.

*

Back then, she and her street friends were picking one of their targets. They watched the man as he went to light his cigarette. 'You got this,' the one girl said as she pushed Miley forward. 'Stupid man doesn't know where he's going either, he's walked past us three times already. Go get him, I think he fancies you anyway. Look, he's staring at you.' He tried again to light his cigarette, but his lighter had obviously run out of fuel. The chilly air bit into her lungs as she inhaled.

Miley stepped forward avoiding the frozen puddle, her heart quickening as she stood before him. He gripped his lighter as he stared at her and a smile beamed across his face. She held out a lighter. 'You want a light?'

'You're a lifesaver. It's my only opportunity to have one in peace, without being nagged.' She could see him looking at her hair. For a moment, she thought he might touch it, but he withdrew his hand and sucked on his cigarette, sending plumes of smoke into the air. She guessed he might be a businessman given that he was wearing a shirt and a designer jacket. He wouldn't miss the few quid he had in his pocket. If she could only find a way of slipping the shiny gold watch from his wrist – no, too risky. She wasn't skilled enough for that kind of trick.

'I don't suppose you can spare some change.'

The man stubbed the cigarette out on the floor after barely smoking half of it. 'Walk with me.'

'I, err, I don't know.' Something felt wrong. She glanced back and saw her two friends giggling behind the barrow, selling umbrellas.

'I don't bite. Do you want a cigarette?'

Miley shook her head as she walked alongside the man. It was a public street, heading up from New Street towards Symphony Hall and walking with him didn't feel dangerous.

They passed a man sitting in a doorway of a long-abandoned shop. Wrapped in a quilt, shaking as he pleaded with his eyes for a bit of change. 'People should work for their money, there are no free passes in life. These people stuffed up, they made their life choices and they ended up in the gutter. We all have choices. Don't you agree?'

Miley reluctantly nodded and wondered if he had a low opinion of her. She had however given him a light, which had benefitted him. He turned slightly, his wallet sitting proud of his back pocket. She could grab it now, make a run for it. She held her hand out as he stared at the homeless man, her fingers almost reaching it.

He turned and she flinched. As her heart rate peaked, she knew her face was reddening.

'I asked you a question. He stuffed up and now he's in the gutter. Don't you agree that it's all his fault?'

She shrugged. 'I don't know. I guess we all have a different story.'

'You can write your own story and someone like me can help you. I can be your guardian angel. I can give you the opportunity to turn your life around. A home, gainful employment, safety from the streets. You would regain your self-respect.'

'What?' Miley was confused. She'd gone from offering him a light while eyeing up his wallet, to being offered a way out. She wasn't quite sure what he was getting at.

'Can you spare some change?' the homeless man called. His chocolate-coloured eyes threw a glassy stare as he pleaded for a few quid. The young man reached out with a dirty hand, smiling with an open mouth, displaying a dirty set of teeth, plagued with chips and gaps. 'Anything will help, even ten pence.'

She watched as the man stepped back, not wanting his smart jeans contaminated by the young man's filth.

She allowed the thought of a new life to run through her head. It seemed he *was* offering her a job. At the moment, she'd have to decline. She had her friends to think of and if they were all to eat that night, she needed his wallet. He was a tough target. Most were easy, a quick distraction and grab. She glanced back hoping to spot the other two. One of them should have caused a distraction by now. Through the corner of her eye, she spotted them giggling. Behind the man's back, she stuck her two fingers up at them. They obviously thought it was hilarious. She was determined to win this one, with or without their help. That wallet was her target.

'Get off me, you scrounging piece of shit,' he said as he gave the homeless man a little kick with his shiny shoe. 'Come on, let's walk.' She gave the young man a glance back as she followed her target up the street. He was clutching a carrier bag. She tried to peer around, into the bag as she kept up with his fast stride.

He continued walking towards Symphony Hall, passing several *Big Issue* sellers. 'You haven't answered my question. I'm offering you a new life.'

She looked away, awkwardly staring into the window of a shop. A warm bed and employment sounded tempting but could she trust him? Most people she'd come across when on the streets had been after one thing, her body. Would he take her to a brothel, force her to have sex for money and trap her, with no escape? 'I don't know.'

'I had someone working for me, she was perfect, but she left for another job not long ago. I know what you're thinking.'

She glanced at him.

'You think I want to get you somewhere and maybe pimp you out. Or you think I'm a nutter, that I might rape you or imprison you. Let me put your mind at ease. I am just a normal person with a position to fill. I have no desire for your body, I just need a carer for a lovely lady whom I care deeply about and you look like a person I could trust. I'm not saying it's an easy job but you could do it. It would be live in as she needs round the clock care.'

As he continued speaking, he told her about the woman who needed care, Jackie. 'Why would you want me to do that? You don't know me and how do you know you can trust me?'

'There's something about you. I feel I could trust you to treat her with dignity. You seem like a nice girl and you don't look like you belong here with all these losers.'

She gulped as she thought of her friends. They worked as a team and that's how they survived. She glanced at his wallet again. There's no way she could snatch it now after he'd offered her such a good opportunity, even though she didn't think she'd take the job.

He checked his watch. 'Come with me. Check out our home and meet Jackie. You will love her, I promise. She's such a wonderful lady.'

Her two friends darted from around a corner and bumped into them. Her distraction had finally arrived. He jerked to the side, to avoid impact. Now was Miley's chance to snatch the wallet. A sick feeling churned in her stomach. The man had a sick relative and he'd approached her with an opportunity that might change her life. She grabbed her friend with the dyed red hair and pulled her close. 'These are my friends. Apologise for bumping into him like that.'

'Sorry, mister,' her red-haired friend said as she giggled. Her other friend gazed through her blonde fringe poking out of her dirty cap and looked on suspiciously. Miley's red-haired friend did her scruffy coat up and shivered as she fidgeted on the spot.

'Forget it, I'm fine. Do you girls want a sandwich? You look hungry.' The man pulled the pre-packed sandwiches out of his bag and thrust one into each of their hands, then passed them all a can of pop. 'Thank you,' Miley replied, noticing that the man seemed to be fixated on her friend's hair.

'You're all welcome.'

Miley's blonde-haired friend burped after swigging from the can.

'Are you all homeless?'

'I might be or I might not be.' Her blonde friend replied as she guzzled more of the drink before taking a bite of the sandwich. As she chewed, bits of mulched up ham filled her mouth, making Miley feel slightly queasy.

'I can help you, well two of you.'

Her blonde-haired friend piped up. 'Really? Because the only help I get offered around here comes with conditions, conditions I'm not prepared to enter in to. So, that's no to the blow job and I will not become your sex slave or engage in whatever perverse plan you think you have in store for me.'

'Really? You're young enough to be my daughter, maybe even my granddaughter if I started young. Life is all about give and take and I definitely wouldn't try to disrespect any of you in that manner. What I have to give might just be worth taking.'

'Go on then. Give us what you've got?'

'I'm looking to employ two people and they will be provided with a room and three meals a day. It is gainful employment and will involve a lot of, shall we say, domestic duties.'

'Domestic slaves, I've heard of them. Do I look like I was born yesterday?'

Miley nudged her blonde friend. She was about to blow it for all of them. 'If you're not interested, go away and give us the chance. If you are, listen to what he has to say.'

He cleared his throat and smiled. 'It's good that you don't trust everyone. There are some dangerous people about, but I'm really not one of them. I'm looking for employees, not slaves. It's a good opportunity to get off the streets and make something of yourself. You'd like to make something of yourself, wouldn't you?'

'Not with your help. Stay away from me.' The blonde girl paused and looked around. People walked by, ignoring them. That was the worst thing about being homeless, no one took a blind bit of notice. Crowds walked past, getting on with their bland lives. Work, shopping, keeping kids placated. 'I've heard of your type before. If you don't go away, I'm going to shout paedophile and point at you before I run. These people don't see a thing all day. They walk past, pretend they haven't seen me but the minute I start drawing attention to you… they'll look at you. They won't believe me, of course, but they will think about it and remember the way you look. If they see you again, they'll make that connection.' She stared at him with her blue eyes and pointed. 'There's the paedo. Do you hear me?' It wasn't quite loud enough for the passers-by.

'Keep it down. He's offering me a job, for heaven's sake. I don't want to be out here, stuck in the cold forever,' Miley said.

'Yeah, me neither,' her red-haired friend replied as she stuffed the rest of her sandwich in her mouth.

'I know you don't know me and you probably don't trust me, but just give me a chance. Come with me. Have a look at the rooms, meet the lovely lady who you will care for and then make your decision.'

'Do what you like, but I'm not going anywhere with him,' the blonde girl said.

'I like the sound of it.' Her friend scrunched up the sandwich packet. 'I hate it here.'

'It's all your fault.' The blonde-haired girl said to Miley as she threw her sandwich packet at her. 'She would never have agreed to this before you came along. Go on then. Go with your new but stupid best friend.' She stomped off. They watched her as she disappeared around a corner. It didn't matter, there were only two jobs going anyway. Miley shivered as it began to rain. A warm bed and a job were all that she dreamed of and the man seemed so nice.

'We'll have a look. If we don't like what you're offering, we don't have to take the job. Right?' Miley asked. Her red-haired friend began to shiver and cramp up. She'd need a fix soon.

'I can help you with that too. You'll soon feel better. This will be a new start. If you don't like it, I'll bring you back here, I promise.' Miley took in his warm smile as he placed a firm arm on her shoulders, leading her back towards New Street. She soaked up his warmth, almost wishing they were in another life and he was her dad. 'My car is just down here. Let's get you both warm.'

She smiled as she urged her friend on. 'We'll be okay soon, nice and warm, I promise.'

*

She opened her eyes, almost biting her tongue with her chattering teeth. She wiped the trail of spit from the side of her face. 'Can I have my medicine, please?' she whispered.

Her memories had been so vivid, it was almost like they were back on the streets of Birmingham. She felt the cold, she could smell the food that was being sold on the streets, and she could feel her red-haired friend leaning against her for support as they headed to his car. She'd promised her that they would be fine as she'd helped her into his warm car.

A tear escaped from her eye. Miley had broken her promise, now her friend was no longer there and she was all alone, trapped.

CHAPTER FORTY-THREE

Heading through the main entrance, with O'Connor in tow, Gina hurried to the incident room. Jacob was sitting at the head of the table. Wyre removed her headset and joined them. Smith entered, carrying a pot of coffee and a few cups on a tray. 'I took the initiative, guv.' Smith let out a small laugh as he placed the tray down and began pouring the drinks. It had been a long, hot day for all of them but the weather was about to break, just like she hoped their case would. In the distance Gina heard a gentle rumble of thunder. A storm was brewing.

They grabbed a drink and huddled around. Jacob leaned in. 'What a discovery. In the depths of her pocket they found a small piece of cellophane packaging.' Jacob held up a photo. It was small, about the size of a baby's fingernail. 'Tests showed that minute traces of heroin were found on the packaging, which ties into van girl's blood results. Here's the good bit, a partial print was left on this packaging. It is currently being run through the database, no match as yet. It may belong to her, before her prints were seared off, or it may belong to the dealer or even to someone else she'd been in contact with.'

Gina smiled. 'Great find, let's hope for a match. Just to update you, O'Connor and I have been to see the Smiths and we have a clearer picture of how life was at home for Simone. I'll be updating the system with my notes as soon as I get into my office. I suggest you read them immediately. I also want to speak with Simone's biological mother, there's a slim chance she may have gone back to her old home. Any light that Miss Duxford can shed on the case would be good. What do we know about her?'

Wyre opened her notebook. 'Cassandra Duxford, aged thirty-five. She's spent the last two years on a methadone and drug rehabilitation programme after being threatened with permanently losing her other two children, twins, aged three. From looking at her record, all the petty crimes she had been involved in before seemed to have stopped. No more shoplifting, no more anti-social behaviour and no more charges of soliciting. She has been off our records for a few years now. It looks on the surface that Miss Duxford is a changed woman.'

'I'd like to see for myself. Did you have any luck contacting her?'

'No. I tried calling a few times but her number keeps going to voicemail. I will keep trying. It's been hard for her too, knowing what has happened to her daughter.'

'Let's hope she hasn't slipped. Inform social services what has happened. She may need further support. We have two other children in her household to consider here.'

Wyre nodded. 'Will do, guv.'

Gina took a swig of coffee as another roll of thunder built up to a clash. She took a few deep breaths to calm down her galloping heart rate. Thunder was always a trigger for her anxiety, taking her straight back to the night when she helped Terry to fall to his death. The thunder that night had been deafening. A flash of lightning filled the room.

As Gina went to place the cup on the table, she spilled the contents everywhere, soaking Wyre's paperwork. 'For heaven's sake, I'm so clumsy.'

'No worries, guv. I can print the notes out again,' she replied as she grabbed a couple of serviettes and began mopping up the mess. 'No harm done.'

Gina stared out of the window, waiting for lightning to strike. Another rumble filled the air. She shook her hands, willing the tremble to go away. Closing her eyes, she counted to ten and breathed in and out. Terry was gone. He could never hurt her again. 'Shall I get you some water, guv?'

'No, I'm fine, thanks. I just felt a bit nauseous,' she lied. 'Right, I'm fine now. Where was I? That's it, the shallow grave. Are we done collecting there yet?'

Jacob put his cup down. 'Yes, I think Bernard has taken all he needed, sample wise. Thankfully, no more bones belonging to anyone else were found in the vicinity. The announcement came at the right time this afternoon as I've had the Norths calling non-stop, saying that we are holding up their development and that time was money in their business. Apparently, they have some new members of staff starting soon. They want them in the property cleaning, ready for viewings. At least they will be able to do that and Mr North won't keep calling all the time. We've maintained the cordon so Mr Tilly won't be building his summerhouse anytime soon.'

'Great. No more results to share as yet?' Gina thought back to their chat with the Norths earlier that day. Mr North had something to hide, she was sure of it.

'That's it for now, guv. As always Bernard and Keith said they'd give us any information they had as they found it, before the official report is written. Bernard seemed very excited about the larvae cases providing the match between the two girls. Could we be looking at a serial killer?'

'We have two dead girls at the moment. I really don't want another to turn up. I don't think Cleevesford could take much more. It's turning into an unsafe place to live. "Help her" – I want to know who Simone was referring to on her deathbed. We're still no further with that line of enquiry. How bad have the press been?'

Smith finished his drink and placed the empty cup on the tray. 'They've apparently come in a couple of times, hoping to speak to one of us. Nick on the front desk gave them Corporate Communications' number. Briggs also said not to tell them anything so we've just been fobbing them off really.'

'Good advice. On to another strand of this investigation, I want to be kept in the loop with the drug problems in Cleevesford. If you get a tip-off, I want to be a part of it. I know it's not my territory but given the drug link I feel we need to stay close on this one, pool intelligence, information, details of arrests. I want to know whose prints are on the cellophane wrapper and we could do worse than pulling in any potential dealers.' The lights flickered as another rumble of thunder filled the room.

'This is going to clear the air. I'm sick of this heatwave,' O'Connor said as he began to doodle on his pad.

'Me too. I'll let you know of anything that comes in with regards to any potential drug busts. I have been in contact with the man who owns the chippy on the High Street. We're on alert, waiting for his call. He said it happens regularly so I'm thinking it could be anytime.'

Gina smiled. 'Great, as soon as you hear, let me know. I'm coming with you. Call me anytime. Wyre, could you dig a little deeper on Mr North? I don't trust the man.'

Wyre nodded and returned her smile. Smith's radio came to life as the operator read the incident out, calling for Smith and his team to attend. 'They're outside the chippy now. We've got to go.'

'That was quick,' Gina replied as she grabbed her phone. 'Let's go.'

CHAPTER FORTY-FOUR

'This girl is useless,' the voice boomed from Jackie's room. 'I can't have her here, looking after Jackie any longer. Have you seen the bruises on her?' He was on the phone.

'I didn't hurt Jackie, I love Jackie. Please, I need my medicine. Help me,' Miley cried, knowing that the boss would never believe her as he spoke on the phone to the very person who had been hurting Jackie.

Jackie began to shout and cry out, louder and louder. Miley flinched as she heard a slap through the thin wall. He was now hurting her.

'Stop yelling,' he called out. 'I'm sorry, sorry, my love. I didn't mean to hurt you.'

'I can look after her. I just need my medicine.' Miley writhed on the floor of her room as another wave of stomach cramps travelled through her, this time stronger. She screamed as her body flushed with heat and sweat dribbled down the side of her face, making the carpet she was lying on, even stickier.

Jackie's yells filled the house again. 'Oh shut up! Shut up, both of you!' the boss shouted.

'Don't hurt her,' Miley cried as she doubled over. Jackie was all she had. She wanted so badly to hug and feel the warmth of the woman who never responded to her need for affection. She wanted to feel what it was like to be hugged by her mother again. She began sobbing loudly as a wave of nausea shot through her.

Closing her eyes, she tried to face the carpet. The light was making her head throb and the room sway. She needed to be in darkness.

Jackie's door slammed and the boss stomped down the stairs, locking the bottom door after him. 'I need my medicine,' she croaked. It was the first time she'd been without since arriving. The boss was punishing her now he believed that she'd beaten Jackie.

Miley hadn't been out of the room all day. The urine in the bucket filled the warm room with an unbearable stench. Rain fell, pattering on the roof above. At least the thunder had stopped. Listening to Jackie's animalistic cries during that time had been torture for Miley.

Her skin began to crawl as she watched the beetle emerge from the skirting board.

She rolled on the floor. 'Leave me alone,' she cried as she scratched. Her worst nightmare was happening. It felt like the insects were all over her, gnawing away until there was nothing left but bone. 'Help me.' She wanted it all to stop. It had to stop. She couldn't live like this any more.

Jackie began calling as the rain outside fell.

She listened as the flapping of moth wings surrounded her. She couldn't open her eyes and be confronted with the creepy crawlies. She scratched and scratched until blood seeped from the tears in her skin.

She awoke to the sound of the downstairs door being unlocked. A heavy foot led the way. Jackie began to call out. He murmured words that she couldn't make out until he reached the landing. 'Jackie, please, my love, stop shouting.' It was the man again.

Back then, he'd promised her everything, a wonderful job, a lovely safe place to live and help with the work. He told her that she'd been just the type of person he'd been looking for. He had made her feel safe and warm.

'Help me. I need my medicine,' she mumbled, as he passed her room. She couldn't shout any more. She turned and forced her eyes open, knowing she had to face whatever was surrounding her. The insect wings flapped louder and the rain sounded like knives on the roof, no longer were they little droplets. Darkness had fallen and the room filled with shadows. Afternoon felt like it was night or was it night? The crawling sensation receded, leaving her with a moment's respite.

Her heart began to pound as she fought to lift her arms up. She could just about see that they were still smooth, except for the occasional spot. Nothing was crawling out of her skin, it never had been. The itching had come from the large spots that she'd been picking. Her limbs were plagued with them. She gazed at the black scabs that had formed on her fingertips.

Her stomach contracted. It was coming again. 'Please stop it.' Her cries were so gentle, no one would be able to hear. Why hadn't Miley realised? She'd become so dependent on them and there was no way out. She'd do anything for a fix. Medicine! It wasn't medicine. There had been nothing wrong with her in the first place. She needed to get out. 'Mum.' Her mum wouldn't hear her calling, but she could hope. She wondered if her mum actually missed her. 'Mum,' Miley called as the man paced behind the door.

'It's me,' he said abruptly.

Her heart misfired, beating irregularly until she realised he was talking on his phone again.

'That stupid bitch has been going mad. I can't deal with her any more. I've had to lock her in her room, just hurry back.' He paused and paced up and down, behind the door. 'Oh shut up. How can you accuse me of that? I've never touched a hair on her head or any of the others. Sometimes you disgust me, I will always love Simone.'

'Jackie loves me,' Miley called, whimpering as she lay there.

'Shut up.' He banged on the door. 'Not you, okay I'm sorry. Just hurry back with the stuff.'

'Who's Simone?' she shouted.

'Got to go,' he said into the phone as he unlocked her door.

'Please, I didn't mean it. Please, I just need my medicine. I'm happy. I never hurt Jackie.'

The man stood before her. He looked so smart and clean. What she'd do to feel clean again. She reached out. 'Please help me.'

'You stupid junkie. Why would I help you? Who's Simone? You really want to know?'

Miley wept as she nodded. The crawling was starting again. The insects were back. 'Simone was the most beautiful girl ever. Kind, gentle, loving. Jackie loved her so much.'

'Jackie loves me—' Her stomach clenched as she screamed.

'She doesn't love you. She has no idea who you are. You're nothing. Look at you. You're useless. Jackie is always filthy. It was your job to keep her clean and safe. Clean, all you had to do was clean. The house had to be kept tidy, your room, Jackie's room or any other room that needed cleaning. Smell this room.'

Miley continued to weep as pain tore through her body, wave after wave.

'It smells filthy, like you.'

'I didn't hurt her.'

'I saw what you did.' He drew his foot back and a kick landed in her gut, taking her breath away. The man jangled his keys and laughed as she writhed around on the floor, gasping for air as he walked over to the door.

'Please don't lock it. I won't leave, I can't leave – look at me,' she whispered.

He grinned as he pulled the door to and locked it. 'Sleep well.'

'No, don't leave me.' She didn't want him to go even though he'd hurt her. His being cruel was better than her lying alone in pain, in the stormy darkness. The flapping wings were back. She scratched her arms and dug her nails under her skin. She'd dig out the intruders, every last one of them. 'Mum! Get them out of me.'

CHAPTER FORTY-FIVE

PC Smith sat in front of the undercover police car next to Gina. Jacob was with another officer on the other side of the road, watching. Another two cars had been prepped and were waiting on side streets. 'Okay, our young man was seen about forty minutes ago, when we got the call. He was loitering by the bus stop.'

Gina watched as Smith spoke. 'I hope he comes back soon.'

'I hope he comes back full stop. There have been so many false alarms.'

Gina smiled. 'I used to love my uniform days. It's like being back. I don't miss Broad Street, Birmingham, on a Saturday night though.'

'I know what you mean. Did it for a long time before being transferred here. Cleevesford sees far less action. We get the occasional bout of trouble, the odd fight at the Angel but nothing too taxing.'

'You're a good copper, Smith. Have you ever thought about becoming a detective? You're always an asset when we have a big case on.' Gina grabbed a chocolate biscuit from the bag in the footwell.

'I did think about it. Unlike you, I love a rowdy Saturday night. I love uniform and front-line policing. I love days like this. Does it sound wrong to love being here to bust a drug dealer?'

'Not at all. It's exciting. Much better than sitting at home watching TV.' Gina crunched on the biscuit and offered the packet to Smith.

He patted his belly. 'Best not. The wife says I'm getting fat. She said I'm not allowed any more of O'Connor's offerings.'

Gina laughed and placed the biscuits back in the bag. 'I best move them out of your way then.' They had been sitting in the car for over half an hour now and no activity had occurred. People waited at the bus stop, ordinary folk going home late from work. People went to the chip shop and left with wrapped up fried food. The drifting smell of chips wafted through the slightly open window. Nothing out of the ordinary stood out. Gina began fanning herself with her hands, trying to battle the suffocating heat.

The radio cracked into action. 'Anything your end?' said PC Kapoor with a high-pitched Brummie accent.

'Not as yet.' Smith paused and stared out of the window. A young man was checking his surroundings as he took large strides towards the bus stop. 'It looks like our guy. Young male, white, looks to be about five ten, shoulder-length, wavy dark hair, twenties. Remember, he doesn't do just one deal then leave. Pick up anyone he's dealt to when they're out of sight. Continue watching him. I want him and all the punters.'

'Understood,' Kapoor said.

Another young male began walking towards the bus stop. Black, greasy hair. It glistened as the light from the chip shop sign caught the top of his head. She recognised the well-built man. 'That's Darren Mason.'

'Darren Mason?'

'The kid we brought in. He was the one who was driving the van in which our girl came from. We found a packet of weed in his van. That must be his dealer. It didn't take him five minutes to break his bail conditions.' Gina grabbed the radio. 'We have our first customer. It's only Darren Mason.'

Jacob answered. 'Bloody hell.'

'When he's made his purchase, get one of the officers on foot to follow him. As soon as he's out of the dealer's sight, arrest him.'

'I'm on it, guv.'

'You're taking over my bust, guv.' Smith held out his hand. Gina passed him the radio.

She laughed and continued watching as the speedy transaction took place. The dealer bent down as if pulling up a sock. Darren Mason bumped into him and it was over. Mason continued walking away. 'I wonder if our dealer has finished for the evening or if there will be others.'

'He hasn't moved. He's not going anywhere yet.'

'We've got him,' Kapoor said through the radio. 'One of the officers is taking Mason in to be questioned now.'

'One down, however many to go.' Gina smiled and grabbed another biscuit. The sugary bakes were set to be her evening meal, she might as well eat as many as she could manage and fill herself up.

'Look at him,' Smith said, his gaze on the dealer. 'Full of it, has no idea we're on to him. I love it when it's like this.'

Gina's stomach began to flutter. She couldn't wait to pounce, to get in there and arrest the man. She couldn't wait to question him, see if he knew either of their girls. Both of them had been discovered locally. There can't be too many dealers in Cleevesford. He could be their man. If not, it was certain that he'd know who his competition was. Whether he'd give that information up was another matter.

'Come on.' She began to annoyingly bounce her knee as she waited. 'Sorry,' she said as she stopped. It was a habit of O'Connor's that annoyed her. She was going to try to not be as annoying as him. 'Who's that?'

A couple that looked to be in their forties were beginning to slow down by the bus stop. 'Going home from work. He's wearing a T-shirt with a logo on it. Maybe they catch the bus.' Smith leaned back and observed.

The couple slowed down and again, they looked like they'd bumped into the young man and it was all over. The woman nudged the man and they laughed as they crossed the road and went into the chip shop. Gina could see the disapproving look on the chip shop manager's face. He looked out of the large glass front towards the bus stop. 'Please don't give the game away.' Gina tapped her fingernails on the dashboard as she leaned forward. 'Stop looking out. He's giving away that he knows we're here.'

'Here's his number. You call him while I arrange for officers to be ready to pick the couple up.'

'Hello, Cleevesford Fish Bar.'

'Hello, this is DI Harte. Please stop looking out of the window. We have this under control, but you will make the dealer twitchy. We don't want him to run. Don't look, but the couple who are next in the queue have just bought something. Serve them, be your usual polite self and we will pick them up. Can you do that?'

'Of course. We are open until eleven every night,' he said as he hung up.

Gina smiled. Another woman approached wearing a rain mac with a hood covering her head. Her shiny heels clacked on the pavement. 'Another customer?'

'Nothing surprises me. Both sides of the street are covered by officers, ready to pick the couple up.'

'Great.' Gina watched the couple leaving the chip shop. They headed off to the left, back past the Angel Arms pub, towards the newer estate.

'They're heading towards King Street,' Smith said.

Gina watched as the next woman pulled her plastic hood further over her forehead. It was too dark to see what she looked like. As she approached the dealer, she held out some cash and dropped one of the notes. She thrust what she had into the young man's arms as she reached for the other note. He frantically looked around as he threw a package towards her, snatching the last note as she stood up from the pavement. His gaze rested on their car. They'd been spotted.

The man darted. 'Dealer heading towards King Street. All units standing by head along the back road and cut him off. He's on foot. The woman has just left in the opposite direction on foot. We're heading towards King Street. Stop the woman.'

Smith set the siren off and pulled out of the car park, speeding onto the High Street. Gina held onto the seat as he took a right onto King Street. She watched as the dealer jumped over a fence, landing in a residential back garden.

Gina darted out of the car, leaving the door open. She heaved herself up over the fence. She was getting too unfit to give chase. She felt a splinter embed itself into the palm of her hand. She landed in a shrubbery on the other side of the fence, flinching as she reached out and grabbed a spiny bush. Rain pattered, bouncing off the wheelie bin next to the back door. The terraced house looked empty and left no way to get out unless he'd escaped over another fence. She got to her feet and stumbled into the overgrown garden. It was silent. Creeping around, she listened for signs of movement.

'Guv?' It was Jacob.

'I'm here. Beware of the shrubs.' She heard a thud as he joined her in the garden, swearing as he landed on the spines. She continued to creep around. She hadn't heard the dealer climb another fence but the garden was empty. As she reached the house, she heard a shuffle. Turning, she caught sight of the young man, crouching behind the bin. 'Here he is.' They had caught their dealer and possibly the person who knew something about their two girls.

CHAPTER FORTY-SIX

Gina rushed through the main entrance with Jacob closely following. The couple from the chip shop were standing in the queue waiting to be booked in. Behind them, their wavy haired young dealer nervously bit his dirty nails. Darren Mason skulked at the back, avoiding her gaze. Desk Sergeant, Nick, began the formalities. 'When they're all booked in, let me know,' Gina said to Smith as he herded them all into the right area.

'Will do.'

She pulled him aside. 'As soon as you have their prints run them and send the results to Bernard. I want them crossmatched against our case.'

'Will do, guv.' Smith went back to the line and gestured for Kapoor to assist him.

As she went to leave, she heard the dealer speak when asked what his name was. 'Westley Young.'

Gina turned back, almost bumping into Jacob. 'Julia Dawson mentioned that her daughter had left with someone called Westley. It could well be him. You don't hear the name Westley mentioned much.' Gina walked over to the desk and checked the paperwork Nick was filling in. Westley was currently living in Worcester. She pulled Smith aside. 'When he's booked in, I want to interview him and then we need to speak to Darren Mason.'

Smith nodded. 'I'll give you a shout when he's ready.'

Gina continued along the corridor towards the incident room. 'Looks like O'Connor and Wyre have headed home.'

'Lucky them. Of course, they have good reasons to want to go home,' Jacob replied as he turned the desk fan on. A few of O'Connor's loose papers flew off the desk. 'I'm just going to head back out the front, keep an eye on what's happening. I could do with getting away some time tonight.'

'Date with Amber?'

'Definitely not. She said we're over. She's apparently met someone else. Oh well. I'm just tired, I guess.' Gina could understand that. It had been a long day for them all.

As Jacob left, Briggs walked in, eating a slice of pizza. 'I heard the place is packed out. Nice operation, looks like we nailed a dealer.'

'Yes. It's was Smith's victory and a good stakeout. Guess what?'

'Go on.'

'The dealer is called Westley. A missing girl, Christina Dawson, left with someone called Westley. It's too much of a coincidence. And that's not all, one of the punters is only Darren Mason. The young man with the van our mystery girl came from. What is going on? They must know something. I'm hoping our partial print found on the cellophane in van girl's clothing matches one of them. Their prints will be going right over to Bernard and Keith for cross-checking.'

'Let's hope for a match. Our dealer may show himself to be the one who supplied the girl in the van.'

'From what I read earlier, we have spoken to a lot of people in the Winyates area of Redditch, spoken to pubs, shops, gone door to door and not one person remembers seeing a girl of her description just before she turned up in Darren's van.'

'It's odd that our Darren turns up again in the same investigation. Coincidence or not?'

Gina looked at the strip light reflected in the darkness of the smeared window before turning her attention back towards Briggs. 'That's what I'm hoping to find out. You look tired.' It made a change, her having to tell Briggs he looked tired. She was almost pleased for getting that statement in before he did.

'I suppose I am. The other night when you called…'

'I hung up, sorry.' She didn't want him to know that she'd heard Annie speaking in the background.

'I can tell when you're hiding something. You forget how well I know you. You heard her, didn't you?'

'Who?' Their eyes met in the silent incident room. 'Okay, chief detective, so I heard her. It doesn't matter. We're friends.'

'Are we?' He smiled. 'Just so you know, it was a mistake.'

'Like we were?' She could have kicked herself. Her jealousy was now showing. He'd know.

'That was never a mistake. You gave me some wonderful memories. The other night was a mistake.'

'You don't have to tell me, really. I don't want or need to know any more, sir.'

'I want us to stay friends. Friends talk about things like this so I just thought I'd tell you. Want some pizza? It was a mistake, but I can't say it won't happen again. I get lonely now and again, what can I say? Anyway, Harte, I have half a big pepperoni in my office and it's just waiting to be scoffed. It will be a good half hour before you get to speak to anyone. They're probably having their prints and mugshots done as we speak.'

'I don't know—'

'It's just pizza. Are you hungry?'

She nodded. 'Starving,' she replied as she followed him down the corridor, the smell of grilled cheese hanging in the air. The biscuits she'd eaten in Smith's car hadn't even touched the edge of her hunger and she'd burnt off a fair bit of energy chasing their dealer. Just as she reached his office, Jacob came running down the corridor.

'Young is ready for his interview.'

Gina took a large bite from a slice of pizza and swallowed. 'Right, I'll interview Westley Young with Smith and you can take Darren Mason with Kapoor? We can pool findings after. It'll be quicker.'

Gina dragged her phone out of her pocket, almost dropping it as it slipped through her greasy fingers. 'Damn.' She'd missed a call from Hannah two hours ago. She read the message.

Why is Gracie using the words bloody hell at the end of every sentence, Mum?!!

Damn it. She should've have known that slip up would come back to haunt her.

CHAPTER FORTY-SEVEN

The recorder was running and the young male was hunched over the table, tracing his finger over the grain in the wood as Gina joined Smith in the interview room. He announced for the tape that she had joined them.

'Westley Young, twenty-two years old. You live in Worcester, is that right?' Gina scraped her chair across the floor until she was positioned comfortably at the desk, placing her notepad in front of her.

'I sleep rough in Worcester.'

Gina pulled out the photo of Christina that Julia Dawson had given her. 'Do you recognise this girl?' The man looked up through his scruffy brown locks. Most of his long fringe was tucked behind his ears. She slid the photo across the desk. He stared at it and looked away.

'Never seen her.'

'Are you sure? Take another look?'

She could tell he was getting nervous. He began to tap his fingers on the desk, drumming away. 'So what if I have?'

'It's a simple question, Mr Young. Have you seen this girl?'

'Okay. Will I be in less trouble if I tell you about the girl?'

'I can't promise you anything but it will be on record that you were cooperative.'

He leaned back and slumped in the chair. As he moved, Gina could smell the sweat wafting from his old grey T-shirt. He clearly hadn't bathed for a long time. 'I haven't seen her for ages. She used to hang out around Worcester, looked a bit lost. A couple of times she gave me some of her food. We chatted and became friends; that is all.'

'Were you in a relationship with her?'

'God, no. She was a kid. I'm not some paedo. She just liked to hang out with me.'

'Do you know her name?'

'I always called her Pipsqueak. I did find out her name after though. I saw her mother putting posters up.'

'And you never called to say you'd seen her?'

'She'd run away. She didn't want to be found. You don't tell on friends. When I left her, she was fine. I thought she'd just go home when she got fed up. Has something happened to her?' Westley couldn't look directly at her. His gaze shifted between her and Smith before resting on the wall behind them.

'That's what we're trying to establish.' Gina opened a fresh page in her book. 'Tell me about the last time you saw her.'

He smiled. 'She's a good kid. She always cheered me up.' Gina noted that he referred to her in present tense. 'It was a few months ago, March, April, I don't even remember, my brain is addled. She did say she'd had another argument with her mother about being grounded all the time. I always hung around by the river come early evening. I like the peace, believe it or not. She had her bag with her and said she was leaving, that she couldn't take any more and would I go with her? I didn't want to go but I didn't want her to go alone either. She needed to get out of Worcester so we went to the station and she bought us both tickets to New Street. I spent a couple of days with her and I suppose I got fed up. I asked about work at the market, had no luck and hated it there. I tried to persuade her to come back with me but she didn't want to come, said she'd go it alone. She got a bit huffy and walked off.' He started twitching. Gina knew he probably needed a fix. She looked over Smith's notes and saw that a doctor had been called to attend to him after the interview.

'Did you sell her any drugs?'

'No, what do you take me for?' He ran his fingers through his messy hair.

'A drug dealer. You were brought in tonight for dealing drugs.'

'I don't sell to kids. She was a kid.'

'A dealer with a conscience.'

'Stuff you!'

Gina ignored him and pulled out another photo, one of Simone Duxford. It was a long shot, but if he was involved, then he'd show some recognition. 'Have you ever seen this girl?'

His brow furrowed as he examined the photo. 'No, I don't recognise her at all. Never seen her in my life.' His reactions matched what he was saying. Gina couldn't even see a hint of recognition in his eyes. He began to fidget in his chair and tapped his foot on the floor as his agitation worsened. 'I don't want to say any more, I feel sick and if you don't let me out of here, I'll chuck up all over the table. I know my rights. Get me a solicitor. Oh, one thing, when I left Pipsqueak in Birmingham, she hadn't taken any drugs and she told me to shove off and that's what I did, I shoved off. All because I didn't want to stay in Birmingham. That's all I know. I don't even know when this was. I can't remember. That's your lot. I need the bog now.'

Gina nodded to Smith. 'Interview terminated at twenty-three fifteen. We'll continue shortly.'

As she left the room, she began collecting her thoughts. He had seen Christina Dawson but she wasn't quite sure how much of what he'd said had been truthful. If he'd left Christina in Birmingham like he'd said, where had she gone? It was as if the girl had just disappeared.

CHAPTER FORTY-EIGHT

'Right, Jacob. What did you get from Darren Mason?'

He entered the kitchen and took one of the coffees she'd just poured. 'With what we have on him already, this is his second offence over the past week and he's breached the conditions of his bail. But it was only weed. The other officers who arrested him, said he was tracked all the way down the street until he was out of the dealer's sight. He didn't offload anything once he spotted them. The area was well searched and nothing else was found.'

'The girl who fell from his van had definitely been on heroin, her blood results have confirmed that. I know we found anabolic steroids in his room but we know where he obtained those from after checking his browsing history. We searched his boyfriend, Callum Besford's flat and again, found nothing.'

'Oh, I forgot to say, his father, Dennis Mason, is waiting for his son in reception with a solicitor and he's in a foul mood.'

'Probably peeved because we still have his laptop and one of his vans. More than likely wants his porn collection back.'

Jacob sniggered as he swigged his coffee. 'Smith and Kapoor have moved on to interviewing the woman and the couple.'

'Do you know any more about them?'

Jacob pulled his little notebook from his back pocket. 'I did grab a bit of info to keep us going before they update the system. Smith assures me it will all be updated as soon as they've finished the interviews. Ellen Simpson and Aaron Dunn, the pair in the chip shop. She is forty-one, he is forty-five. It looks like they'd prepared for a good night in. A bag of beer, bottle of vodka, kebab and chips and a few grams of cocaine. Ellen Simpson is carer to her elderly mother whom she lives with. Aaron Dunn stays with her most of the time but lives in a bedsit at the back of the High Street. He works at a biscuit packing factory on the industrial estate. That's all I have on them so far. The other woman was scoring heroin. She looks high functioning, maybe she's a new addict. She's in her late fifties, at a guess. She's also refusing to speak at the moment. Won't even confirm her identity. I'm sure a night in the cells will change her mind. We'll know more tomorrow. I seriously think we should be going home and getting some sleep.'

'I seriously think you're right,' Briggs said as he entered and threw his empty pizza box into the bin. 'I'll catch you both tomorrow. If you want to run anything by me, call me when you get home.' Briggs smiled at Gina and left.

'"Call me when you get home." I think he likes you.'

Gina playfully slapped Jacob on the arm. 'Don't be daft.' If only he knew how right he was.

As Gina headed towards the door, car keys in hand, she passed the corridor to the cells. She headed down towards where Darren Mason was being held and opened the flap on the door.

'Oh, it's you,' he said as he lifted his head off the thin mattress. 'When's my dad getting me out of here?'

'I can't answer that, sorry. I just thought I'd check on how things went with the council. I did call them to mention the abuse, you know the kids with Callum.' Despite what was happening, she wanted to make sure Callum had been looked after.

'You're concern overwhelms me. I told my dad about Callum. You should've seen the disappointment in his face. That look will stay with me forever. Are any of you surprised that I need weed to escape, that I take steroids to make myself fit in with what a proper son should be? What my dad thinks I should be. Macho tree surgeon. It's him. My dad's a twat. Mommy saved the day though, couldn't bear her boy being unhappy and moving out to a place where other people want to hurt him. She let Callum move in to ours for a bit until the council find him somewhere.' He paused and smirked but Gina could see his eyes watering up. 'It's far from pleasant. My dad keeps scowling at him. You've met Callum, you know what a quiet, person he is. He was upset. I thought I'd score us a bit of weed so we could chill. He doesn't deserve to be treated like that.'

'People come round. Your dad just needs time to take it in.'

All of a sudden Darren Mason looked like a scared child. He drew his legs up and hugged his rolled up hoodie. 'I doubt it, but thanks for calling the council.'

'Goodnight, Darren.' She closed the flap and left him pondering about all that had happened as she headed out past the front desk.

'I hope you're getting my computer back to me soon,' said Dennis Mason. Some of the buttons on his shirt had come undone, revealing his bulbous hairy belly. His dirty work shorts skimmed his dusty knees.

'Don't worry, Mr Mason, we'll get your porn collection back to you very soon,' Gina said as she left, giving him no opportunity to answer back.

It was the end of a long day. She checked her phone as she walked to her car. A woman stared back from another car. She'd recognise that face anywhere. Lyndsey Saunders, reporter for the *Warwickshire Herald* was topping up her red lipstick in her rear-view mirror. Gina had no idea why. Lipstick or no lipstick – that woman would have to go through the right channels to get a statement. The reporter caught her eye and quickly got out of the car. 'Detective Harte, could it be that a serial killer is lose in

Cleevesford? The public have a right to know. Human remains. A girl, emaciated, falling from a van, since died. Too much of a coincidence, I'd say.'

Gina could easily punch the woman after the last case she worked on. She had no empathy for the people whose lives she reported on and that included Gina's. Lyndsey Saunders was never getting a morsel of information from her lips. 'You know the score. Contact Corporate Communications. Don't call me or approach me again or I will haul you in for harassment.'

'It's a free country and I'm on public land.'

Gina walked up to the woman. 'The world doesn't need people like you. I will never tell you anything. Do you hear me?'

The woman grinned. 'Oh, I hear you. It's all right when you need us for your appeals, one sniff of a real story and you shut us out. I'll call you.'

Gina got into her car, slammed the door and drove off, knuckles gripping the steering wheel, revving the engine as she exited the car park. Maybe Lyndsey was right. What if they were looking for a serial killer? And van girl's last words were telling them of girl number three. All girls involved had red tones to their hair and insect cases had linked their two dead girls. She shivered, wondering if the insect cases had been picked up accidentally or if a kidnapper had left them deliberately for forensics to find. Her head was awhirl with all the information.

As she sped down the country roads, a fox darted from the bushes, its eyes fixed on hers as she slammed the brakes on, stopping just in time. She gasped for breath as the creature ran, disappearing in the hedge. *Calm it down, Gina.* She put the car into first and started driving again as jumbled elements of the case flashed through her mind.

There were too many people involved. The drug dealer, the Masons, the others who had been booked in. Images of distraught parents flashed through her mind. There was Josh and Angela

Smith, Simone's foster parents. Julia Dawson and her boyfriend, Roy, and she had yet to visit Simone's biological mother. Bryn Tilly and the Norths. What was Mr North hiding? That was a question that kept playing on her mind. Her own daughter – she'd let her down again. She couldn't bear for Hannah to be mad at her forever, but she couldn't face her either. As she pulled up on her drive, the security light came on. She fiddled with the splinter that was now causing a major irritation.

'Got you, you bastard,' she said as she slid the splinter from her hand and flicked it out of the window.

CHAPTER FORTY-NINE

Thursday, 19 July 2018

Julia placed her rucksack on the floor and pulled out the sunscreen. The overnight storms had cleared the humidity but she still felt the morning rays penetrating the back of her neck. Her long summer dress reached the floor, covering her legs. She spread the cream over her arms and nose then stopped. The back of a thin scruffy girl wearing a cap stood beside the bull statue. It had to be Christina's friend, the one the homeless chap said had been hanging around with her. She was skinny and she looked young. Julia grabbed her rucksack and darted as fast as her sandals would allow.

The girl started to walk away. 'Wait,' Julia called.

The girl turned. Julia stopped, open-mouthed, staring at the woman who had to be in her sixties. From the back, she looked so young and tiny. 'Sorry, I thought you were someone else.'

'Nanny!' a child called as she ran from her mother, into the woman's arms.

Julia half smiled and half wanted to cry. She held her hand up and left the family to continue with their day out.

Grabbing the paperwork from her bag, she read the first address on her list. It was for a small homeless centre that offered food and was only two streets away.

She brought up Google Maps on her phone and followed the directions, weaving through the crowds of people trying to get to work in the centre of Birmingham. As she passed, she made a mental note of where the *Big Issue* sellers stood. 'You have reached your destination,' her phone told her.

Entering through the main door, she was faced with a makeshift cafe in some sort of small community hall. 'Can I help you?' a woman asked as she placed a knife down. The tower of buttered bread balanced next to the chopping board almost toppled. She grabbed half and placed it safely down.

'I… err… I'm looking for my daughter. You help the homeless people around here. Have I got the right place?'

'We're underfunded but we do what we can. Offer advice, washing facilities, connection to other services and—' she held her hands out, 'food.' The middle-aged woman wore her hair high on her head in a messy bun.

Julia pulled the photo from her backpack and passed it to her.

She removed her blue gloves and put her glasses on.

'Have you seen her? She's been missing since the fourth of April. I've been told she came to Birmingham.'

'I see so many people and a lot of them young. It's so sad. How old is she?'

'Fifteen. She's just a kid.'

The woman bit her bottom lip. 'She looks familiar. I don't know where from or when from but I feel as though I've seen her at some point. I don't think I've seen her here. I normally remember the people who use the centre. We do go out on food runs. Actually, the more I look, the more familiar she seems. Before you go, I'll give you a list of places that we deliver to.'

'That would be really helpful, thank you.' Julia felt her heart rate pick up. She might actually find her daughter that day. Her slight smile turned back into a frown. What if her daughter ran from her? What if she was still angry? For so many years, Julia had felt needed by Christina but, recently, Christina hadn't wanted a thing from her, apart from more money and freedom. She had left their home in search of her freedom with the small amount of money that she had access to, and now she was gone. 'What's your name by the way?'

'Cynthia. I work here part-time, well three days a week.' She began noting down some locations on a pad.

'Can you remember when or where you saw her?'

'I couldn't swear that I did. There were two girls, they used to hang around together either by the bull statue outside the Bullring, by Symphony Hall or by New Street Station. I haven't seen them for at least a couple of months, but as I said, I can't be sure that one was your daughter.'

'Do you remember seeing her with a man?' Maybe this woman had seen Westley.

She shook her head. 'I don't recall.' She paused in thought. 'Wait, I saw a younger man, probably in his early twenties with one of the girls at one point. He was very unkempt, like he lived on the streets too. Thin, dark messy hair, shoulder-length. I can't recall any more as I didn't speak to him at all.'

'Did you hear the name Westley mentioned?'

She shook her head. 'Sorry. I really wish I knew more. It must be awful for you. I can only imagine what you must be going through.'

'It's hell.' Julia forced a smile. The more she smiled the more she trembled. Tears began to spill down her cheeks. She wiped them away and turned to face the door.

'I'm so sorry. I didn't mean to upset you.' Cynthia came from behind the counter and pulled out a chair. 'Here, would you like some water?'

Julia shook her head. Not wanting to lose any more time she thanked the woman, took the list and left for the first place at the top, the bull. The homeless man she spoke to in Redditch had also mentioned the bull statue.

Fifteen minutes later, she reached the statue. Back where she began her search. A middle-aged woman in a headscarf called out as she passed. '*Big Issue.*' Julia pulled a few coins from her pocket and walked over. 'Have you seen this girl?'

The woman began speaking in a language she didn't understand but the woman was shaking her head and shrugging her shoulders. Julia pointed at the woman, then at her eyes, then at the photo of Christina. The woman shook her head again. Julia gave her the change and left. After waiting by the bull for twenty minutes she went to leave for New Street. The *Big Issue* woman ran over with a man and shouted. 'Symphony Hall.' She shrugged her shoulders again. Was she suggesting that she try by Symphony Hall or that she'd seen her daughter at Symphony Hall? Either way she didn't want to waste any time, so she ran as fast she could.

CHAPTER FIFTY

Miley opened her eyes to another stuffy bright day. 'Jackie,' she said as she turned. The woman was sitting in the middle of the room on the filthy wooden floor, wiping her hands through the dust. Her bruised face now framing her eyes. Miley shuddered as she thought of what the male boss said. He thought she could actually do that to Jackie and that stung more than any amount of pain she was going through. She could never harm her only friend.

She couldn't remember coming into Jackie's room but the calmness that washed over her meant she'd had some form of medicine. It didn't feel like her usual stuff. Something didn't feel right, the crawling was coming back as she rubbed her eyes. Her stomach went into a spasm, causing her to double over. 'Help me,' she called. Staggering across the room to the door, she tried the handle but her sweaty hands slipped.

Jackie's murmuring filled the room.

'Come on, Jackie, let me help you back onto the bed.' She leaned down, tears of pain streaming down her face as she grabbed the woman's hands and tried to haul her up. A sharp pain shot through her back, almost causing her to topple as she pulled Jackie up to a standing position. As Miley turned her, ready to sit on the bed, she almost gagged as she caught sight of the yellow, pus-filled flesh on the woman's bare buttock. Dropping Jackie on the bed, she darted to the other side of the room, trembling and gasping for breath.

Jackie screamed, no words, just sounds, like those she'd heard in horror films. The woman clumsily lay back on the single bed, one leg hanging off. Miley ran over and hoisted her leg up as Jackie continued to yell. 'Please, Jackie, I know it hurts. Please don't cry.'

Tears streamed down Miley's face as she stroked the woman's hair. She grabbed the unravelled, grubby, knitted doll from the bedside table and placed it in Jackie's arms. 'She'll look after you,' she said as she kissed Jackie's forehead and staggered across the room. Jackie gripped the doll and the cries simmered down to a murmur.

She needed to get out before she passed out – the room was getting hotter and little black spots teased her vision. The more she thought about the flesh, the more she could now tell that the sickly smell in the air was coming from it. She reached for the door handle and almost fell into the hallway as the door sprang open.

'Hello,' Miley called. 'Simone?' She had heard that name in the midst of her confusion, before the boss had drugged her. She hadn't slept that deeply for a long time. Had he hurt her? Apart from the twinge in her back, she didn't feel any other injuries that had come on since yesterday. Her heart began to pound as her mind flashed with possibilities of all he could have done to her when she'd been asleep. She reached down and exhaled. He hadn't raped her.

She staggered in the other direction, towards the top of the stairs. She didn't want to eat but she knew she needed to keep her strength up if she were to ever see her mother again. They wouldn't forget to bring Jackie's breakfast, surely. If there was only one portion of breakfast, they would share.

As the top of the stairs became visible, she could see that there was no food. 'We're hungry,' she yelled as she slammed her body into the bannister. It was all for nothing, no one was coming. She reached the top of the stairs and took the first step. Her weak body slipped down several more before she grabbed the rail.

Shaking the bottom door, she sobbed as she realised it was locked. 'Let me out. I want to go home.'

Heavy footsteps made their way across the floor. She began to shiver and needed to pee. The shaking became violent as the door unlocked. 'Stupid junkie,' the man said as he stepped over her and pulled her back up the stairs by her skinny, needle-marked arm. As he dragged her back up, she felt the skin on her bottom burning on the coarse carpet. He flung her across her bedroom and filled the doorway with his imposing frame.

'Please, can we have some food?' If she didn't eat, she would die and she wanted to see her mum again. 'Please, anything. I'll do anything.'

The man slammed and locked the door. She listened to him pacing along the creaky landing. 'Answer your phone,' he yelled as he kicked the door. The old floorboards squeaked as he walked across the landing.

Jackie began to scream out again.

'It's okay, my love. It will all be okay, I promise,' he said as he ran into her room. He let out a roar that almost shook the building. As he thundered out of Jackie's room and along the landing, Miley felt her stomach drop as she shook uncontrollably. He was coming for her.

'How dare you?' he yelled as he ran in and kicked her hard in the buttocks. 'Call yourself a carer?'

'I didn't hurt her. I love Jackie. I didn't do anything.' Her breath was that erratic, words were barely forming. Spittle landed on her face as he seethed and held a fist above her. She closed her eyes. 'It was the other boss, not me. Please. I didn't do it.'

He roared again as he hit the bedframe, left the room and thundered down the stairs.

The crawling started again, under her skin, inside her, in all of her. Even her eyes itched. She used all her strength to push her little finger from her tense fist.

A little beetle crawled around it, until it reached the skirting board and escaped through a gap, through the gap where all its friends lived. 'Come back.' Tears fell down her cheeks. She clamped her eyes closed and cried as sweat drenched her old T-shirt. 'Don't leave me alone to die.'

CHAPTER FIFTY-ONE

Sweat began to drench Julia's hair as she lugged the rucksack towards Symphony Hall. Almost there, she thought as she grabbed a flyer and stuck it to the window of a vacant shop. She spotted the grand building with its mirrored glass frontage up a flight of stone steps. She scanned the area, looking for anyone who might be loitering. Passing the art museum, she spotted the blonde girl lying in the sun on one of the steps. Her head was resting on a rolled-up hoodie as she slept. The dusty shade of blonde that only came with not washing it stood out, as well as the tears in her clothing.

Julia pulled a flyer from her bag. 'Hello.'

'I'm not moving. If you think you can move me on, you've got another thing coming. Go away.' The girl didn't even open her eyes.

'I'm not here to move you on. I'm looking for my daughter and I thought you might have seen her.'

Dazzled by the sun, she sat up and rubbed her eyes. 'You'll be lucky if I can remember her, they come and go all the time. Some go home, some get mopped up by the pervs, and some get off the streets – not many though. You all come around, trying to gain my trust. What for? You all pretend that you can help or you need help. I don't fall for that sort of thing.'

'Please.' Julia thrust a flyer into the girl's hand. 'She's fifteen. Christina and I argued. School wasn't going too well. I suppose things just got her down. She met a man. From what people tell me he's in his early twenties with brown shoulder-length hair. She came with him. Maybe you've seen them. He is called Westley.'

The girl sighed and looked at the flyer. 'I don't remember the man but I remember her. She and Erin left me on my own. We met late last year, when it was freezing – broke into places together to find warmth and shelter. I got sick of hanging around with Erin anyway, stupid cow was a junkie.'

Julia almost stopped breathing knowing that her daughter had gone off with a junkie. 'Was my daughter taking drugs too?'

'How would I know? I only knew about Erin because I saw her doing it. She didn't shoot up in the street, nothing like that, and I made her take her needles to the exchange. I wouldn't know about your daughter.'

Exhaling, Julia scanned around for somewhere to sit. 'Can I buy you something to eat, if you don't mind talking to me? I really need to ask you a few things.'

'There's a cafe inside Symphony Hall. I haven't had anything decent for ages. Buy me a dinner and I'll answer all your questions. Ask me to get in a car and go somewhere with you, I'll scream paedo. Don't test me.'

The girl scoffed the sausage and mash meal in front of her, stopping to reply to Julia's questions with an open mouth.

'When did you last see my daughter?'

'A couple of months ago.' The girl began licking gravy off the plate.

'That long. I thought you'd seen her recently.' Julia gripped the edge of the table and fought her tears back.

'I never said that. I said I remembered her and she took my place as Erin's best mate. We shoplifted together, made a pretty packet at one point. They used to try and sell their goods by the Bull outside the Bullring. There's always a buyer if you've got good gear. If trainers are a hundred pound, someone will always give you thirty for them. We got hold of perfume, even meat. Yes – you'd be surprised. A piece of beef for Sunday dinner that cost fifteen quid – some cheapskate in a pub will buy it for eight quid. I taught Erin all she knew.'

'What did Erin look like?' Julia pulled her old diary from her bag, the one she had for 2014 but had never used. It would be good enough to take some notes in.

'Skinny, but aren't we all? She had brown hair but she'd run a red colour through it. Stupid cow used to make me help her dye her hair in the bogs at Selfridges. We got chucked out a few times, once before she'd managed to swill it out. She had brown eyes, bags under them. The drugs had given her a sunken look. She was always toying around with the thought of prostitution until she tried it once and some shitbag beat her up. I told her not to.'

Julia's heart began to race. Had Christina got embroiled in drugs and prostitution? She could be working out of some massage parlour at night. Her daughter didn't belong here, she had a home. She looked at the girl sitting before her. Did she belong here? How had she ended up on the streets? Julia wondered if she'd left to escape abuse or had just fallen out with her parents. 'Can you tell me anything else? I really need to find her.'

'The last day I saw them, a man came along. I think he was in his fifties but he might have been a little older. We'd been begging and thieving by New Street, by where the trams pass. There was something about the man. I've seen him since, looking for people to work for him. He gives me the creeps so I avoid him if he's around. He came back with a woman a couple of weeks ago. I never trust people like that. There's always someone offering me *work* but it's never the kind of work I want to get involved with. Your daughter and Erin went with him. I told him to stick his job.'

'What was the job?' Her heart sank as she thought of her daughter in some seedy brothel.

'Care work, domestic work, he said. They all lie though. I knew he was after a slave.'

She swallowed. Getting het up and panicky wouldn't help. She needed information. 'Can you tell me what he looked like or the woman?'

'I remember thinking he looked really well off, fancy clothes and all that. I didn't take a great deal of notice and they were quite far away. I just remembered his jacket, a really nice cut, looked designer. The woman came a little closer to me at one point, almost stared me out. Creepy bitch.'

'What did she look like?'

'Her roots needed doing.'

'Is that all you remember?'

'Yes. I see people all day long. How much do you expect me to remember? They are a posh-looking couple, with money and the woman's roots needed doing, I remember that much. That's all I have. I didn't want to catch the man's attention. He gave me the creeps when Erin and your daughter went with him. The last thing I wanted was for him to come over and speak to me. I walked off and haven't seen them since.'

Julia ran her fingers over her own roots where the grey was coming through. 'Please try to remember something.'

The girl closed her eyes as she thought back, frowning occasionally as she did so. 'The first time I saw him he was smart, wearing a crisp light-coloured shirt, trustworthy looking. I hate that I didn't take any more notice now. I just wanted him to piss off. I'm really sorry, I can't remember any more.'

'Did he have an accent?'

'Not much. He was quite well spoken. Can I have a dessert?'

'Of course.'

'I'll have one of those?' Julia hurried to the counter and bought the large slice of chocolate cake.

'So you have no idea where she went after that? Are you sure you haven't seen her since?'

'I'm sure. I would have asked her about Erin if I'd seen her around. I sometimes go to some of the shelters for a free meal and I haven't seen her there either.'

The girl filled her mouth with cake and licked her lips. 'This is so nice, thank you. Aren't you having any?'

Shaking her head, Julia felt a tear slip from the corner of her eye. The girl in front of her was just a little older than Christina. She acted like she knew it all but underneath, she could sense her fragility. 'Can you go home?'

The girl placed the fork down and stopped eating. She shook her head. 'I'm never going back there. They can never find me. I mean it. Soon, I'll find a job. I'm a survivor. I've enrolled at college in September to do hairdressing. I have an interview at a bar next week. The centre gave me an address I could use and they take my post in. They are also helping me with clothes for my interview. It's a start. I stay at a hostel overnight now. I'm slowly getting on my feet. I stay away from weird men and I stay away from drugs. I may look like some sort of vulnerable street urchin but I have my shit together. The only thing I'm always short of is food, as you can probably tell.'

'Thank you for talking with me. I'll go back to the police and tell them about the man and woman you mentioned.' She paused and looked up, trying to suck the tear back into her tear duct. 'Can I leave you my number? If you see her or hear anything, can you call me?'

The girl nodded.

'If I can ever help you, just let me know.' She couldn't leave the girl without at least offering to be there. She'd felt a connection. This girl was someone's daughter. She was scared to go back home and she was slowly crawling out of the gutter. If Julia could help her to escape the last bit, she would. Deep down, she knew the girl would never trust her. She pulled all the notes out of her purse amounting to forty pounds and placed them on the table. 'Please buy food with the cash.'

'I only ever buy food with the cash. Thank you. I hope you find your daughter. She's lucky she has you. My mother would never come looking for me. There is just one more thing. Your daughter didn't go by the name of Christina.'

CHAPTER FIFTY-TWO

Gina's phone buzzed. She hoped that it wasn't Hannah with another annoyed message. She exhaled as she saw it was Jacob, telling her that he'd got her something exciting, punctuated by a laughing emoji. She got in her car and drove to the station.

'Morning, guv,' Jacob said, sitting with his head in hands at the main table in the centre.

'How long have you been here?' she asked.

'About half an hour. There's no point lying in when you're on your own. I woke up hungry, grabbed a buttie on the way and thought, why not, I'll come in early, show willing.' She spotted the sandwich bag on the table, grease absorbed into the paper.

'I hope you got me one.'

'That's what's exciting. Fried egg.' He grabbed the bag and passed it to her. 'Slathered in ketchup.'

'Yum.' She pulled the sandwich from the bag and bit into the cold sandwich, yolk running out of the sides. She was sure it would have tasted better half an hour ago. 'Thanks.' She noticed Jacob's tie looked a bit wonky and one of his buttons had been pushed into the wrong hole. He'd made light of his break up with Amber but she knew deep down he was missing her. Maybe when the case was over, she'd see if he wanted to go for a beer, maybe they could all go for a beer and Gina might get another chance to try and blend in, act like a normal human being, enjoying a drink with colleagues.

'My arm and hand are red raw from climbing over that fence. How are you?'

Gina rubbed her arm. She had a bruise and a few scratches from the bush she landed in. 'No serious damage. I think I've survived the splinter. After the last case, this seems tame. At least no one's trying to murder me.' She took another bite of the sandwich and looked away as she recalled the attack in her home. Her attacker's red mask flashed through her mind as she remembered her airways being restricted. As she swallowed a lump of mulched up bread, it wedged in her throat. She tried to gasp, failing and panicking.

'You okay, guv? Need the Heimlich manoeuvre?'

Shaking her head, she tried to swallow and her eyes began to water up. It wasn't going down. She dropped the sandwich on the table and darted to the ladies, almost choking as she heaved the sandwich into the bin. Shaking, she stood up and stared at her smeared reflection and kicked the bin. How dare her attacker and Terry still make her feel like this? She kicked the bin again and wiped her eyes before straightening up. There was a knock on the door. 'What?'

'Just making sure you're not choking to death.'

'I'm good.' She burst through the door, almost crashing into Jacob. 'I just got a bit of bread stuck in my throat. I'm okay now. Coughed it out.'

He followed her back to the incident room. Wyre and O'Connor were just turning their computers on.

Grabbing a tissue, Gina cleared her throat and wiped the grease from her fingers. 'As you know, we found Westley during our drugs bust last night. You probably saw the email I sent you. He knows Christina, one of our missing girls. The last he says he saw of her was when he left her in Birmingham. Smith will be along in a moment to update us on the other interviews that took place last night. Darren Mason was also arrested as a buyer. Another couple were pulled in, along with a woman. All buyers, only one buying heroin.'

Smith entered. 'That was a long evening. I did manage a few hours' sleep. Lovely to be back so soon.' He rubbed his eyes, rustled in the pocket of his fluorescent jacket for a mint and took a seat at the table.

'How did the interviews go?' Gina grabbed the rest of the egg sandwich, scrunched it up in the bag and threw it at the bin, missing. She'd pick it up later. 'I still can't help but feel there's some connection to our case. Darren Mason and Westley Young turning up has almost sealed the idea for me. Tell me about the others.'

'The woman is giving us real trouble.'

'Which one?'

'The one who was buying alone. She seemed a bit spaced out, refusing medical assistance and not speaking. We don't know her name and she isn't on our database. We ended up just having to leave her in a cell for the time being. I'm going to try interviewing her again this morning. If she carries on like this, I'll have to ask the Superintendent for an extension.'

Gina picked at the sore flap of skin on her hand, where the splinter had been. 'Have we offered her medical help? If she is on heroin, she may be withdrawing soon.'

'She's as cool as an iceberg, definitely not withdrawing. I did offer though. She just shook her head and said she was fine. She didn't even make her phone call when it was offered.'

'How about the couple?'

'Ellen Simpson cracked. She's prime carer for her elderly mother who is completely immobile and has dementia. They live at the big house at the end of King Street, the one with the large garden on the far corner. She said all she wanted to do was get her mother ready for bed and chill out and we'd apparently

ruined her evening. Aaron Dunn virtually lives with her and helps
her a lot too. The woman was constantly in tears, kept saying
that she's never been in trouble with the law and she just needed
a little pick me up.'

'Has she been in trouble before?'

'Yes, fight in a nightclub when she was eighteen.'

'So she lied about that?'

Smith leaned back. 'She did.'

'How about Aaron Dunn?'

'Works in a biscuit factory on Cleevesford Industrial Estate.
Seemed calm under interview and kept going on that all he had
was a bit of coke for personal use and that we were being tossers
for bringing them both in.'

'Does he have a record?'

'Yes, an incident in his twenties. It looks like he once had
everything, a good position in the family business, some small
chain of computer accessory shops, until he fell out with his dad.
His first wife divorced him and he ended up on the scrap heap,
working for one of these awful companies that sell orthopaedic
chairs to elderly people and refuse to leave the house until they've
signed their savings away. The company he worked for got closed
down, Trading Standards were involved. As for his criminal past,
yes, he's had a minor run in with the law when he bricked the
windows of his parents' house.'

'Nothing bringing him back to the girls?'

'Nothing as yet.'

'Keep me and the system updated every time you have new
information.'

Gina checked her emails on her phone. 'Right, Bernard has
messaged. He's hoping to come to the next briefing to talk over
his findings. He and Keith are searching for a match for van girl's
dental records. Here's something for you to work on, O'Connor.
I know you and Wyre have been narrowing down a list of missing

girls. Apparently our van girl had a broken finger that had long healed. Liaise with Bernard to narrow your list down.'

'Yes, guv. The list is only standing at just under sixty now. We've been researching each one in turn until new information came in. All brunettes with red tones, and red heads. We have to consider that some people dye their hair. How many of the blonde or mousy haired girls had dyed their hair? This could take our figure back up.' O'Connor tapped his left foot on the floor. Gina tried to ignore it.

'I know it's a tedious task but it needs doing. Any other information?'

Wyre looked up from her pad. 'We're on it, guv, the tasks I mean. It's just taking a long time to go through everything. There has been nothing useful from the door to door interviews or the CCTV.'

'Okay, have all the samples gone to Bernard from the drugs bust?'

Smith nodded. 'All completed last night.'

'Right, back to it. I need results,' Gina replied. 'Jacob, you and I can head over to speak to Simone Duxford's biological mother.'

All the different strands of the case weren't coming together at all. Something needed to give. Once the unravelling began, she knew it wouldn't stop. She just needed to find the starting point and hope that she wouldn't unravel with it. She coughed again, making sure that her throat was still clear.

CHAPTER FIFTY-THREE

Gina pulled up on the narrow road at the back of Redditch Town Centre and backed into the tiniest of spaces. A young boy, with what appeared to be chocolate smeared over his face, lifted the net at the window. Another child, a girl with pigtails climbed up to the ledge and pushed him out the way. As they knocked on the door, Gina could hear what sounded like a newborn baby screaming.

Cassandra Duxford wrestled with the door, eventually managing to open it. 'Come through,' she said as she twisted her greasy looking blonde hair into a makeshift bun. 'Crystal, Kyle, get off that bloody window ledge. Kids!' A man stood in the galley kitchen, holding the baby against his greasy overall. The newborn screamed, almost wriggling out of its small nappy. As the man held the bottle to the baby's lips, it began gulping the milk.

'I bring new life into the world just before I find out my daughter has died. She'd have been better off with me but no, they dragged her from my arms and out of her home. Do you know, I never saw her after that? They said she didn't want to see me but I know that can't have been right. Those bastards robbed me of my chance to be her mother.'

Gina wasn't going to get into the ins and outs of why Simone had been removed, she'd seen the girl's file. She'd seen the photos of her bruising. She'd read about the extent of abuse the girl had endured. Jacob squeezed into the tiny kitchen. The bathroom door stood open. The older houses around this way quite often had bathrooms coming off the end of kitchens. The smell hit her, first urine, then faeces. Her gaze stopped on the stained carpet surrounding the toilet. She wondered how the family could cook in the kitchen, knowing that their bathroom was that filthy.

'It's cosy in here,' Jacob said as he pulled out a notebook and stood behind the boyfriend. 'Sorry, your name is?'

'What's it got to do with you?' the man asked.

'Please just tell us your name,' Gina replied, wondering why the man seemed so uptight.

'Steve Bell. Mechanic. I have a garage just two streets back. Thirty-two years old. These are my kids and I love them. I've been with Cassie for five years. Enough?'

'Thank you,' Jacob replied as he shifted the pan of cold beans to make room to write.

'Steve, can you take Matty into the other room for a minute, so we can talk?'

The man nodded and left the room. 'Don't you upset her. She's been through enough!'

'Miss Duxford, we're not here to upset you. I know the news about Simone must be hitting you hard but we want to find out how she ended up in a shallow grave in Cleevesford. Do you know how she might have got there?'

Cassie Duxford wiped a tear from the corner of her red puffy eye. She grabbed a cigarette with her chubby fingers and lit up. 'Do you mind? I need a smoke.'

Gina shook her head.

'I didn't want to lose my daughter but back then…' She paused and looked away, taking a deep breath. 'Back then I was a different person and in a really bad place, not like now. There was a string of men, I admit it, and drugs were a problem. I would have done anything for a fix. I did do anything for a fix but I always protected Simone, as much as I could anyway.' The woman sobbed. 'I found out my boyfriend at the time had been abusing Simone. I told him to go but he wouldn't. Eventually he wouldn't allow me to go out, even pimped me out to his friends. I didn't know what day it was back then.' She paused and inhaled on the cigarette, blowing smoke into the small room. 'I barely remember the raid. That wasn't me back then. I don't know to this day how I became that woman. I wanted him to leave but I ended up being his prisoner. The thing that hurt more than anything was when they took Simone. I swore I would get off drugs and get her back, but she didn't want me, refused to see me.' The woman broke down, tears spilling onto the pile of dirty plates in the sink. 'I'll never see her again. Never get the chance to make things up to her.' As the woman sobbed, she hyperventilated.

'I know this is hard, Miss Duxford, and we're so sorry for your loss.' Gina paused for a moment while the woman blew her nose and wiped her eyes. 'Do you know where Simone may have gone when she left her foster home? Could she have gone looking for her dad?'

'He was a waste of space. I was fifteen, he was about twenty-five when we met. We used to meet in Redditch at the weekends. His name was Gareth. Simone knew his name was Gareth, I never hid that from her. She knew he was from Cleevesford. Has that bastard done something to her?'

'We don't know that. Do you know where he lived?'

'King Street, just off the High Street. I don't know the number. He never took me home to see his parents. I don't think I was posh enough for them. I think they had money. Bastard dumped me. He didn't even know he had a daughter and I never told my parents his name.'

'Do you know his surname?'

She shook her head and wiped her eyes with a piece of kitchen roll. 'I was with him three weeks. We had sex a couple of times in his car. After that, he didn't want to know. That was the end. He got what he wanted and left.'

'Did you ever tell anyone?'

'No. I told Simone he was my boyfriend and his parents didn't want us to be together. I also told her it was a long time ago and I hadn't seen him since, and I haven't – that was the truth. Back then I went to Cleevesford, hung around in the pub there. Not once did I see him. I even went to the road he lived on and looked for his car. This was when I was pregnant. I didn't see it. Maybe he'd lied about living there. Either that or he sold his car. I wasn't going to humiliate myself any more and start knocking on doors. He didn't want me and I had some pride left. After that, I eventually told my parents about the baby. Couldn't stand the lectures any more so I ended up in a mother and baby unit in a hostel, then got a flat in Redditch. My life slowly went down the pan after that but I'm clean now. I love my children and I love Steve. I've changed so much. Please don't let anyone take my other children.'

The woman looked broken – a teary mess that could barely stand, leaning over the sink sobbing.

'Are you okay?' Steve called from the other room. The children began running around, playing a loud game.

'I'm fine, love.'

Gina imagined what might have been going through Simone's head. Maybe she'd been looking for her father. Had she found him or had he found her? She sent a quick message to O'Connor as the woman composed herself, asking him to get onto the council and find out anything he could about anyone named Gareth that had been registered as living in King Street. It was a long time ago now but Simone may have found something out and gone looking for him. She followed the message to O'Connor with another.

Contact the press. Put Simone's photo out there. See if anyone has seen her in Cleevesford. We need people to come forward. There may be a connection to King Street in Cleevesford.

'You've got to find out who put her in that grave. Please find out.'

Gina wanted to find out but not solely for Simone's mother or her foster parents. She owed this one to Simone.

CHAPTER FIFTY-FOUR

The fans whirred away in the incident room. Briggs and Annie sat at one end, smiling as they whispered words back and forth. O'Connor and Wyre sat at opposite sides of the table and Jacob sat between O'Connor and Bernard. Gina stood in front of the board. One of the walls was taken up with the map, showing the original route that Darren Mason had taken in his van. That same map had been plotted with the shallow grave that they'd found Simone in. She could see clearly that the route Darren taken hadn't been close to the grave.

She grabbed another pin and placed it in the middle of King Street. 'We have to consider that Simone Duxford may have come to Cleevesford to look for her biological father. After speaking to Cassie Duxford, we know that Simone's father, a man called Gareth, lived on that street. That is, unless he lied to her. Have you started the ball rolling, O'Connor?'

'Yes, guv. I called the council after you messaged. They are looking into it and calling me back in a bit.'

'For heaven's sake. Haven't they got all this information at hand?'

'They said it was on a previous computer system and they'd have to delve into the archives. They managed to tell me that no one called Gareth has lived on King Street over the past ten years.'

Another stumbling block. Gina began to pace. 'We need some officers to get down to King Street with a photo of Simone. Maybe she knocked on someone's door asking for Gareth. If any of you can cancel any plans this evening, I'd be hugely grateful. I know you all have a life but we need to get to the bottom of what's happening and that's going to involve a lot of groundwork. Has the other press appeal gone out?'

'As soon as O'Connor came to me, we prepared it and sent it out. It should be on the news this evening and is probably already online,' Annie replied, twisting her hair between her fingers as she doodled over the page, waiting for further instructions.

Bernard cleared his throat and perked up, presuming he would be asked to speak next.

'What have you got for me?' Gina asked.

'Keith has just messaged me. We've identified our van girl. Erin Holden, aged sixteen. Her dental records match and she is registered as having broken a finger as a child. Also, the cut to her side was made by a tool in Darren Mason's van. Traces of her blood were found on this. The wound appears to be accidental. It looks like she scraped across it, probably as the van took a corner. We know who she is. Yes.' Bernard punched the air and dropped his pen on the table.

'That name is on my list of missing girls,' O'Connor said. 'I was almost getting to her. She left home just before Christmas with a lad. Her mother is from Kings Heath in Birmingham.'

'I need to speak to her. Who's coming?'

Jacob looked up and smiled.

'At least I can lose the list now and get on with the door to door on King Street,' O'Connor said as he closed his notebook and turned back to his computer.

All the other families she'd been speaking to had been devastated but this time, she would be the one to deliver the bad news. Her phone rang and she walked towards the window. 'Hello.'

'I know the name of the girl my daughter hung around with on the streets. Her name was Erin,' she heard Julia Dawson say. 'And there's more, the girl who I've been speaking to said Erin and Christina had been approached by a man, probably in his fifties and he was trawling Birmingham recently with a woman. She hasn't seen the girls since.'

They *were* after another girl. Gina knew it. She grabbed her pad as the woman began relaying all the details.

CHAPTER FIFTY-FIVE

The maisonette on the main road of Kings Heath stood back, behind a clump of unruly trees. After spending several minutes struggling to find a space to park in, Jacob and Gina settled for a space five minutes down the road. The heat hit like a wall and the petrol fumes from the rush hour traffic was nauseatingly thick. The smell of weed filled the air, a smell Gina was coming across more often over the past couple of years.

Belinda Holden eventually opened the door. Her sunken eyes and slight frame almost shook Gina to the core. She had no idea how the woman was still alive. Her wrists can't have been thicker than a tube of toothpaste. Belinda wobbled as she stood aside, staring into space through glassy eyes. Gina could see she'd given up a long time ago. She glanced back at Jacob as they stepped into the stuffy hallway, so dark their eyes had to adjust. She wished she hadn't seen the masses of cobwebs, the piles of clothes and empty takeaway wrappers that filled the hallway. That was where the stench was coming from. A large bug fled behind an old wooden unit as they entered the living room.

'Why are you here?' the woman mumbled.

'Please sit down, Miss Holden. I'm DI Harte, this is DS Driscoll. Can my colleague get you a glass of water?'

The woman went to sit and almost missed the edge of the old torn settee. After recovering her position, she shuffled back until she was safely seated. Greasy strands of dirty blonde hair stuck to her lips and mingled with the sweat on her face. Gina watched as the woman tried to wipe them away but missed each time. She could see why Erin had left. 'I don't need water. I need to know why the police are here bothering me. I haven't done anything. You lot are always on my case.'

Gina had taken a quick look at Belinda Holden's record. She'd been arrested on numerous occasions for soliciting, drug use and anti-social behaviour. The last she read was that Belinda was meant to be on a programme for users to get clean.

'We are here about Erin, Miss Holden.' Gina sat on a chair opposite. Jacob remained standing beside the door frame.

'Erin? She left. I often wonder about her.'

Wonder about her! Is that all Miss Holden did? Her sixteen-year-old daughter had run away from home and this woman was doing nothing to find her. She thought back to all that Mrs Dawson was doing with the posters and asking people on the streets. Gina was aware that people had their issues, but they were talking about her daughter, her flesh and blood. She bit her lip. 'I'm really sorry, Miss Holden. You may have read that a girl had been found in Cleevesford and had been taken to hospital after falling from a van. It's been on the local news. We don't as yet know what happened to her but she was in a bad way and has subsequently passed away. Our tests have come back and we've identified the girl to be Erin. I really am sorry.'

The woman stared blankly at the curtain-covered window and wiped her eyes. 'You mean Erin's dead?'

'I'm sorry. Can we get you a drink?'

The woman shook her head and pulled a half bottle of vodka from under a cushion. Unscrewing the cap, she took a long swig. 'I'm never going to see her again, am I?'

'Is there anyone we can call? Do you have any family?'

'I don't want any of them.' The woman took another swig.

'Can you tell us about when Erin left? You reported her missing last November.'

'And what did you do? Stuff all. People like me, like us, don't matter. Just piss off out of my home.' The woman grabbed the cushion and threw it to the floor.

'It's important that you tell us if you know anything. We need to catch the person who did this to Erin. Can you tell me how things were when she left?'

The woman took another swig of alcohol. 'Are you going now?'

'Can we offer you any support?'

'I've got all the support I need,' she said as she held the bottle up. Her sleeve slipped. Gina caught site of all the open sores and track marks on the woman's scrawny arm. Poor Erin had no chance in life. She swallowed, choking back her emotions. Maybe the system had let them down somewhere along the line. How Erin had been left in a hovel like this made her want to punch something.

There was a knock at the front door. The woman dragged herself up and staggered along the hallway. A man wearing glasses followed her in. 'Belinda?' he said. Gina leaned forward to get a closer look.

Belinda grabbed his arm and led him into the kitchen. 'Just wait a minute. You here for a good time?' She thought that Gina and Jacob couldn't hear from the living room. Her skin began to crawl. Had Erin seen all this going on?

'A friend?' Gina asked as Belinda re-entered.

'Yeah. What of it? We're good friends. I want you to both leave now so I can grieve. Get out.' Belinda held out a shaky finger and pointed towards the front door.

'If you remember anything when we've left, give me a call. If you need any support, I can put you in touch with the right places. You can get help. We'll be in touch when your daughter's remains are released.' Gina placed her card into the woman's hand.

'Goodbye.' Belinda screwed up the card and opened the door, watching as they made their way down the path before slamming the door. Gina wondered if the woman would arrange a funeral for her daughter or even attend if one was arranged for her.

'It's no wonder some kids run away. Imagine having to live like that?' Jacob said as they took the long walk back to the car.

Gina kicked a lamp post and flinched.

'You okay, guv.'

'No, I'm not. Erin didn't stand a chance in life.' Traffic zoomed past, horns beeped as drivers took liberties, not waiting their turn. This wasn't one of her favourite places to be in rush hour and today wasn't one of her best either. 'I wonder if she was on drugs when she left the household or if she started using when she began life on the streets. I somehow think we're not going to get any more from Miss Holden. I don't think she's capable of giving us anything further. On another note, I called Christina's friend. The one Mrs Dawson told us about. Her family are back from their camping trip late tonight. I'll call her parents later, see if they can come in first thing to speak to us. I know we have found Westley Young but you never know, she may be able to give us a bit more of an insight into Christina's life.'

Gina's heart rate picked up. Dare she hope that Christina would turn up safe and sound? They'd identified their two dead girls and neither were Christina. Her mind wandered back to the Norths. Mrs Dawson mentioned a couple, a well-turned-out couple. She needed to get home and get the laptop on, check out the updates.

CHAPTER FIFTY-SIX

'Bye,' Elisa shouted up the stairs. As she left the farm shop, she checked her messages. Her mother was running late picking her up. It was only a couple of miles, she could walk home. It's not like it was raining. She messaged her mum.

I'll start walking. See you at home. X

She kept close to the grassy verge, walking along the single-track road. A car slowed down and passed her carefully. It was going to be a long walk she thought as she looked down at her thin-soled dolly shoes. She stepped onto the grass and plugged her earphones in, selecting her Little Mix album to listen to. As she walked she bobbed her head and stepped in time with the beat. Ethan hated her music, always removing her CDs when they went out in his car. She sometimes won the battle but more often than not, they had to listen to the Foo Fighters. She smiled. In a couple of hours he'd be picking her up and they were heading into Stratford to park up by the river and meet up with friends. They'd go to McDonald's, grab some food and hang out.

Her heart skipped a beat as she spotted the silver car pull up alongside her. She noticed that it was a Mercedes. The creepy man who bought the honey was driving at walking speed. She snatched one of the earbuds out. His window came down. She knew he was a weirdo when he came into the shop. Had he been following her and waiting for her to finish work? Her amble became a fast walk, then turned into a light jog. The man drove a little faster. She looked for a gap in the verge but there wasn't one. She began to sprint but her shoes weren't the best to run in.

'Wait,' he called.

'Get away from me.' He pulled up and began to chase her. She ran until she reached the woodland. A shiver ran through her body. She was running through the same area that the girl had been found in the shallow grave. She should have waited for her mother to pick her up. 'I'm calling the police,' she yelled as she held her phone up. Then she tripped, hitting her head on a tree. Through woozy vision, she watched as the man caught up and kneeled beside her. 'Please don't hurt me,' she whimpered as she drifted out of consciousness.

CHAPTER FIFTY-SEVEN

Gina threw her keys onto the worktop and booted the laptop up as she filled Ebony's dinner bowl. The cat darted in through the cat door and began chewing the meat. She grabbed the glass of warm juice from the side that she'd started at breakfast and took a swig.

Sitting at the table, she checked her emails and logged onto the system. Wyre had uploaded all the information they had on the Norths. They were worth over six million pounds as per their reported figures, all made from investments and property. As mentioned, Stan North had known Bryn Tilly since childhood. They'd attended Cleevesford Junior and Cleevesford Senior together. There was a close history. She could see that he may want to help his friend enter the property business, especially as Bryn had building and project management skills.

She clicked on the tab that would show up any previous. Mr North had been charged with buying cocaine after being caught a third time. One of the charges was with Mrs North. Cocaine use was becoming as prevalent as weed use in the area, especially amongst those who could afford it. A problem that was only escalating. The thought of drug use and the two girls flashed through her mind. Heroin was found in Erin's blood. Maybe the Norths were making money from illegal trades too.

Her mind went back to Mrs North. The woman with everything. She'd never seen so many photos up in a workplace of one person. Each photo a different hairstyle or colour, the trendiest of cuts, the latest designer clothing. Gina knew expensive clothing when she saw it. She used to browse the racks of John Lewis, wishing she could afford to buy from there one day and never being able to. Mrs North even smelled of quality. She hadn't bought her perfume from the market. Gina shook her head and laughed as she swigged the rest of the orange juice, grimacing as it swished around her mouth. Everyone had a past and some people had things in their past they wanted to forget, her included. The Norths hadn't done anything wrong for the best part of twenty years.

Apart from the minor drug charges, there was nothing else that stood out. They were rich, they were business people, she supposed a lot of people loved to hate them. They also looked perfect which made it easier. They weren't entirely likeable though. Her mind flashed to Julia's boyfriend, Roy, the man with no record at all.

She jumped as her mobile rang.

'The plot thickens, guv,' Jacob blurted out. 'Bryn Tilly has just called in. He went over to the property that he and the Norths had invested in, where we found Simone Duxford's bones, and he found a girl holding her head. She said she'd been chased through the woods by a man in a silver Mercedes. He took her to Cleevesford Hospital for a check-up and her mother has been called.'

Gina stared at Stan North's notes and smiled.

'Bring Stan North in now.'

CHAPTER FIFTY-EIGHT

Friday, 20 July 2018

'Did we get hold of Stan North last night?' Gina asked Wyre as she stepped into the incident room, sipping her first coffee of the day.

'No, AWOL. We went over to his pad, and I'm telling you, it's a big pad. It's the type of place you'd expect the likes of Posh and Becks to live in. I took a few photos for evidential purposes. Elizabeth North didn't object. Big kitchen, pristine with a banquet table that could host a huge party. How the other half live? Anyway, he didn't go home last night. Mrs North is going berserk and keeps calling the station.'

Gina carefully studied the photos. The rooms were almost clutter-free except for a few jars on the side, and a spice rack. 'Did anyone speak with her?'

'We asked her a few questions. In summary, he'd left work earlier that day, saying that he was just off to pick a delivery up. It was probably about teatime but she couldn't be sure when. That was the last she saw of him. She's been trying to call him since but he hasn't been answering his phone.'

'And the girl?' Gina rubbed her tired eyes.

'Seventeen-year-old Elisa Stanford. Smith went over to the hospital and spoke to her last night. Her mother was with her and she had been placed in a side ward, being monitored for concussion. She'd fallen and knocked her head after being chased by a male that fitted Stan North's description. Her mother was going to be late picking her up from work. She works at the Taste of Nature farm shop. She left at around five o'clock and began walking home along the country roads. Next thing she remembers is his car pulling up alongside her. She said he'd come in and bought some items from the shop a couple of days earlier and he'd seemed creepy then, so she ran into the woodland. The only thing she remembered after that was Bryn Tilly finding her in the woods with a bleeding head and taking her to the hospital. She called her mother who met her there.'

'Thanks, Paula. What colour is her hair?'

'Smith said she had mousy brown hair.'

'She doesn't fit the description. If our theories are right, our perpetrator likes red haired girls.'

'Maybe he's changed.'

'Maybe.'

Jacob walked past with Smith. Gina listened as Smith spoke. 'We've charged the woman with being in possession of a class A drug and she's still not talking. We've run her DNA, prints and mug shot – nothing.'

'Who's this?' Gina asked as Smith took a seat with Jacob around the main table.

'That woman we pulled in, at the drug bust. She still won't say a word. We're applying to the courts for a further extension this morning. We need to identify her.'

'Has her swab been fast tracked? Was there a match on the prints?'

'It's all been catalogued and the swab has been sent to the lab. There's something you need to know and I was just getting to this.'

Gina took a step closer, eager to hear what Smith had to share. A smile beamed across his face. 'The partial print that was recorded, from the cellophane packaging that was found on our van girl, Erin – it matches our silent woman's print.'

'I need to speak to her.'

'Good luck with that, guv.'

O'Connor stepped into the room with a tray of coffees just as his phone went. He slammed them down, steaming brown liquid sloshing over the side of the cups. 'O'Connor,' he said as he took the call. 'Okay, thank you.' He placed the receiver down. 'Guv, Stacey has arrived with her father – Christina Dawson's friend.'

She'd almost forgotten that Christina's friend was coming in but speaking to her wasn't at the top of Gina's list now. Their silent woman was definitely connected to one of their victims. How? She had no idea. 'It's all happening at once. Can you and Wyre speak with her? Take her to the family room, it might put her at ease. Jacob and I will attempt to speak with this woman. Did she have anything on her when she was brought in?'

'No, guv. Just the heroin that we seized and about another thirty pounds in cash. The rest of her cash probably made up the pile that we confiscated from Westley Young.'

'She didn't have a phone?'

'No. It was just her. We are reviewing what small amount of CCTV footage we have in the area, trying to locate if she has a car. If she has, it would have been left there since the bust.'

'Has she spoken at all?' Gina felt her muscles tensing up. If only she could storm in there and shake it out of the woman.

'She's asked for coffee. She understands, she's just refusing to speak. She grins occasionally as if to tell us where to go. I had the medical officer take a look at her, she spoke to him and she's in good health.'

'Why is this job so damn hard? I mean, how long does she think she can sit there without saying a word? Keep on with the CCTV footage. If we can find a car, we can identify her. Right, let's do this.'

CHAPTER FIFTY-NINE

The recorder rolled and Jacob was fiddling with his pen lid. Five minutes had passed and the woman remained silent. Gina rolled her stiff ankles and flexed her legs under the table. Climbing over the fence the other night had awoken muscles that hadn't been used for a while and her ankle was now slightly puffy.

The young duty solicitor had a slight curl to the edges of his moustache. He fiddled with it as he waited with his client for the interview to begin.

'Here's what I have.' Gina stared at the woman. Her long dyed brown hair with obvious grey roots fell just over her shoulders. The woman leaned forward and sighed. 'We have matched one of your fingerprints to one found at a serious crime scene. Do you know an Erin Holden?'

The woman began staring at the wall, her gaze fixed on what Gina knew was a bit of chipped plaster.

'On Saturday the fourteenth of July, a young girl was discovered escaping from a van in Cleevesford. You may have heard something on the news. Her name was Erin Holden. She was only sixteen years of age and had a beautiful red tone to her hair.'

She watched as the woman's eyes began to water in the corner. Gina struggled to tell if the woman was making an emotional connection to what she was describing or the tearing was a result of the woman's direct stare.

'Why would an item that Erin was carrying have your fingerprints on it?'

The woman wiped her nose with her arm and stared into her lap.

'Where do you know Erin from?'

The air went silent and the solicitor began to style the one end of his moustache. From what Smith had told her, the woman had refused to speak with him, even though he was there to represent her.

'It's going to be a long day. Do you want a drink?'

The woman shook her head.

'We're going to find out who you are eventually.'

The woman shrugged her shoulders. She then caught an expression that said it all. The woman had nothing left to lose. This was her last stand. Or was she protecting someone else, hiding something more? Maybe she was protecting Stan North. The woman hunched forward and continued looking into her lap. Gina stared at her hair. If her prints matched those that were found on Erin, her hair might match the hair that they also found. The DNA results would be back soon enough. What had this woman done to Erin Holden?

'Tell us about Simone Duxford.'

Gina watched as sweat beads began to form on the woman's forehead.

'Simone Duxford, aged eighteen, found in a shallow grave in the woodland. Long gingery-red hair and carefully placed in the foetal position. The grave was a little bit small but we could see that some care had been taken in placing her. Dressed in a white nightdress, underwear. Someone had tried to preserve her dignity. Tell me about Simone.'

The woman began to hyperventilate.

'Tell me about Simone!' Gina pulled Simone's photo from her notebook and slid it across the table.

As the chair slid from under the woman, she clutched her chest as she tried to stagger towards the door. Gasping for breath, the woman yelled and fell to her knees. 'I need an ambulance.' She began ripping her blouse buttons as she gasped for air.

'Tell me about Simone!' Gina yelled.

The woman writhed as she gasped for breath.

'Guv.' Jacob placed a hand on her shoulder. Sweat dripped from her brow onto the floor as her body shook. She was so close to getting the woman to speak.

'Call an ambulance and get Smith here immediately,' Gina said to Jacob, also knowing Smith was their best-trained first aider. There was no way she was getting the information she needed from a woman who looked like she was having a heart attack. The solicitor grabbed his pad and headed to the door, clearly worried about getting his pristine suit dirty as the suspect struggled for breath. Gina daren't push for another question with him watching. She'd already come close to pushing her luck. She only hoped their suspect wouldn't keel over and die. 'Interview terminated at nine forty-five.'

'We were so close.' Gina slammed her hand on the wall as she seethed. 'Give me something good. What did Stacey say?' Gina asked as she left the medics to deal with their mystery woman. Wyre had just come from seeing the girl out.

'She had nothing new to add. The only piece of information she had kept a secret was that she knew of Westley. She hasn't been in contact with Christina Dawson since. What's happening in there?'

'I think our mystery woman is having a heart attack.' They entered the incident room.

'Did you get anything out of her?'

'Not a jot. You should have seen her face when I mentioned Erin Holden and Simone Duxford. Simone's photo sent her off the scale and left her struggling for breath. I think she had an anxiety attack but we have to be sure and get her checked out. They're seeing to her now. I'm just hoping they don't admit her to hospital but I suspect they may want to run an ECG. She looked rough.'

'You think she knows Simone?'

'I know it. I'm sure she knows all the girls. She's the key to cracking this case. If she gets admitted, I want her watched like a hawk. She's a suspect and I'm not giving her the chance to escape, especially as we still don't know who she is.'

'She's stable but they're taking her in,' Jacob said as he ran into the room.

'Great. I'll head to the hospital. I want to speak to the girl, Elisa, about her run in with Stan North. We need him found. Wyre, ask Smith to provide someone who can follow the ambulance and guard mystery woman's room while she's there. I don't want her giving us the slip.'

'That'll make his day,' Wyre replied.

O'Connor walked in eating a biscuit, holding the packet in his other hand. 'I just went to grab a snack. What happened?'

'Wyre will fill you in?' Gina grabbed one of his biscuits and her bag, before heading out to the car park. While fishing through the rubbish in her bag for her car keys, she watched as the paramedics wheeled their suspect into the ambulance. The woman wasn't getting away from her that easily. She would wait as long as it took to get the answers she needed.

Gina checked her messages as she inhaled the summer air. Dandelion seeds gave the dried out townscape a surreal look. All the patches of grass had turned into a golden colour and leaves had begun to fall from the trees prematurely. It almost looked autumnal. The stifling weather was set to continue. Gina took a step back into the shade. A call was coming in from Wyre. 'What have you got for me?'

'It's Mrs Dawson. As you know she's been doing a bit of investigating herself and spoke to a homeless girl in Birmingham who recognised her daughter as being with a girl called Erin. She forgot to mention another detail, which is that when the girl saw the man return to Birmingham, with a woman, she said that the woman needed her roots doing. Not much to go on but I thought—'

'Or it might be everything.' She grinned as she thought about the mystery woman. Had she always left her roots a little too long before dying her hair or were her roots just shorter when she went with Stan North to Birmingham, possibly on the lookout for another girl. Had her hair grown a little more since? All evidence was pointing to Stan North. He was looking more suspicious by the minute. She needed to find out how he was connected to the mystery woman, the girls and the drugs.

CHAPTER SIXTY

Julia paced back and forth across the kitchen floor and flinched as the door slammed.

'What is it, what's happened?' Roy asked as he placed his arms around her.

'I know something happened between you and Christina and I want to know what. I search for her, I talk about her and I think about her all day, every day. You... you just get on with life like it's perfect. She wouldn't just leave the way she did and, as it happens, I don't trust you. What did you do or say to her? She wouldn't do this to me, she just wouldn't.' She sobbed into her hands as she pushed him away.

'Why do you always blame me? She was the one who started all the rows in the house, not me.'

She coughed and spluttered as her nose began to fill. 'And you didn't help. Did you know she was being picked on at school? No. You never asked or cared. I know she acted out but she needed our support and I failed by listening to you all the time.'

He kicked the chair as he headed into the dining area. 'I could never do anything right. She hated me.'

'You made her hate you, always on at her. She was a child and you were the adult.' She walked over to him as she wiped her face with the back of her hand. 'What did you say?' She pushed him. He held his hands up and looked away. 'What did you say? Why did she run away? Tell me,' she yelled as she brought her open hand back and slapped him across the face.

He grabbed both of her hands, pushed her back against the worktop and stared into her eyes, his face reddening. 'You really want to know?'

She nodded as she expelled a loud cry.

'I told her the truth, that she was a spoiled little cow and that she was making us miserable. I told her the best thing that could happen was for her to get out of our lives and I didn't mince my words. That girl made my life a misery with all that she put us through. I thought if she left, we could be happy and live in peace. I thought she'd plan to move in with a friend after her exams and get a job, not run away with some stranger.'

She fought against his strength, wanting to hit and punch him but he had her hands pinned to the worktop. She writhed and wriggled until she ran out of steam. 'I want you out of my house. Get out.'

He let go, allowing her to slump to the floor in floods of tears.

'No problem. Just remember one thing, you let her come between us. You were too soft on her. All this is your fault.'

'How dare you. Just get out of my house. I never want to see you again. Ever. I hate you.' As she sobbed, she heard the front door slam and his engine revving as he sped down the street. Knowing her daughter had been driven out of her home by the man she thought she loved was too much to bear. She needed to find her, tell her she loved her and wanted her to come home.

CHAPTER SIXTY-ONE

'I said eat. Come on, just a little bit,' he yelled at Jackie. Miley listened to the sounds emanating through the walls. Jackie began choking on whatever he was feeding her. The sound of a plate slamming on the chest of drawers made her flinch. 'I said I'd get the best for you and I let you down.' He cried as the woman wheezed and then gasped for breath. Jackie was okay, this time. Even Miley knew that Jackie could only take in little amounts on a spoon and quite often struggled to swallow. 'I'm so sorry, my love. Why did this have to happen to us? Why?'

Miley lay on the floor. As she listened to the chaos unfolding outside her locked door, she had a vision of her mother standing against their front door refusing to let her out. She remembered the names she'd called her as she stormed back up to her bedroom. She only hoped that one day she'd get the opportunity to apologise and go back home. She remembered the last words her mum's boyfriend had said to her. Did her mum still love her? 'Can I go home?' she whispered. She didn't have the strength to yell.

She smiled as she thought of her grandma and grandad. Maybe she could go and live with them. Grandma Emilia, whom she was partly named after. It seemed silly to shorten it to Miley the more she thought of it, but she had been a fan of Miley Cyrus since watching re-runs of the *Hannah Montana* series. She had so wanted to become Hannah Montana.

When she was about nine, her grandparents had taken her to a farm in Evesham to pick strawberries. She ate most of what they'd picked as they walked around and her grandma had turned and said, 'Christina Emilia Dawson, what a mess you are!' Just after, Grandma licked her embroidered hankie and began to wipe the stain, only making it worse. Miley began to weep as she thought of all the lip she'd given her lovely grandma and grandad. They were always so kind and loving towards her, but she'd pushed them away too. She wanted to go to Grandma's and go strawberry picking again. She wanted to hear her grandma call her Christina Emilia again.

A wave of nausea swept through her. She wiped the sweat from her brow. 'I need my medicine,' she tried to yell. There was a bash on her bedroom door as he passed and went down the stairs. 'Please,' she called. Yelling as a cramp doubled her up, she began to shake so uncontrollably she smashed her frail wrist on the corner of the wardrobe.

He'd refused to give her the medicine she needed. He'd locked her in her room to die. 'You're killing me,' Miley cried.

She lay there, thinking she might not even survive the day let alone escape her living hell. The crawling sensation under her skin returned. A little beetle emerged from the gap in the skirting board. 'Hello,' she said as she began to claw at her flesh, rolling on the floor in her damp clothes. Her heart pumped so fast she thought it would suddenly stop, become all used up. She had once thought that every person was born with a specific number of heartbeats. She didn't know if it were true or not but if it were, she was fast running out of beats. She closed her eyes and imagined her heart was a ticking clock, getting faster and faster. She gasped for breath as her muscles went into a spasm. It was happening, her end was near.

She opened her mouth to speak and the moth flew in. The moth was back and it was choking her. As she caught sight of the sun-drenched window, the moths emerged through the vent, filling the room, entangling their wings in her hair, rubbing their

tiny scales onto her body, scuffing her skin. She coughed and
spluttered, trying hard to shift whatever was choking her. The
moths were everywhere. She knew they couldn't be real but they
looked and felt real. Her fear was real. Her itchy raw skin was
real but her eyes were deceiving her.

CHAPTER SIXTY-TWO

Gina sprinted across the car park, watching as they wheeled their mystery woman into the accident and emergency ward. Smith pulled up behind the ambulance and caught up. As she turned to enter through the main hospital entrance, she almost bumped into a girl with a dressing on her head. 'Sorry,' she said as she stepped past and walked through the main door. A woman sitting by the reception desk glanced up. 'DI Harte, I'm looking for an Elisa Stanford, brought in yesterday.'

'She's my daughter,' the woman said. 'We're just waiting for the discharge papers.' The woman stood up from the plastic seat and threw her empty styrofoam cup into the overflowing bin.

'Would it be okay if I spoke to her? I know she's had a tough night but it's important that we find whoever chased her in the woods.'

'Bastard, I hope you catch him quick. She was so upset when I arrived. After a tough night, she's calmed down a lot now. She's just outside, said she hated the hospital smell. It was making her nauseous so I told her to wait out there while I got her papers.'

'Mrs Stanford—'

'Gillian, please.'

'Gillian, shall we go outside to speak, if that's where Elisa's comfortable?'

The woman nodded. Gina followed her out, into the sunshine. She caught sight of the shimmering horizon over the houses in the distance. The girl she'd almost bumped into was staring at the ambulance across the path. 'This is Elisa.'

The tiny girl only looked about thirteen but Gina knew from her notes that she was actually seventeen. Her petite features made her seem even more delicate than the dressing to her head did. 'I'm DI Harte. Sorry for nearly bumping into you a moment ago. Are you okay to talk about what happened yesterday?'

The girl nodded and sat on a bench beside the sliding door. Every time Gina took a step back, the door opened. She stepped into the sunshine, away from the annoying sensor, and grabbed her notebook.

'My mum messaged me to say she'd be late so I messaged back to say I'd walk home. I wanted to get back so I could get ready to go out with Ethan—'

'Ethan is Elisa's boyfriend. I don't approve when he races off our drive in his souped-up car. I do worry.' Gillian Stanford pulled a pack of cigarettes from her bag and lit one up. Gina remembered having the same worries when one of Hannah's first boyfriends passed his driving test and whizzed off their drive.

'I understand. Could you please tell me what happened next? You started walking home?'

'Yes. I was listening to my music and I didn't hear him pull up. It was just before I reached the woodland. As soon as I spotted the car, a silver Mercedes, I got scared. I'd heard something on the news about a girl being found in a shallow grave in the woods and I ran.'

'Did you recognise this person?'

'Yes, he'd come into the shop before and creeped me out. He was just walking around, not really looking at what was on the shelves. He asked me if I worked there alone. I just wanted him to leave. I was working alone in the shop but one of my employers was upstairs. I remember hearing the printer chugging above. It wasn't the first time the man had come to the shop. I spotted his car on the drive a couple of days before. Do you think he'd been watching me?'

'We're not sure yet, that's what we're trying to find out. Did he buy anything?'

'He bought a few jars of honey. He overpaid too and didn't want his change. Really odd. He looked me over before leaving. Creep.'

Gina almost gasped. Her mind flashed back to the photos that Wyre had shown her, from the Norths' house. The jars on the side were jars of honey. They had been so easy to spot as the rest of the house had been uncluttered. Along with the description that Elisa had given them, she was now even more certain that the man who had chased her was Stan North. 'So you ran, what happened next?'

'I almost reached the scary house, the one near where the girl was found buried. We all think it's scary anyway as the old woman was found dead there not long ago. Everyone says she had been left there ages and was all scabby and mouldy. They say that her ghost wanders the grounds, looking for souls to devour. I know it's just a scare thing but it still freaks me out. When it first happened we used to go up there and dare each other to stand in the garden alone and try to conjure her spirit.'

Gillian Stanford pulled a grimacing face as she sucked on her cigarette and exhaled a plume of smoke. 'Elisa!'

'Sorry, Mum, we were just mucking about.'

'You were running and—' Gina wanted to bring the girl back on track. For someone who looked so poorly, she could talk and Gina wanted to hear what she had to say.

'He kept telling me to stop. There was no way I was stopping in the middle of the woods so that he could rape or kill me. I saw the house and the police tape.' She paused in thought. 'I lost concentration and was wearing those stupid flat dolly shoes. They're no good for running in. I lost my footing and went flying into a tree trunk or something, hitting my head. I blacked out for a while, possibly only a couple of minutes. When I came round, he was gone. Another man was calling me and said his name was Bryn.'

Gina recalled that Bryn Tilly had gone over to the property and found the girl. It was at least forty-five minutes after Elisa finished work. Gina had seen the call logs. Maybe Elisa had been unconscious for longer than she'd thought as there had been at least a twenty-minute time gap that hadn't been accounted for.

'I heard him calling an ambulance too. I called Mum from his van. Then he took me to the hospital, my mum met me here and that was it.'

'You've been really helpful, Elisa. Thank you for speaking with me. Here's my number if you remember anything else.' As Gina handed her card to Gillian Stanford, the receptionist came out with Elisa's discharge papers.

'Thank you.' Gillian stubbed her cigarette out on the wall, took the papers and placed them in her bag. 'Right, home we go and it's straight to bed for you, young lady.'

Elisa smiled as her mum placed an arm around her, obviously enjoying the loving attention she was receiving after her injury. 'Can I just see if Mrs Hanley is okay?'

'We're not dropping by the farm shop today, sweetie. You're just going to have to call in and tell them you're not well enough to work for a couple of days.'

'No. You're not getting me, Mum. I just saw her being wheeled into A & E. Something's happened to her. I wondered if she was okay.'

'When did you see her?' Gina asked, her heart drumming away.

'Just as you bumped into me. The woman that was being wheeled out of the ambulance. That's Mrs Hanley, my manager at the Taste of Nature farm shop. I just hoped she was okay and wondered if Mr Hanley knew as he wasn't with her.'

'You've been really helpful, Elisa. Take care. You'll be hearing from us soon,' Gina said as she hurried across the car park, phone in hand. Their mystery woman had been identified and Gina knew where she worked. O'Connor answered her call. 'Find out all you can on Mrs Hanley, the one who runs or owns the Taste of Nature farm shop. Our mystery woman is only Mrs Hanley.'

'I was just about to call you too. A car registered to a Mrs Hanley was ticketed in Cleevesford. She'd parked in a resident's only space. It has been there since the drug bust. I'm on it now.'

'Any news on Stan North?'

'Nothing. He's completely off radar. He hasn't made any phone calls or been home. His car hasn't shown up anywhere and Mrs North is still calling every five minutes. She's doing our heads in with her whiney voice and patronising tone. She called me an incompetent muppet.'

'She sounds a handful. I'll be back in five. Gather in the incident room, I'm leaving the hospital now. Call everyone in.' As she ended the call, she noticed a missed call from Bernard. He'd only call if he had forensics results.

CHAPTER SIXTY-THREE

Flinging her bag to the floor, Gina hurried to the boards at the one end of the room. Sunlight filled the room. Gina pulled the blind across, blocking out the sun and heat. The fan whirred behind her, wafting the musty smell around.

'As you probably all know, we have identified the mystery woman as Mrs Hanley, co-owner of the Taste of Nature farm shop. On the way back, Bernard called. We also have a match on the hair that was found on Erin Holden's clothing. As well as Mrs Hanley's prints being found on something connected to Erin, we now know that the hair found on Erin also belongs to our Mrs Hanley. I called Smith. Last he heard, she was receiving treatment and our Doctor Nowak had pushed him out of the room. Let's just hope she doesn't have a heart attack and peg it. In the meantime, we need to make a plan of action. What did you find out about Mrs Hanley, O'Connor? Wyre?'

Wyre draped a stray hair behind her ear and O'Connor tapped his foot on the floor as he flicked through the pages of his note-filled pad before speaking. 'She co-owns the shop with her husband. They were easy to find, their house is about a ten-minute walk down the road from their shop. Clover Farm, it's called. It hasn't been a working farm for over forty years. Their full names are William and Jaqueline Hanley. William is fifty-nine, Jaqueline is sixty-two. There was something else—'

'Spill it out,' Gina replied.

'Jaqueline Hanley has late stage Huntington's disease and from what the doctor at Cleevesford Surgery said, she can't communicate any more and is totally incontinent. He didn't recognise the photo of our mystery woman that I emailed over. Shall I go back to calling her the mystery woman?'

'This is all we need. Didn't we say that traces of blood and faeces were found on Erin's clothing and that they didn't belong to Erin?'

They all glanced over at the board. 'Yes, guv,' Wyre replied.

'What if the bodily secretions belonged to the real Mrs Hanley? Who is this woman and why is she purporting to be Mrs Hanley?' Gina began to pace in front of the board. 'We need to get a warrant for that house. Wyre, make it so. We still have a missing girl, Christina Dawson.'

'I'll do it now.' Wyre swivelled her chair to the side and slid across the floor to her computer.

Briggs entered, holding a takeaway coffee. 'Any updates?'

'It's all happening, sir. I think we're onto something and it's all leading back to Mrs Hanley and Stan North. We need a search warrant. As soon as we have it, I'm sure we'll have the answers.'

'There's another thing, guv,' Wyre said as she did a half turn in her chair, her ponytail slapping her shoulder.

'Go on.'

'If you look at the map and all the points I pinned.' Everyone's gaze was on the map.

Gina walked over and pinned Clover Farm and the Taste of Nature farm shop. 'I see. Erin could have come from Clover Farm, run across this field, alongside the brook, over the style, through this gate that leads to the pull in parking place, which is just a short drive from the garage. Darren Mason said he stopped at multiple places and this was one of them. It would have been hard for her considering what a state she was in but she did it.

Let's run this through. She'd have got into the van while he was arguing with his partner, Callum Besford. Darren also said that the van may not have been locked. She simply opened the back door to the Transit van, climbed in and waited for him to drive off. She must have been scared to death, hoping to get as far away as possible. He drove for a while. Maybe she was clinging to the back door of the van and the door flew open at a bend, which is why she may have fallen out. Who was she running from? And what has the fake Mrs Hanley got to do with all this?

'I'm grabbing a quick drink and I want all the paperwork in order to go to the farm and the shop. Get back-up units on standby. I want you all ready to go and storm the place but we must tread carefully.' She paused. 'Erin wanted us to help someone. We don't want to put her at risk by storming in too hard.' Gina stomped over to her bag, popped a paracetamol into her hands and swallowed it down with Wyre's glass of water. Her head was beginning to throb as more information filled it. 'Were the others taken to replace Simone? Why? Erin was found in dirty clothes, not all secretions her own. Julia Dawson said the girl she'd spoken to on the streets had been approached about a job, the same job that Erin and Christina had left the streets of Birmingham to do. What was that job? Care work, domestic work?'

'Domestic slavery, guv?' Wyre said.

Gina grabbed a marker pen and wrote domestic slavery on the board and stabbed a full stop at the end before flinging the pen onto the table. 'Yes! The heroin is used to control them. They don't necessarily always need to be careful about locking the doors, at least they might not have thought so, until Erin ran away. William Hanley has a wife who, from the sound of it, needs round the clock care. She'd need feeding, toileting, and washing, everything that she can't do herself any more. Is our mystery woman his live-in lover, taking Jaqueline Hanley's place? Maybe they just couldn't cope any more.'

'Where does North fit in with all this?' Wyre asked.

Gina paced back and forth. Her heart rate began to pick up. Excitement or anxiety? She couldn't be sure. She began to breathe in and out, trying to intercept a potential anxiety attack before it forced her to leave the room. 'I don't know. I can't think. Damn it.' She balled a fist and slammed it on the windowsill, her hand shaking.

'Guv?' Wyre said as she stood.

Gina exhaled and wiped her brow. 'However hard I try, I can't think how North fits into this, I just know he does. I want to know what he's hiding. If he wasn't hiding anything, he wouldn't have absconded the way he did. I'm missing something. We're all missing something.'

Jacob stood and left the room to take a call. They all awaited his return. 'Stan North's car was spotted by a mobile camera unit on the carriageway that runs from Alcester to Stratford-upon-Avon, the A46. He's been pulled over and they're bringing him in as we speak.'

'Yes,' Gina said as she punched the air and swallowed. She turned, took a final deep breath and discretely checked her pulse. It was normal. Everything was fine. She was fine – wasn't she?

Briggs flung his cup in the bin as he finished his coffee. 'Good job team. Let's hope our theories are right.' Gina looked across and caught his eye. He smiled as he left the room.

'Be ready. As soon as the warrant is granted, we have to leave. I'm heading off to the interview room to wait for Stan North's arrival. We're going to nail him, and when we do, we're going to find out once and for all what he's been hiding.'

CHAPTER SIXTY-FOUR

Stan's designer suit was creased and he filled the small room with the smell of stale sweat. The tape had been rolling for a couple of minutes. Jacob leaned back in the plastic chair, creaking with every small movement. The man removed his glasses and placed them on the table. She could tell he was tired. The length of his stubble and the greasy bit of hair he had showed he hadn't seen a bathroom that morning. 'What were you doing after five in the afternoon yesterday, Mr North?'

'Not what you think I was doing.' The man shook his head and rubbed his eyes.

'So enlighten me.' Gina threw her pen to the table and folded her arms.

'You think you have me all worked out? You haven't. I had no intention of hurting the girl. I went back to the farm shop. You showed me a photo of a girl the other day.'

'Simone Duxford?' Jacob pulled the photo from the file and slid it across the table.

He nodded. 'That's her.'

'You recognised her, didn't you?' Gina unfolded her arms. He nodded again. 'Why didn't you say anything?'

'I couldn't.' The man leaned his head in his hands and sweat began to roll down his forehead. 'I didn't want my wife to know.'

'Know what?'

He looked away.

'We're going to find out, Mr North. You need to tell us how you were involved or you could be charged with obstructing an officer in the course of their duties.'

'I had sex with her.' He rubbed his temples as tears began to run down his face. 'She was out of it, on something. I went to the shop, the farm shop, and Mr Hanley served me. This was back in December last year. I bought a holly wreath for my wife, as you do. I remember feeling sorry for him. He and his wife were caring for a relative in a wheelchair who looked totally incapable of doing anything for herself. I gave them a twenty-pound tip. They had her at the back of the shop, and she was calling away. I saw the red-haired girl leave through the back door. I swear, I'd never seen anyone so captivating, so beautiful. She had this almost translucent skin and looked so pure. The woman in the wheelchair began screaming, reciting the same noises over and over again. It made me jump and I'm embarrassed to say, slightly uncomfortable. Anyway, at that point, I left the shop.' The man wept into his hands.

'Go on, Mr North.'

'I've never done anything like this in my life and I'm so ashamed. For all my years of marriage, I've not once cheated on my wife, except for this one time. The girl was outside, it was dark. She basically offered it to me on a plate, said she needed to *feel something* and she could tell I'd noticed her. She beckoned me over to a shed at the back of the car park. She pulled down her thick tights and hitched up her denim skirt. I stupidly followed. I remember her kissing me and cupping me, rubbing and gyrating against me. I wanted her so badly. She wanted me. I never assaulted her. I even asked her if I could see her again. The way things were at home, with Elizabeth, I'd have left in an instant, but she just pulled her tights up and told me to leave.'

'She was young enough to be your daughter. She was eighteen.' Gina watched as he breathed a sigh of relief. Gina could tell that he hadn't been sure.

'I haven't done anything wrong then?'

'If you say so, Mr North.' Maybe he hadn't legally been out of order with Simone but there was always that moral question that would haunt him. He hadn't known her age. She looked younger than her years. He couldn't have been sure. 'So, why were you chasing Elisa Stanford through the woods yesterday?'

'That really wasn't what it looked like. I only went back to the shop this week to see if the new girl remembered the red-haired girl. I couldn't ask her when I got there. I don't know why. Maybe I thought she'd link her death to me. Anyway, it played on my mind and when I saw her walking alongside the road, I pulled over. It wasn't planned. I just had to ask if she knew anything. I thought if I said something to you, you'd think I did it. I didn't mean to chase her. She got scared and ran. I kept telling her to stop. I just wanted to explain myself. I messed the whole thing up.'

'You left her in the woods, unconscious, with a head injury!'

'I called Bryn Tilly, asked him to check on something at the house. I hoped he'd find her and he did. I didn't leave her.' He wiped a tear from his eye.

'How well do you know the Hanleys?'

'I don't.' Gina kept her gaze on him. 'I've seen them once, that time when I bought the wreath.'

'Interview terminated at fifteen twenty.' Gina checked the time and she was running short of it. She glanced back at Stan, his head in his hands. He knew his wife would end up finding out his sordid little secret. She wondered if he was truly ashamed. She felt he was more likely upset that he'd been found out. A message from Wyre flashed up on her phone.

We have the warrant and all units are on standby. We are in position to take the farm shop at the same time.

She nodded and closed her notebook. They had to get to Clover Farm.

CHAPTER SIXTY-FIVE

As Miley shook violently, the boss dragged her from her room, into Jackie's room. The delicate crepe-like skin on the back of her legs began to peel away as he pulled her faster.

Jackie was sitting in the middle of the room with her legs splayed out. The smell hit Miley and almost made her heave. Her friend Jackie hadn't been washed or changed all day, she could tell. Jackie rocked back and forth, shouting meaningless words.

'You need to deal with her now,' he yelled.

The shakes began to build up again and the spasms caused her to arch her back. Her body jerked and foam began to seep from her mouth as she heaved. Hell, that's where she was, and things weren't set to get better. Her heart rate sped and she scratched. 'I need my medicine, please.'

'There is no more medicine and you don't need any more. Look at you. Do your job and take care of Jackie.'

Do her job! She couldn't even move, let alone work. The moths began to crawl from the walls. 'Get them away from me.' It was all happening again and Miley didn't know how much more she could take as his shouting mixed with her screaming. His words sounded like a record being played backwards and she could barely make them out. Help Jackie, she needed to help Jackie. As she tried to sit up, spasms flashed through her body.

'You're just another useless piece of shit, like your stupid friend, Erin. Did I tell you she was dead? Poor, stupid, little Erin. I gave you an opportunity and like her, you blew it. What thanks do I get for taking you off the streets? Nothing. A big fat nothing.'

Through her warped vision she saw him standing over her, his head backlit by the sunshine flooding through the window. As her eyes focused, she noticed the deep creases that gave him a harsh look. Through his thin lips, a curl developed at one side as he grinned. His green-eyed stare met hers. She looked away. As she inhaled, she caught the smell of washing powder coming from his casual shirt. She'd forgotten what it was like to feel clean. He used the same powder as her mum, she recognised the smell and tried to breathe it in again. Her abdomen felt like it was being sliced apart. She leaned to the side and screamed as she avoided the moths that came for her. *They're not real, they're not real. Imagine they're beautiful butterflies.* The shivers were coming again. She braced herself as the biggest tremble she'd ever felt in her life travelled through her body. The moths were around her, they were in her, scratching away under her skin. She jerked and coughed as she gasped for air. She couldn't breathe properly. The light room became speckled, like it had filled with murky pond water.

'Good for nothing,' he yelled as he kicked her in the side. 'A good for nothing junkie. Why couldn't you be more like Simone?' He turned to Jackie. 'Our lovely granddaughter. She came to find us and she loved you so much.' He kneeled beside Miley as she jerked and writhed in pain. 'You were never going to be Simone. I'll make sure you have a dignified send off and then I'll go looking for your replacement. Give up. Death is inevitable. It will be less painful if you don't fight it, then you can be at peace.'

She coughed and gasped as he kneeled on the floor until she closed her eyes and floated off into another world with a smile on her face. *Don't fight it.*

She was back at home, sitting at the dinner table, contemplating whether to do her English literature essay. She had to write a critique on *Jane Eyre*. As she walked along the corridors of Mr Rochester's old house, dare she enter the attic and face her own ghost? She closed her eyes, took a deep breath and reopened them. She was back at the dinner table. Her mother Julia, scooping potatoes from a pan onto her and Roy's plate. She would leave *Jane Eyre* until the weekend. She wanted to go to the park with Stacey. She wanted to write silly messages under the slide and play around. She wanted to pinch one of Roy's cans of beer from the fridge so that they could drink it together and giggle the evening away. Her homework could wait. Life was too short. 'You know, your mother would be so much happier if you left,' Roy said, smiling as he shovelled mashed potatoes into his mouth.

A flash of pain filled her head and her family were gone. The grey-black speckles filled her eyes. She was gone, just like Roy had wanted.

CHAPTER SIXTY-SIX

Gina stepped out of Jacob's air-conditioned car into the sweltering heat with the warrant in her hand. A couple of police cars pulled up behind her. The ambulance came up the windy country road, ready for any casualties.

The house stood on a slight hill, with brown patchy fields stretching way into the horizon. The heat had made the usually lush landscape look almost post-apocalyptic. The sun was just coming over the house and Gina felt sweat begin to absorb into the waistband of her grey trousers. The house itself was quite large, five windows spanning the upstairs, three windows and a bay on the downstairs level. She tried to get a look inside. Whether it was the glare or the dirt, she had no chance of seeing much.

'Follow me.' She beckoned to Jacob. Two further officers followed behind, another two waited with their car. Wyre and O'Connor had gone and led the search of the farm shop.

The weed-sprouted path led the way through the dead-looking garden to the main door in the centre of the house. A gargoyle with a metal ring in its mouth stared back at Gina. She almost wanted to smile at the irony. Weren't gargoyles meant to warn evil off? In this case, if they were right, evil had been residing in the building. Vulnerable girls had been invited in with the promise of work, food, a warm bed. She lifted the heavy ring and tapped it several times. There was no sound. She lifted the letterbox and peered in.

'Mr Hanley? We have a warrant to search the premises. Open up.' A thudding noise came from inside. 'There's someone in there.'

*

Wyre walked up to the farm shop and stopped to read the notice that had been pinned to the door.

Closed due to unforeseen circumstances. The management.

Wyre banged on the door. 'Mr Hanley, open up. We have a warrant to search the premises.' She placed her ear by the door and listened. A shuffling noise came from behind the wooden panels. She held her hands over her eyes and peered through the small window. 'I heard something.' She stepped aside and an officer stepped in with an enforcer.

'Shall I?'

She glanced towards O'Connor. 'Do it.'

After three smashes against the door, it finally rattled as it sprang open. Wyre flinched and held a hand to her chest. The rat scurried along the floor and escaped behind the French dresser stacked with chutneys, its tail disappearing into the darkness. 'If nothing else, I think environmental health need to come and check this place out.'

O'Connor followed her closely. They both stopped and listened, adjusting their stab vests as they approached. She led them behind the counter and through to a small staff room. At the end of the room was a small bathroom with a toilet, a shower and a washbasin. Wellies lined the walls. The side door was covered in cobwebs and insects. Spiders hung from the frame, waiting patiently for passing flies. Between the bathroom and the staffroom was a set of stairs.

'Mr Hanley. We have a warrant to search the premises,' O'Connor called. There was no reply.

With every step Wyre took, another creak interrupted the silence. Her heart began to pound slightly as she reached the top. She bent down and peered round the wall, nothing. She flinched as the office phone beeped with a message. With a gloved hand, she pressed the red button to listen to the message. She checked her watch against the displayed time. It had only been left ten minutes before.

'All right, Dad. I've just finished my contract in Spain and I'm finally coming home to meet my daughter. That's the good news. No need to pick me up at the airport, I've booked a taxi. Get some beers in and give Mum a kiss from me—'

The message ended. The caller had run out of time. 'That must be Mr Hanley's son,' Wyre whispered. 'Mr Hanley,' she called out. No one answered. 'There's no one here.'

More officers followed and began searching the smaller rooms. She gazed out of the window as another officer entered the shed at the back of the car park. The officer exited the shed and headed towards the car. She opened the top drawer. It contained a photo of Simone and a small tea light candle in a holder that said *thinking of you* on the side. She pictured Mr Hanley getting the photo of Simone out and lighting a candle in her memory. She pulled her phone from her pocket and dialled Gina. 'Hi, guv. There's no one here but I just found a photo of Simone in one of the desk drawers. Thought I'd let you know. Mr Hanley's son, Gareth, just left a message on the shop answerphone to say he was coming back to visit them, and Simone. He has no idea that she's dead as yet.' She paused. 'If Hanley's not here, he must be there.'

CHAPTER SIXTY-SEVEN

Gina placed her phone back in her pocket, stretched in her stab vest and allowed the officer with the enforcer to step forward. She'd given enough warning. She'd called through the letterbox, telling the occupants that they had a warrant but no one had answered. Several bangs later, a section of the door caved in. Gina pushed her arm through the gap and opened the door from the inside before she and Jacob stepped over the threshold. Dust motes filled the sunlit stairway and the sun shining through the window at the top of the stairs almost blinded her.

To the left was a dining room. She crept forward, heart hammering against her ribcage. She gulped a mouth full of air and tried to swallow but her throat refused. She needed to swallow quickly, either that or she might choke. She loosened her shirt and coughed slightly. Now was not the time to have an anxious episode. Sweat beads formed along her hairline and began to stream down her forehead. As she stepped closer to the kitchen table, a flashback to her last case almost caused her to stumble. An image of her being dragged under her own table by her masked attacker filled her mind. Clenching her fists and swallowing again, she took a step back. Just like she'd been told, slow breath in, hold, slow breath out.

'You okay, guv?' Jacob whispered. The other officers turned right by the door and entered the lounge.

Gina felt her blood pumping hard, the dust motes turning into the speckles a person sees just before they pass out. It was hot, so hot. She inhaled sharply. *Not now, not today.* 'I'm fine.' She crept towards the kitchen and opened the door as she continued to breathe in and out. Flies buzzed around a cracked Belfast sink. The dark oppressive wood on the cupboard doors made the room feel dingier than it really was. The stink of rotten food and onion skins filled her nostrils. 'Mr Hanley,' she called. He wasn't downstairs. She proceeded back towards the main door. She was going up. 'Mr Hanley. Christina or should I call you Miley? You call yourself Miley now. Just shout if you can hear me.' She crept up another step, listening for a noise, any noise.

A woman began murmuring and shouting incoherently.

'Mrs Hanley?' Gina took another step.

'Guv, you have to come out,' their most recent recruit, PC Kapoor, called as she slammed through what was left of the front door. Crying came from the right side of the building.

'You go back out,' she said to Jacob. She beckoned to Kapoor to back her up. The young woman crept up the stairs, crossing Jacob as he ran back down.

'Mr Hanley, stay right there,' she heard Jacob shouting.

Gina hurried up, passing a small bathroom. She gently pushed the first door. The smell hit her. A slop bucket sat in the corner of the room. A pile of several sheets that had once been white sat on top of an old torn mattress. Carpet fibres were dug up all over the room and she saw a couple of beetles making their way towards the skirting board. She remembered the cast skins that forensics had found. The girl cried out and another woman kept shouting the same incoherent sound over and over again. She heard Jacob shouting outside but she couldn't make out what was being said over the noise.

'The next room,' she whispered as Kapoor trod gently behind her. There were two more doors but it was obvious that the screaming was coming from the door she and Kapoor waited behind.

'Mr Hanley, don't jump. Please let Miley get back into the bedroom,' she heard Jacob saying.

'We have a hostage situation,' Gina said. Sweat filled her eyes. Every time she brushed it away, more replaced it, almost clouding her vision. She untied her stab vest and threw it to the floor.

'Guv?'

She knew she was putting herself in danger but she couldn't work in the heat. It was sending *her* mad and *her* heartbeat erratic. 'I'll be okay.' Her hand rested on the door handle. If she pressed it down, would she alarm the girl's captor? If she didn't, would she miss her chance to save her? Her mind flashed to Julia Dawson. More than anything, she wanted to find Christina and reunite the family. 'What do I do, what do I do?' she whispered.

Kapoor wiped her head with her sleeve and returned a nervous smile.

'Mum.' Gina listened to the girl choking on her own tears as she forced her words out.

She had to get into the room. Gently pressing the door handle, she gave Kapoor the nod, letting her know that they were going in. Another officer hung back on the stairs. As Jacob called out again, Gina opened the door.

'You don't have to do this, Mr Hanley. Come down so we can talk about it,' Jacob said.

'This was never meant to happen,' the man yelled as he stood on the ledge, the other side of the window.

Jackie Hanley kept repeating the same sound as she sat on the floor in the middle of the room.

Gina nodded to Kapoor who knelt down to see if Mrs Hanley was okay. The sick woman was gripping a knitted doll and strands of wool were tangled in her hair and around her legs as the doll unravelled with every movement. Christina was sitting on the window ledge, her legs dangling outside with Mr Hanley's hand snaked around her waist, squeezing her as she screamed. The girl turned, gazing at Gina as if trying to focus. Gina held her finger to her mouth and watched as tears slipped down the girl's cheeks.

'You have to let the girl go. Let her get back in the bedroom,' Jacob called. 'We can talk about this. I know you don't mean to hurt her.'

'I didn't mean to hurt anyone. I didn't hurt Simone. I loved Simone. Jackie loved Simone being here. I tried to help her, took her in and paid her to look after her grandmother. The drugs took her, not me.'

'And you don't want to hurt the girl. You didn't hurt Simone so please let the girl go. She's scared. Please step back into the room.' She could tell Jacob was running out of ideas. If William Hanley jumped, depending on how he fell, he might make it. He may break a leg or even both. He may fall badly and end his own life. From what she remembered, the outside of the building was slightly larger at the bottom. Mr Hanley probably had a plinth about a foot long to stand on. He was a big man and by the way he was holding the girl, she could tell he was jittery.

Gina stepped past Jackie and Christina tried to reach back to grab her hand, but the girl had no strength and her hand dropped before Gina could grab it.

'I am never going with you. You can all go to hell. I've lost my granddaughter, when my son finds out what happens, I'll lose him too. I'm not losing my freedom. You think I don't know that you're trying to come here, be all sympathetic, telling me we can talk about it? Like hell. There will be no talking.'

'No, please let me go,' Christina whimpered. Mr Hanley turned and caught a glimpse of Gina creeping up behind him. Their gazes locked. She felt her heart almost beating out of her chest as she realised he was going. He propelled them both from the window, letting go of the girl once his feet left the plinth. Gina's eyes met Christina's as she reached out and grabbed the girl's desperate hands. She heard a thud as Mr Hanley hit the stone porch, face first.

Christina sobbed as her weak sweaty hands began to slip out of Gina's. Jacob and the two officers linked hands below them.

It wasn't ideal but it had been all they could probably think of given the time in which they had to react. However hard she tried, it was no good. Kapoor pushed in and leaned out, grabbing Christina's wrist, just below where Gina was holding. As Kapoor held onto the girl, Gina inched forward and grabbed her other wrist. Between them, they slowly pulled the lifeless girl up and through the window, laying her on the floor. Pale and clammy, Christina jerked and screamed before shaking and passing out. 'Get a paramedic up here,' Gina called as she held the girl. 'We have a vulnerable adult and an unconscious girl.'

Footsteps stormed the house and filled the room.

She watched as another paramedic inspected Mr Hanley's body. They would never hear his full version of events. She did know that the house would give up his secrets. Once forensics came in and examined everything, they would have a clearer picture of what had happened to Erin. Out of the corner of her eyes, she noticed that Christina had stopped moving.

A young female paramedic darted in and knelt before the girl. Gina crawled across the floor and sat beside her, stroking her hair. 'It's okay. You're okay now. Wake up.' Gina couldn't feel a pulse. 'Wake up,' she yelled.

'Could you please move back, Inspector?' the paramedic asked.

Another paramedic entered and helped Jaqueline Hanley out of the room, slowly steering her towards the stairs while trying to unravel the woollen doll from her.

'Your mum loves you very much and she just wants you home safely,' Gina whispered, feeling a tear welling in the corner of her eye.

'Inspector, I need you to get back.'

Gina hit the door frame knowing in her heart that they had been too late for Christina. Her phone went. 'Smith?' She paused and looked up at Kapoor. 'I've got to get back to the station. Our fake Mrs Hanley is being discharged from hospital and then being brought back to the station for interview.' She gazed back at Christina as the paramedic tended to her. She so wanted to stay with her and will her through whatever was happening, but she had no option but to hurry back.

Another officer ran out of the house, holding a passport. 'Look what we found in the bedroom.'

CHAPTER SIXTY-EIGHT

The phone next to the incident board rang. Gina snatched the receiver. 'Harte.' She made notes and listened before placing the receiver down. 'A Mr Patel called in after recognising the photo of Simone Duxford in the online local paper. He lives with his family on King Street. Sometime before Christmas last year, he said, a girl knocked on his door asking if a Gareth lived there. She said that Gareth was her father and she'd been trying to trace him. Mr Patel said his kids were a little scared by her and she looked to be on something. He told her the man she was looking for had moved years before and that he had bought the house off a Gareth Hanley. He also said he used the farm shop and it was owned by a Mr Hanley. He thought Mr Hanley may know of Gareth. He gave her basic walking directions and ushered her off his pathway.'

'That all makes sense with the answerphone message that we heard, back at the farm shop. Mr Hanley's son is coming home and expecting to see his daughter,' Wyre said.

'That would make Simone William Hanley's granddaughter. She would have taken the walk.' Gina looked at the map and followed the route with her finger. 'We're talking a good hour of walking from King Street to Clover Farm. It would have been dark, wet and cold and there is barely a footpath for most of the route, especially as she left the town. She must have been so desperate to find her family. What the hell did they do to her once she arrived?' Gina felt her hands twitch as she balled her fists. Poor Simone had gone to them, searching for her father, finding her grandfather and possibly seeing her sick grandmother. 'Right, let's go and get this interview done.' She beckoned Jacob to follow her.

The recorder had been rolling for several minutes. Their fake Mrs Hanley had now been identified as Vanessa Tranter. Gina glanced at the passport, which confirmed her identity. The woman looked paler than before. Gina suspected that the severe anxiety attack she'd been diagnosed with had left her exhausted. The photo of Simone sat on the table, neither her, the woman, or Jacob looking at it. 'It's over,' Gina said.

The woman began running her thick fingers through her straggly hair, trying to comb it through. The ticking of the clock seemed louder than before. Seconds and minutes passed. Gina just hoped that hours weren't going to pass without as much as a word.

'Vanessa Tranter. Did you understand what I said? About the house and William Hanley.'

Vanessa nodded. Gina watched as a tear slipped down the woman's cheek.

'Elisa Stanford recognised you at the hospital. She thought you were Mrs Hanley. Funny that, we found Mrs Hanley at Clover Farm. Dirty, uncared for and covered in sores. You know what else we found out?'

The woman looked away and wiped her eyes.

'You let your own sister live in that state. You and William Hanley lured those girls in with the promise of work, then you imprisoned them and pumped them full of drugs to trap them.'

Vanessa's voice began to crack as she muttered through her tears. 'I've always loved my sister.'

'It looked like you did.'

'I did!' She slammed her hand onto the table. 'We'd already lost her to this awful disease. He couldn't cope.'

'So you came along to help?'

Vanessa's breathing became erratic as she let her tears flow. 'You just think you know it all. You don't know anything about me.'

'So tell me, because from where I'm sitting, you have nothing to lose. We have two dead girls and you are implicated in both deaths. We have a girl in hospital fighting for her life and I must say, it's not looking good. You best tell me everything, Vanessa.' Gina's mind flashed back to the room in which Christina was found, being pulled out of the window by William Hanley.

'Tell us, Vanessa.' Jacob shuffled on the plastic chair.

The smell of body odour filled the room. Stale and ripe. All three of them were suffering because of the intense heat and it wasn't set to get any better. The small fan in the corner of the room was barely making a difference. The woman shook her head and began to sniffle. Gina pushed a box of tissues in her direction.

'I came to help him care for Jackie. My sister had been getting worse for years and, you know something, William had devoted everything to caring for her. Money had been an issue. The shop hadn't been doing well. He couldn't afford to place her in a home or employ carers. He tried to get help but as long as he coped, no one helped. Eventually no one even cared or contacted him. When he called me he'd been desperate, on the verge of a breakdown so I moved in with him, to help.'

'So you moved in to help care for your sister, Mrs Hanley. Why were you pretending to be Mrs Hanley then?'

Vanessa cleared her throat and blew her nose. 'It wasn't intentional. Elisa started working for us and she just called me Mrs Hanley after William told her he was Mr Hanley. I liked it, liked hearing it.' The woman paused and pulled a piece of stray hair from her sodden cheek. 'We'd had a relationship before he met my sister, when we were kids really. I never stopped thinking about him and when he needed me, I thought I had the chance to be happy. I would have become Mrs Hanley one day and I liked her calling me Mrs Hanley. I can't believe he's dead.' The woman began to weep once again.

'You took her place in her home, you took her home, you took her husband and her name. Tell us about Simone.'

'I never had kids and I found out I had a great-niece. When she turned up I felt like all my Christmases had come at once. She came looking for Gareth, William's son. She was so sickly looking when she arrived. It was then we discovered she had a drug problem, heroin. I think she was hoping that finding her father would turn her life around. She was introduced to her grandmother, Jaqueline, and she was so sad. She then asked if she could stay and William was delighted. She said she'd help to care for her grandmother in exchange for bed and board. She made us swear not to tell her biological mother or foster parents where she was. Said she needed time away from it all and that the streets had been hard on her. We were really worried about the drugs. She begged us to get her some, said she'd die without them. We found a local supplier, the man you caught me buying off, and we were giving her what she wanted. William would have done anything for her. We thought we were doing the right thing. One day, last winter, something went wrong. She'd just shot up and she began convulsing, foaming at the mouth, making choking noises. We tried to resuscitate her but it was no good.'

'Is that when you buried her in the woods?'

Vanessa nodded. 'William did. He gave her a good send-off. Even bought some flowers and chose a lovely spot in the woods. Then we cried for her. She was my sister's granddaughter for God's sake. Gareth, his son had been irresponsible as a young man and got her mother knocked up. He found out he was a father years later through a friend of a friend. The woman moved and he never knew where to. He hadn't even known her full name so he couldn't trace her. William and Gareth hoped that his daughter would find a way back to them one day. We didn't plan what happened.'

'What happened after that?'

The woman sighed. Jacob grabbed a tissue from the box and wiped his head. 'Without Simone, we couldn't cope. Every minute of the day was consumed with Jaqueline's care. You wouldn't understand how hard it was. She'd be sitting on the floor. Between us, we'd struggle to get her up. She fell down the stairs a couple of times, needed constant supervision. She was totally incontinent and always needed toileting and hand feeding. We looked to each other for support through this and became even closer. He couldn't afford round the clock nursing care. She really needed to be in a home, but he couldn't afford that either. It would have meant losing the house and the shop. We had no choice! That was when William had the idea of taking a street kid in, giving them work – to help a kid like Simone. He became obsessive though, looking for red-haired girls. I realised then he wanted to replace his granddaughter. They never lived up to his expectations though, never quite the same, never good enough.'

Gina slid the photo of Erin Holden across the table. 'Tell me about Erin.'

'Her and Miley,' Gina noted down that Miley's real name was Christina, 'he found them together in Birmingham. They were so keen to get off the streets, Erin had dyed red hair and I could see William's eyes light up when he brought them home. Our intentions were good, you have to believe me.'

Gina remembered when she saw Erin lying in the hospital bed, tubes coming from everywhere. She looked like the living dead. So thin, it was hard to imagine how she'd summoned up enough energy to escape. 'Erin was in a bad state, Ms Tranter. She escaped from you and William and her last words were "help her". We now know she was referring to Miley whose real name is Christina Dawson.' Gina paused. 'We saw the locks on the bedroom doors but that day, you'd both slipped up. Erin found a way out and she seized her opportunity. What did you and Mr Hanley put her through?'

'We gave her everything she wanted. All she wanted was drugs and we gave them to her.'

There was a knock at the door. O'Connor beckoned her out. 'Excuse me.' She left the room and followed him down the corridor.

'Do you want the good news, guv?'

'Hit me with it.'

'It's Christina Dawson. She's come round and is responding well to treatment. Her mother was called and the reunion brought Wyre to tears. That doesn't happen often. She spoke to Wyre, told her exactly what she'd been through. Basically, the woman you have in there and Mr Hanley were locking her in her room, forcing her to work for them, to look after Jackie Hanley. At first things were good, she and Erin arrived together, were treated well and given a room. Erin was an addict already and Vanessa Tranter was bringing drugs back for her. Then, one night while Erin was out of it and Christina was sleeping, Christina was woken by a sharp pain. She remembers seeing the other boss, who she describes as Vanessa, holding her down before the effects of the heroin kicked in. Since then, she's been begging them for her fixes and working hard to pay her debts for the drugs back to them.'

'The sick bastards,' Gina said as she massaged her aching temples.

'Christina keeps asking to see Jackie, says they were friends even though they couldn't communicate. I think Jackie was all she had. She felt they were prisoners together.'

'Thanks, Harry,' she said as she walked back to the interview room.

'Miss Tranter. We've received a full statement from Christina Dawson. You know her as Miley. We know everything. The way you and William told her that she'd have to pay her drug debts by working. There was no way she'd ever be able to repay you both. You planned it that way, didn't you?'

She shook her head and began to sob. 'No—'

'She told us of the night you first injected her, against her will. You turned her into an addict, didn't you?'

The woman shook her head and screamed. 'No!'

'You and William Hanley used her as a slave, imprisoned her and pumped her with drugs. We know all about it, Vanessa.'

'I didn't want to do it. It was William.'

Gina wasn't having any of it. Vanessa Tranter was fully complicit in everything. She believed Christina. The girl had no reason to lie. 'You injected her.'

'I didn't mean it. I didn't want to.'

'But you did—'

'Yes,' the woman cried between sobs. 'I just wanted to have some time with William. Jackie had everything. Back then, William dumped me as soon as he saw her, all sweet and innocent. She made me like this—' The woman gasped for air as she broke down.

'Did you always want everything your sister had?'

'She took William from me, he should have been mine. He liked me first. Even Daddy loved her more but she was his. Jackie's poorly, Jackie needs help, how dare you hurt Jackie, our poor little premature baby,' she mimicked in her father's voice. 'Me, I just got punished all the time, like now, just because my mother had a fling soon after Jackie was born. I got punished because my mother was a slut!' she spat. 'He locked me in a cupboard with spiders and insects – you wouldn't have guessed. Daddy hated me and I couldn't wait to leave home. When I met William, he promised to take me away from it all until *she* came along and ruined things. She took everything of mine—' Vanessa could no longer speak as violent sobs consumed her. 'She had it all.'

'Vanessa Tranter, I'm arresting you on charges of Manslaughter and Keeping Someone in Servitude…' She continued reeling off the charges whilst looking the woman in the eye. 'You do not have to say anything, but it may harm your defence if you do not mention something now which you may later rely on in court. Interview terminated at nineteen ten.'

'She took everything—' the woman yelled.

As Gina left the interview room, she heard Vanessa's sobs echoing throughout the building. The thought of what those poor girls had been through made her skin crawl. As her heartbeat raced, she ducked into the toilets and ran the cold tap, splashing her sticky face with water, taking a few deep breaths. They'd finally caught the people who had caused so much misery to those girls. Some people would never be brought to justice. Mr Hanley had died, never to be punished for what he did to Simone. Had he supported his granddaughter properly, taken her to the doctor and enrolled her on a drug rehabilitation programme, things could have been different. He'd never be punished for the way he'd treated Erin or Christina.

She slammed her open hand onto the mirror several times, full of hatred at what she was seeing. She was like them and it sickened her. She'd never been punished for the death of another. She retched and ran to the toilet, dry heaving. This case was almost over but the case of her stuffed-up life would never be over. One minute she'd forgiven herself and tried to forget, the next Terry was in her dreams, in her thoughts, guilt gnawing away at every fibre in her body.

Wyre entered as Gina was swilling her mouth out. 'Good job today, guv. Are you okay?'

Gina caught her reflection. Pale, sickly-looking. Her sweat-drenched knotted hair, half tied back in an elastic band. 'No. I'm hot, bothered and tired, plus I have the headache from hell.'

'Is there anything I can get you? Water?'

She forced a smile and shook her head. 'Honest, I'm feeling better now. It's just this headache. I'm going to head over to the hospital before it gets too late, then I'll be back for a catch up.' Gina dabbed her face and threw the paper towel in the wastebasket.

'Are you sure you're up to it?'

'It's something I need to do. I'll call the Crown Prosecution Service to go over the charges first, then I'll see you tomorrow.'

'Why don't you go home and get better, then go to the hospital tomorrow? Christina will still be there. You look like you need to rest. I think we're all feeling it.'

Gina stared at her reflection, trying to figure out the wreck of a woman who stared back at her. 'You might just be right. I'll go tomorrow.'

Wyre placed a friendly hand on her shoulder then nodded as she left the toilets. Gina tidied her hair with her fingers and blew her nose. *You can do it, Harte.* She wasn't going to let her anxiety win.

CHAPTER SIXTY-NINE

Saturday, 21 July 2018

Visiting times had long been over and the hospital seemed quiet. The canteen had been closed since teatime but a family were sitting around one of the tables, drinking machine coffees and eating a pizza that they must have ordered in. Gina had left the station late the previous night, but had managed to lie in until almost lunchtime before continuing with the case paperwork.

She headed towards ward twelve, where she knew Christina Dawson was.

All she could hear was her shoes tapping on the floor as she headed towards the ward. She squirted a bit of alcohol rub on her hands before pressing the buzzer. A nurse let her in. 'DI Harte. I've come to see Christina Dawson.'

'Private room, first on the left.'

She passed the nurses' station and glanced through the wards that branched off. Most patients were watching the screens over their beds. Her gaze was drawn to Julia Dawson who was texting outside Christina's room. 'How is she?' Gina asked.

'Asleep,' she replied with a smile. Gina glanced through the window in the door. The girl had a drip going into her arm and seemed to be sleeping soundly. 'They've given Christina a mild sedative. She's malnourished so they're tube feeding her. They told us about the drugs and they are dealing with that too. I don't understand these things. I can't believe what those animals did to her.' She closed his eyes and held on to the wall to steady herself.

'Are you alone?'

A tear slipped down the woman's cheek. 'I threw Roy out. It's just the two of us now. He drove her away and I'll never forgive him for that.' Julia pulled a crumpled tissue from her pocket and wiped her chapped nose. 'I found out he told Christina that she was making me miserable and that she should leave. She'd taken it to heart and done exactly that. He drove her away.' The woman sobbed. 'How did I not see it?'

'All that matters now is that you're there for her. What you've been through is one of the hardest things a parent could ever experience. She's suffered a lot. She will need you to be there through every step of her recovery. Just be there, give her a lot of love and support. She needs you to be strong.'

A smile spread across the woman's face. 'I'm going to be so strong. I'm determined to be everything she needs me to be. Thank you for coming and thank you for what you did today. We've been told. Christina was exhausted after talking to the other detective, Wyre. She wasn't really with it but she was so happy to see me. She held me so tightly, I thought she'd never let me go. Thank you so much for finding my daughter,' Julia said as she wiped a tear away.

Gina glanced through the window at Christina. Yesterday she hadn't known if the girl would pull through. She wanted to go home and celebrate too. Before popping back to the station for the debriefing, she was going to go to the wine shop, buy a nice red and a large bag of crisps. She was going to go home, run a hot bath and enjoy the wine.

As she left the hospital, her phone beeped. It was a message from Briggs.

Fancy a curry in a bit? You must be hungry. I'm starving after today. We can have a catch up. No funny business – friends.

She placed her phone in her pocket. She didn't need a curry and she didn't need him. She was going home to call her daughter. Their stand-off had lasted long enough and Gina was going to be grown up enough to break it.

EPILOGUE

Saturday, 11 August 2018

It was a lovely morning, the birds sang in the trees, the smell of freshly cut grass filled Gina's nostrils and wild flowers dotted the gardens. She swallowed as she stared up at the large mansion-like nursing home on the outskirts of Cleevesford.

Another case had been solved and she could rest in the knowledge that Christina had been reunited with her mother. If only Erin and Simone had made it. The thought of the two young girls and their unimaginable suffering sent a shiver through her body. She closed her eyes behind her sunglasses as she thought of them. All of her wanted to scream and cry for the Erins and Simones of the world. It was a cruel world and most people glossed over the realities that she saw on a day-to-day basis. They preferred not to think about the suffering of others, suffering on their own doorsteps, on their streets, in their neighbourhoods.

She turned to look through the window of the home, spotting several elderly residents watching television in the lounge. She stepped forward and rang the bell.

'Who are you visiting?' the middle-aged woman asked as she opened the door and led Gina into the hallway.

'Jackie Hanley.'

'Oh, our new lady. She's just been dressed and is in her room, waiting to be brought down. Are you a relative?'

Gina shook her head and pulled out her identification. 'I worked on her case and just wanted to see her.'

'We heard what had happened. I'm sure she'd love to see you. Just go up the stairs and take a left. It's the last room along the corridor.'

Gina continued through the large house until she reached the last room. A little plaque had been pinned up on the door with Jackie's name on it. She knocked and entered. 'Hello, Jackie.' The sun's rays lit up Jackie's light grey hair but there was no mistaking the occasional rosy tinge that had once been red. Her genes carried all the way to Simone.

Gina sat on the edge of the bed, next to Jackie's chair and smiled. 'Looks lovely here.' The woman brought her hand from her lap and flung it on the arm of the chair as her gaze moved from the window to the wall. She began murmuring under her breath, over and over. It was obvious that there was no communication going on between them. Jackie had no idea what had happened to her.

'You've been through a lot but you're safe now. We are safe.' Gina took a deep breath as she fought back a tear.

With the case over, she had finally felt that she could now take time to look after herself. She'd called Hannah and although the reception hadn't been warm, at least the call had ended with a date in her diary to take Gracie out.

'The view's great.' Gina stood and walked over to the window, admiring the fields that stretched all the way to the horizon.

'I'm as bad as them,' she continued, as a tear trickled down her cheek. 'I really am no better. I've done things that I've never told anyone about.' Her heart began to pound as she darted over to Jackie and kneeled before her. Maybe, just once in her life, she had someone to confide in, someone who would never tell. 'I killed my husband,' she whispered, finally saying those words out loud to another human being.

Her mind flashed back to Briggs and when she was telling him about how Terry had abused her. Now their relationship had ended, he still carried some of her secrets around with him. She had to trust that he'd never tell anyone.

Nothing would take away the fact that she pushed Terry down those stairs and cut his life short. 'Do you hate me? I hate me.'

Jackie remained motionless, then her hand left Gina's and flew up before it landed in her lap. Whether that was her answer or just another involuntary movement, Gina would never know. All she knew was that she really hated herself. She wiped a tear away and stood just as someone came through the door.

'Jackie,' Christina shouted as she ran across the room. The thin girl wrapped her arms around the woman and hugged her tightly. 'I'm back home with my mum now but I'm going to visit you all the time, I promise. Mum doesn't mind dropping me off.' The girl pulled a knitted doll from her handbag. 'I got this for you, it's like your doll. I hope you love her as much.' She placed the doll in Jackie's lap, held both of the woman's hands and squeezed.

'I think I should get going now. It's great that you could make it while I was here, Christina. I hoped you'd pop by which is why I left your mum a message. It's lovely to see you looking so well,' Gina said as she headed towards the door.

The girl placed Jackie's hands in her lap. Jackie grabbed the doll and squeezed.

'I have a long way to go but the doctors say I'm doing well.' Christina paused. 'I heard what happened. I was so out of it I just can't remember, but thank you. Thank you for coming for me and thank you for taking me and Jackie away from that place.'

Gina tried her best to hold the tears back but one drizzled down her cheek.

'Have I upset you?'

Gina shook her head. 'No, it's just lovely to see you visiting Jackie.'

'She was my best friend for ages. I don't think my will to live would have been so strong if I didn't have Jackie to care about, would it, Jackie?' She placed a hand on Jackie's shoulder. 'She kept me going, didn't you?' The girl kneeled before Jackie and began tidying her hair as she chatted about her mum and her friends. 'Maybe Stacey and I can bring Jitterbug one day. You'd love Jitterbug.'

Gina slowly backed out of the room and closed the door as she left them to it.

As she reached the car park she noticed a man sitting on the bonnet of a car. 'Gareth Hanley?' His red hair gave his identity away and he had similar features to Simone and Jackie. Wyre had been the one to speak to Gareth so he'd never met Gina.

'Yes.'

'DI Gina Harte.'

'Your DC said you found my mother and the girl. I was working on a contract in Spain and wanted to see Simone badly. I'd never met my child before and I begged my dad not to lose her.' His face reddened as he grabbed his hair and let out a frustrated roar.

'Mr Hanley, it's not your fault.'

'I thought they were all living happily together: him, Mum and Simone. Dad said that Simone was helping to care for Mum, which I thought was lovely. I can't believe he did this to her! And Vanessa? I hope she dies a horrible death. That woman always hated my mum, always resented my grandparents for apparently loving Mum more. She always wanted what Mum had and it's not the first time she came between Mum and Dad. I can't believe my dad did all those things, with that woman.' The man's glassy stare had a haunted look. 'My last words with him will always haunt me. I begged him to keep Simone there until I could get home. I didn't mean for him to trap her, just make her really happy so that she'd want to stay.' He paused and stared out at

Carla Kovach

the tree-lined drive. 'I never even got to meet my daughter. I'd have been a great dad.'

William Hanley may just have taken his son's request literally. Gina felt her face burning from the midday sun.

'I begged him to keep her and he imprisoned her—' The man broke down. 'He did what I asked. They killed her and it was my fault.'

There was nothing Gina could say that would ease his pain and guilt. There was nothing she could do to ease her own. Maybe, given time, he'd accept that it wasn't his fault.

Confessing was meant to help but it hadn't helped Gina. Telling Jackie hadn't taken her pain away at all. She still carried it with her like a rucksack full of bricks. It came everywhere with her and she knew one thing for certain, it would never leave.

A LETTER FROM CARLA

Dear Reader,

I'd just like to take a moment to thank you for choosing *Her Pretty Bones*, book three in the DI Gina Harte series.

If you enjoyed *Her Pretty Bones* and wish to keep up-to-date with my latest releases, please sign up at the following link. Your email will never be shared and you can unsubscribe at any time.

www.bookouture.com/Carla-kovach

This book covers themes that are close to my heart. Homelessness being one, and how hard carers work, another. Huntington's disease has personally affected my family and I've seen first-hand what this does to a person and the impact it has on the rest of the family. If my book has raised even a fragment of awareness, I will feel as though I've achieved something good.

Being a writer, this is where I hope you'll leave me a review on Amazon, iBooks, Google or Kobo. Reviews mean so much and I'd be hugely grateful.

I'm also an avid social media user and love hearing from readers on Facebook, Instagram and Twitter.

Once again, a huge thank you!
Carla Kovach

 CKovachAuthor

 CarlaKovachAuthor

 carla_kovach

ACKNOWLEDGEMENTS

Firstly, I have to thank my editor, Helen Jenner. I love working with her and truly appreciate all the work she does. The hours, the fantastic edit notes and all her suggestions really made *Her Pretty Bones* shine. I appreciate everything she does and look forward to working with her again soon.

Kim Nash and Noelle Holton, the publicity team, you are both amazing. You tirelessly work hard, spreading the book word on social media, arranging publicity opportunities and you do it all with enthusiasm. Huge thank you!

Bloggers, what you do is fabulous. I fully appreciate the time you give and the effort involved. I'm so glad you do what you do and I'm grateful that you chose to review *Her Pretty Bones*. I also need to thank all the other Bookouture authors. We really are like a lovely little family. I've never felt so welcomed into a fold before and I'm really honoured to know you all.

The world of policing isn't something I've ever directly been involved in which is why I need to thank DS Bruce Irving. Not only is he a good friend, he advises me on the police procedural side of things. Thanks Bruce. May we long continue having our gory chats over curries.

I have a core of friends who give me their thoughts on my stories. I'd like to thank authors Derek Coleman, Vanessa Morgan and Brooke Venables, and friends who love crime fiction, Su Biela and Lynne Ward. Your continued support means a lot. I love chatting with you all about books, writing and everything else and I value your friendship.

Lastly, thanks again to my husband, Nigel Buckley. He really is my rock and is always there. I truly appreciate all that he does for me.

Printed in Great Britain
by Amazon

57899329R00187